11/2/99

Eric & Erin Haas

With deep thanks

Daniel Pauger

# SOLDIER BOYS

# SOLDIER BOYS

# DANIEL PANGER

Resource Publications, Inc.
160 East Virginia Street, Suite 290
San Jose, California 95112

Editorial Director: Kenneth Guentert
Production Editor: Elizabeth J. Asborno
Cover Design and Production: Andrew Wong
Production Assistant: Allison Cunningham

5 4 3 2 1

**Library of Congress Cataloging-in Publication Data**

Panger, Daniel.
    Soldier Boys.

    1. United States—History—Civil War, 1861-1865—
Fiction. I. Title.
PS3566.A57S64 1988 813'.54 87-62533
ISBN 0-89390-102-4

For my son Jim Panger,
with deep love and appreciation.

# I

The sky was black except for a scattering of stars. It was still too early for the rooster's crow, yet two young men were walking along a muddy dirt road and had been traveling east for almost three hours. Each footstep was accompanied by a squish as their boots sank to the instep in the sticky mass. The shorter youth carried a coal-oil lantern that cast just enough light to guide them around the large boulders and deep ruts. The taller held a bundle slung over his shoulder and his free hand gripped a smooth-bore rifle.

"Slow down, hoss, that lantern ain't got 'nough light for the two of us do you be in such a hurry."

The smaller youth turned back smiling. "Sorry, Josh, I jus' don' wanna be late. Do we miss the train, no tellin' how long 'fore we get to Montgomery."

The sky started to brighten in the east and the taller youth noticed the change. "Luke, you right. We had better hurry. Mus' be close to six and that train is boun' to be there by seven."

By the time the boys reached the railroad, the sun was clear of the hilltop and the air had lost its icy snap. They walked several hundred yards along the single track until they came to the water tank where the engine would have to stop. There was no sign or sound of the train. The only sounds came from insects hovering around the pool formed from the tank's drippings.

Josh sat down heavily on a stump and sighed, closing his eyes against the brightness of the sun. His powerfully-built body sagged, but his hands stayed busy fingering the firing mechanism of his rifle.

Luke remained standing, the lantern tightly gripped in his hand, its little flame lost in the shimmer of the morning. He walked onto the roadbed, dropped to one knee and put his ear to the track. "Nope, can't hear a thing; maybe somethin' happened to her. They say they was some fightin' hundred miles to the north; she mighta been wrecked or captured."

Josh opened his eyes and squinted to the north. "Nothin' we can do 'cept wait; if she ain't here by noon, we'll have to hoof it."

"Man, that's more 'an a hundred fifty miles and part uphill. I jus' don' know if I'm gonna walk that far for anyone, even for ol' Jeff Davis hisself. If they need soldiers, they can come out and get me." Luke glanced at his friend. "No sir, I'm not walkin' no hundred fifty miles for nobody — not for Jeff Davis, not for Lee, not for Jackson, not for . . ." Luke fumbled as he searched his memory. ". . . Not for Jesus Christ Almighty," he said proudly.

"You blasphemin'," said Josh. "No call takin' the Lord's name like you do." He smiled, showing a set of white, even teeth, but his wide-spaced, smoke-gray eyes were heavy. Thoughts of the clapboard shack in which he had been born and had lived all his life, yet might never see again, oppressed him. He had wanted to join the Army from the day his older brother Ben left home to fight. But his father needed another hand to help him work the farm. After he turned nineteen, there was no way of holding him. His father argued and then threatened to whip him, but it was an idle threat and they both knew it. Now, waiting for the train to come down from the north, already further from home than he had ever been, he almost wished he had stayed with his folks another year or two before testing his manhood. Josh sighed and glanced at his friend. His lumpy, irregular-featured face did not show a care. As far back as Josh could remember, Luke had been happy-go-lucky. They had been friends all their lives and a week ago, when Josh had told him of his plan to go to the city and enlist, Luke declared that that was for him, too. Josh sighed again. He was certain if he started back home Luke would come along without a word of protest.

Luke again walked out on the roadbed and put his ear to the track. Then he pulled out a shiny silver watch from his shirt pocket. From his earliest childhood, this timepiece had been as much a part of his father as the old man's gray-streaked whiskers. Each night before sleep his father would carefully wind the watch then rub its shiny silver case with a soft piece of cloth. The night before, at bedtime, Luke's father had given him the watch. He placed it in his son's hands and without a word went into the bedroom before the boy had a chance to open his mouth.

The watch showed 8:30; the train was one and one half hours late. Luke suddenly didn't care. The sight of his father's gift reminded him of his new position in life. He settled down next to Josh and opened a package wrapped in oil paper. It contained some cold side-meat, half a loaf of bread and several onions. Their appetites readied by the long walk, they ate with satisfied grunts. Josh wiped his greasy hands on his shirt. Luke sucked each finger clean before he wiped his hands and then carefully took the watch out again. It was nine straight up. "She's two hours late," he murmured. Josh shrugged. Luke started to polish the watch with the tail

of his linsey-woolsey shirt. After shining the timepiece, he
held it to his ear and listened to the tick. He had listened
for more than a minute when his other ear picked up
another sound. The train was coming from the north and
Luke thrust the watch in his pocket, jumped up and
started hopping from leg to leg. Josh, too, had heard the
rumble and was trying to rub the sun's glare out of his
eyes.

The engine came to a stop directly under the water
tank and the engineer and fireman climbed down after
first shouting hello. As they attended to the needs of the
hissing locomotive, the conductor swung off the single
passenger car and walked up to the two friends. "You
boys figuring on coming aboard?" he asked. They
nodded. "Where you goin' to?"

Luke, unused to talking to strangers, turned to Josh
who answered, "Montgomery."

"What you want to go there for?" asked the conductor, who considered himself a representative of law and
order and carried a loaded Navy revolver strapped to his
waist to back up his self-designated authority. Taking
the man's questions as a sign of neighborliness, Josh
smiled and told him that they were going to Montgomery
to join the Army and fight. The conductor stared hard at
the boys. He saw their fuzzy homespun clothing and the
open, friendly look of their sunbrown, beardless faces.

"Hop on and find yourself a seat," he boomed. "I'll
be by in a little for the fares." Then in a half-whisper, "If
you keep you' lips buttoned and don't let on, I won't col-
lect no fares at all, seeing how you is off to fight."

This being the first trip aboard a train for both, their
excitement was mixed with apprehension as they climbed the metal stairs. But each being unwilling to let the
other know of his anxiety, they whistled and grinned as
they moved out of the sunlight into the car. It took
several moments for their eyes to adjust so they hesitated

in the entranceway, but before their vision was completely adjusted, the conductor shouted a warning that they had better find seats. In response to this, they stumbled into the aisle.

The car was half filled with passengers and the commotion caused by the boys' entrance made them all turn around and stare. Most wore city clothes and smiled at the coarse dress and awkward manners of the the two hill-country boys. Josh and Luke felt their faces burn as the strangers stared at them. Then the train lurched forward and the boys stumbled against some of the seated people. Several grabbed the boys' arms to help them. When they were finally adjusted in their seats, they sat stiffly, looking straight ahead as they forlornly blinked back tears of embarrassment.

# II

All the recruiting for the city of Montgomery took place at the courthouse, a massive, white stone building sitting ponderously in the middle of a park. Before the war, the park had been filled with carefully lettered signs warning everyone to keep off the carefully-trimmed grass. But these were gone and now scores of white tents had been pitched on the lawns and piles of equipment and provision leaned against the walls of the courthouse.

As they approached, the boys could see dozens of small cookfires, each tended by several soldiers. And everywhere they looked there were lines from which flapped an endless variety of laundry and gear. The bright fires, the white tents, the groups of young men and most of all the flapping of the hanging laundry blended to give the scene a carnival appearance.

The well-lit courthouse showed scarcely a darkened window. Men in and out of uniform came and went. Dozens of horses hitched to a low iron-work fence fronting the building stamped and snorted.

As the boys hesitated at the bottom of the imposing marble steps, they were scarcely noticed. Several times they were elbowed by hard-faced individuals intent upon the transaction of their business. To these shoves, the boys responded with shrugs and grins.

There is no way of knowing how long the two boys might have stood there, interfering with traffic, had not a full-bearded, massively built, fierce looking man in the uniform of a master sergeant come to their rescue.

A quick glance told the sergeant what he needed to know. "So you want to join up?" They nodded and he motioned them to follow him.

They walked down the main corridor of the building to an unmarked door which the sergeant opened without knocking. He executed a perfunctory salute that was scarcely returned by a middle-aged, balding man wearing a poorly fitting, soiled uniform of a captain. Both boys stiffened as they entered the room, throwing their shoulders back and pressing their arms to their sides. The captain smiled at this, showing brown-stained teeth and dribbling tobacco juice down the corners of his mouth, which he casually wiped away with his sleeve.

"Cap'n, these boys want to join up," said the sergeant.

The officer nodded, then turned his head and spat a mouthful of brownish liquid into the corner. He rearranged the glob of tobacco then addressed the boys. "I'm Cap'n Carter. Lieutenant Rawlins be your platoon officer. You all will like Lieutenant Rawlins." He grinned and winked at the sergeant. "You both over eighteen?" Without waiting for an answer he pulled some papers from a drawer which he began to carefully fill in. "These here are your muster papers," he said. "Soon as I get you names and a few other things I'll swear you in so's you can get yourself some victuals and a place to bunk."

The papers were quickly completed, but not without some damage from dripping tobacco juice. The oath delivered by the captain in a wet mumble, he turned his attention back to his work, dismissing the boys with a gesture of his hand.

They meekly followed the sergeant down the hall, each boy in his own mind just beginning to realize the impact the past fifteen minutes would have on his life. And there was a feeling of disappointment. They both had expected a ceremony. But instead there had been nothing. In and out and now they were soldiers signed and sealed until the war was won or lost.

They had no time to share their thoughts as they tried to keep up with the sergeant who was leading with great strides. He made his way to a tent not far from the courthouse and ordered its occupant, a young, broad-shouldered, towheaded private to provide beds and food for each. Before the sergeant left, he turned to the boys, and in a tone less cordial than that used when they first met, ordered them not to wander off on pain of desertion. Then he said with emphasis, "You may not have uniforms, but you're soldiers 'spite of that. I'll be by after reveille, and I want you dressed and ready, understand?" Josh and Luke both nodded and the sergeant walked away, leaving them in the charge of the private.

"That ol' mule's bray is wors'n his kick," said the private as soon as the sergeant was gone. He smiled and a fine web of tiny lines formed around his eyes. "He don' allow no tom-foolery but do you get into trouble he most-ly handles it hisself. He ain't one to be runnin' with stories to the cap'n or puttin' a fellow on report." He paused, still smiling — the web of tiny lines aged his face ten years from his twenty — then said, "I'm from Tuscombia. Up near the Tennessee line. Name's Davy Medlock." With that they shook hands all around — each squeezing the other's hand hard.

"They is rebuildin' the regiment," Davy went on. "Most-a the men were one year men and they be gone home. We lost plenty from fightin', then some jus' took off when they had a bellyful. A batch came down with the fever and the pukes so they pulled us back here for a time 'til we get more men and have a chance to train 'em."

"How long you reckon we gonna stay here trainin'?" asked Josh.

Davy shrugged. "No tellin' — I ain't in no hurry. I'm the oldest enlisted man in the regiment, 'cept for that sergeant, so I sure ain't in no hurry." Realizing he might be confusing the two boys he added, "I mean I'm the oldest in time in this regiment. I first joined up when she was formed and stayed right with her. They ain't many of us originals lef', no sir. Like I said, they is all gone one way or another." He paused. "'Spect you boys know how to handle a rifle," he went on. "That's the main important thing; the rest is mostly learnin' to march and take orders. But when the outfit was formed, we didn' have no time for trainin'. We didn' even have no regular uniforms, jus' our rifles and blankets when they took us north. We was plenty green when them Yanks started shootin' they minnie balls at us. But we learned quick, you bet."

Davy spoke some more about the early days of the regiment and might have continued for another hour had he not been interrupted by snores — Luke had fallen asleep.

Davy grinned at Josh, who struggled to keep his eyes open, then with a nod left the tent and, after a slow stretch, sat down by the fire. Gently massaging an injured leg while exposing it to the warmth of the whitening ashes, the young man's craggy-featured, almost handsome face settled into sad lines.

The stimulation of his two new companions had brought back faces of men with whom he had served and who were now dead. As he thought of his old companions he wondered where he would be in a year. Would he be sitting by another campfire thinking about the new dead? Would these include the two eager young men

from the northern hill country? Davy sighed, started to
kick out the fire, but then through force of habit covered
it with dirt. He crawled inside where he lay on his cot listening to the even sounds of breathing, his wide-opened
eyes staring into the blackness of the tent. Outside it
started to rain, a slow steady rain that was to last all
night and well into the morning.

# III

In the light of day the sergeant looked even fiercer than he had the night before. He was a bull-chested man with a mass of bristling hair on his face including thick black eyebrows that had no beginning or end. His nose was broken. A straight nose would have looked strange on such a man. Yet for all its harshness his face was softened by two gentle, deep-set eyes.

The two friends followed the sergeant to a tent larger than the rest. There they were issued uniforms and rifles. The uniforms were poorly tailored and an awkward fit. However, they were new and were made of good cotton cloth. The rifles were not new. They showed heavy use. Their mechanisms were rusted and their barrels clogged with dirt. These weapons had been rescued from the battlefield and it was impossible to say if they were even capable of firing.

"You country boys know how to use a rifle," the sergeant glowered, daring them to contradict him. "I'm gonna order drill in the afternoon and I expect these guns to be clean and in firin' condition." Noting their expressions, he frowned. "You lucky to have rifles at all. They is damn few left." Then taking a step toward the boys he said, "I don't expect any sass out of either of you. You get these rifles cleaned and workin', understan'!" The boys shuffled from foot to foot, confused, not knowing what was expected of them next.

"What the hell you waitin' for? I tole you somethin', didn' I?" The sergeant took another step toward the boys. At this they turned and ran, carrying their gear as best they could. Luke dropped his rifle as he tripped over a guy rope in front of the tent, but snatched it up and moved even faster as he heard the sergeant bellowing threats.

Sergeant Benjamin Graves stood at the entrance of the supply tent watching the two new recruits stumbling away. His angry expression changed to one of amusement. On the muster rolls of the regiment was listed the name "Graves, Benjamin S., Master Sergeant." Next to it the date: "January 11, 1861," for the unit was organized the same day the ordinance of succession had been ratified by the Alabama State Legislature and the sergeant was the first man to sign its rolls. Other than this brief entry there was no further written indication of the man's true function in the company and regiment. But in a very real sense Sergeant Graves ran his company, and was at least partially responsible for making regimental decisions.

Captain Carter, the company commander, functioned well enough in bivouac. However, as soon as there was a chance of fighting he would lapse into indecision. At these times he turned to his master sergeant whose advice he followed without question. This incompetency was no secret to the men.

After Josh and Luke were out of sight, the sergeant stood musing in front of the supply tent. The two young men were among the last few recruits that would be assigned to his company. The new boys now outnumbered the veterans by more than two to one, yet the sergeant was not too displeased with the situation. "Those hill boys don't take much trainin','" he said to himself. "They are natural wonders with a rifle; take to life in the field real easy; only thing you got to make 'em know is they is part of the outfit and must learn to do together with the rest of the men." He slapped his thigh with determination as he decided, "Some hard drillin' and a few forced marches and the company's bound to shape up real good."

The supply sergeant came to the door of the tent and Graves turned to him as if the man had been listening to his thoughts. "Yes sir, a little touchin' up here and there and we boun' to have a first-class company." The supply sergeant shook his head.

"You ain't gonna have much if all the new chickens is like them two." He jerked his thumb in the direction the boys had gone.

"You wrong there," the master sergeant said with a chuckle. "Those boys gonna make first-class soldiers. They may act simple, but they came down from the hills to fight, and they is used to a gun and I never saw a hill boy as would take water."

The supply sergeant shrugged ending the discussion with, "I hope you right, Ben."

By early afternoon the intermittent rain had stopped. The gray, cheerless day still refused to brighten, but the soldiers had a chance to work the dampness out of their clothes. About forty of the new recruits, including Josh and Luke, gathered in the clear area directly in front of the courthouse. Sergeant Graves, flanked by two corporals, stood in front of the group bellowing threats and curses at whatever man happened to catch his eye. The new soldiers had no idea of what was expected of them and to a man were cowed by the sergeant's fury.

"I never seen a bunch of lummox like you," he said and spat on the ground. "What the hell you think you joined, a Sunday School study class? This ain't no Sunday School, no, nor no ladies' missionary society! You s'posed to be soldiers! I seen wooly-head field hands shape up better'n you!''

The men shuffled uneasily under the sergeant's barrage. "What you fidgetin' and squirmin' for? You brace up you backs and stand steady! You is at attention! Some of you think that all they is to it is going off and fightin'. Some of you think that jus' because you joined up to defend this State of Alabama you is heroes. I got somethin' to say to you. First, you gotta learn to fight! You gotta learn discipline. You gotta learn you a part of an army. This ain't no private war. An' I'm gonna tell you somethin' else. Jus' because you signed the army rolls you ain't heroes — you ain't nothin'. When this company goes into battle, then we see who is a hero and who shits his britches. Until then you trains and drills and marches!''

For hours, supported by the two patient corporals, the sergeant tried to shape the group of men into some sort of working unit. His commands were simple. "Left turn, right turn, forward and to the rear march." But for all their results, these might have been instructions for passing through the Labyrinth. Periodically, he would stop, hands on hips, and stare at the group with disgust. Several times he threw up his hands and walked away only to stop halfway across the field and return, sputtering a series of pungent oaths.

Finally he dismissed the men with threats that all would face transfer to an outfit of road builders and ditch diggers if their performance did not show a remarkable improvement the next day.

Josh and Luke limped back to their tent, and when they reached it, sprawled exhausted on the ground. Both had grown a crop of blisters inside their new stiff shoes. But, too tired to invest the effort to gain relief, they just lay with closed eyes while their feet continued to ache and burn. Davy, who had watched them limp back, after several headshakes, helped them off with their shoes. He looked at their faces. Their hopeless expressions were proof that the old sergeant had given them hell. "In a week or two you'll get used to it," he said with a smile. "You shoulda seen my feet after my first day's drillin'." Still smiling he got up and returned to the cookfire where he was preparing supper.

Davy held the needs of his stomach in the highest possible regard and whenever he had an opportunity, which was anytime he was not actually in the field, he devoted much of his time to the preparation of food. At times the dishes he developed could only be described as exotic. Yet mostly they were tasty, so he never had any difficulty when he desired company to join him at mealtime. This night he had been experimenting with salt pork which, by a process of his own particular brand of logic, he was stewing with apples. If roast pork was enhanced by applesauce, he reasoned, why not improve the flavor as well as the odor of salt meat by actually stewing it with locally gathered apples?

As they ate, the two boys' grunts and finger lickings were sufficient compensation for the shared meal. By the time they finished it had grown dark. With the coming of night the clouds and overcast disappeared and the sky filled with stars. Murmurs of well-fed men filled the camp.

Josh enjoyed his achy tiredness. He lay on the ground and stared upward. The sky looked exactly as it looked at home. His favorite stars were where he had left them two nights before. He wondered at the sameness of the sky. His home was far away yet here was the same sky, the same stars. It was a comfort to him. His thoughts drifted to the hill country. About how his mother would be banging with her heavy iron pots as she prepared dinner. His father would soon come out of the barn carrying a pail of steaming milk. In the deep of his chest Josh felt the tug of homesickness. He was glad that it was dark. He didn't want his friends to see the moisture filling his eyes.

Perhaps the mood was infectious. For Luke too began to think of home. But his was not a feeling of homesickness. Rather, one of guilt. He pictured his father trying to do the work of two. Luke also was glad for the dark.

Davy, months ago, had put thoughts of civilian life out of his mind. He lay on the ground and just gazed at the sky, enjoying the feeling of being alive. As it grew cooler his wounded leg began to throb. Then he hobbled to his feet and moved close to the fire where he pulled up the leg of his trousers, exposing the wound to its warmth.

"Does is still smart?" asked Josh with forced casualness.

"How did you get it?" said Luke. "Looks like it near tore you' leg off."

Modesty having not yet become fashionable, Davy enjoyed talking about his experiences. He lightly tapped his thigh. "It wasn't hardly nothin'." No story, however harrowing, could begin without this or some similar statement. "I guess I was lucky — three times this regiment fought the Yanks and each time I came out without hurt." He stopped speaking for a moment and took in a deep breath — almost a sigh. "So many didn' have the luck." He paused for another moment. "I don' rightly know how many we lost. Some I didn' know too good. They jus' came and went and some never even made me acquainted with they names. All told I guess we lost 'bout a hundred — if you count the missin' and the boys as died from the sickness. Each time we fought, they sent new men to take up the places that were made empty, and it was hard to know them all.

"The fourth time we went up against the Yanks I

didn' worry none 'bout myself. It seemed that I was different — grape and cannister would knock a fellow down
both sides of me, but I wouldn' be touched. A minnie ball
might pass through the sleeve of my tunic or take away
my cap. But nothin' ever touched me. It seemed that the
good Lord had decided to give me His Own special protection, so I didn' fear battle no more 'an I would taking'
a swim in the creek.

"We was in the Valley of Shenandoah and for days
we was playing fox and hounds with the Yanks. First, we
would chase them, then they would chase us. You might
say we was feelin' each other out. Each to get the advantage of the other. This company was in a small woods.
We had snuck in durin' the night, and lay mighty still
so's the Yanks wouldn' know where we was at. The rest a
the regiment circled 'round to the other side and we had
them Northern boys between us. Musta been four, five
hundred of 'em in that field, and they had their backs to
the woods. They never had no idea of what was gonna
happen. 'Bout an hour after sunrise some cavalry joined
our regiment and they attacked 'cross that big field
pushin' them Feds closer and closer to the woods. We
was ready to give them a surprise, I reckon, when some
field pieces were brought up from the other side of the
field — Northern guns. We was gonna give them a
surprise, but they turned it into a surprise on us. They
musta knowed all along we was in the woods. Like I said,
as soon as the cavalry showed up we started to push them
Yanks to the woods. It was then they opened up with
them parrott guns and started to raise the very Ned.

"I was crouched down in a hollow, but could see
through the trees into the field. At first I couldn' tell what
was happenin'; our horses started to come 'cross that
field followed by our boys in butternut. I saw them
Union soldiers in blue slowly move down that field
towards the woods. It was hard to see — it was dark and

cool in the shade and the field was bright and shiny with the air sorta dancin' like it does when it gets heated. It was noisy out there in the field and they couldn'a heard us no ways, but I breathed soft and stayed still as a log. The first I knew somethin' was wrong was when I heard a kind of swish high up in the trees and then an explosion as loud as you could ever believe. This was jus' the start. One after the other them thirty pounders came sockin' into the woods and they seemed to have eyes in they middle 'cause they sure did find out where we was hid. Near ever' explosion was followed by a groan or a yell and some poor boy was hurt. I scrunched up tight hopin' the shells would move away from where I was at. It's a terrible peculiar feelin' to hear them things a' whooshin' through the air. You don' know if they be comin' at you or goin' away. The firin' stopped for a bit and I rose up and saw that now them Yanks were movin' away from the woods and our boys were being pushed back.

"The next I knowed I way lyin' face down; I didn' hear nothin' or feel nothin', but I knew some time musta passed 'cause the sound of fightin' was far away. I remember tryin' to get up and feelin' a strange thing in my leg while my head buzzed and I couldn' see — like there was ink in my eyes." Davy stopped talking and rubbed his injured leg. The fire cast patches of light on his sharp-featured face. Several minutes elapsed. Then Davy started talking again.

"It didn't hurt too bad at first. It jus' felt warm and sticky like when you sit too long and you' leg goes to sleep. I was plenty weak, I'll tell you. Almos' couldn' move my hands, but I took some soft earth and put it into the hole in my leg — piled it in thick so's the bleedin' would stop. The blood and dirt made a kinda brownish mud, and I remember thinkin' how funny it was that I was bleedin' mud, not blood."

"Didn' no one come to help you?" asked Luke.

"The ambulance wagon came for you didn' it?" said Josh.

To both questions Davy shook his head. "Nobody came and soon it was night. My leg began to hurt worse and worse and I remembered hearin' that George Washington's men chewed on lead bullets when they was in pain at Valley Forge, so I tried bitin' on a ball, but instead a stoppin' the hurt it made me want to yell and scream. Sometimes I would hear a scream and I would wonder where it was comin' from 'til I realized that it was me screamin'. Sometimes I could see myself lyin' there just as plain — I could see me hurtin' and screamin' and dyin' jus' like I was two different people. Sometimes it all went away and I would feel all warm and good and dark. Sometimes I thought I was dead and it seemed funny I could still think, me being dead and all."

Davy suddenly stopped talking and went back to rubbing his leg. After another several minutes, with a shrug, he continued.

"I remember waitin' for the sun to come up — I couldn' know if it was still night or almost mornin'. But the sounds and the smells of the woods reminded me of the mornin'. So I lay there starin' up at the tall, black trees and at the sky. Then the trees began to be shiny and I could feel the sun on my body and my leg. It felt good for a little, then as the mud began to bake dry it felt like burnin' ashes was in my leg. And I could hear that man screamin' again.

"I saw someone standin' there, and I knew I mus' be crazy because he was black and now he was kneeling an' washin' my face with a wet rag. I screamed louder 'cause I didn' want to be dragged to hell by that black devil. I don' know what all I said 'cause he took my hand and said, 'It's all right, mister, it's all right; I ain' no devil. You ain' gonna go to hell. I'll take you back to you' folks and you'll be all fixed up.'"

Davy struggled to his feet and yawned. It was clear that the story had come to an end. Almost as an afterthought he said in a matter-of-fact voice, "He was a free nigger who lived in them woods. I guess he was lookin' for loot or somethin' when he heard me. He carried me back to the rest of the men." With that, Davy stopped speaking and went inside the tent.

Josh hesitated a moment, then called out after him, "Did you ever see that nigger again?"

From inside the tent Davy replied, again in a matter-of-fact voice, "Never saw him no more. If I knowed his name, I might send him some money." The boys shrugged at this and were about to join their friend in the tent when they heard a muffled sound. Instead of going inside, they sat down again in front of the fire. Only when Davy's soft sobs were replaced by the even sounds of sleep, did they enter the darkened tent.

# IV

The morning broke crisp — the sky brushed clean by the wind of the rain of the day before. It was one of those special days that only comes five or six times a year. There was no wind, yet the air was not still.

The diamond clearness of the sky allowed streaks of light from the not yet risen sun to find their way across to its western limits.

Josh and Luke stood before their tent, yawning, stretching, and from time to time, with grins on their faces, breaking wind. Each breath of the freshly-washed air made them feel more and more euphoric until they found themselves engaged in a horseplay that involved modified attempts to grab each other's buttocks. Who cared about the crabby old sergeant? Who cared that two hundred miles separated them from their homes? They were young and strong in the first flush of their manhood. And they were soldiers!

Just as the sun began to edge upwards over the roof of the massive courthouse, the echoing notes of a bugle turned the sleeping camp into yawning, stretching wakefulness. Soldiers came to the openings of their tents, tasted the air and were glad. Even those who had caroused or gambled the night before. The day captured them all.

Lieutenant Rawlins joined his company as it formed ranks on the green. In contrast to the stained careless attire of Captain Carter, the Lieutenant was meticulously dressed. His British-made boots had a high polish. His buttons and braid sparkled. Not a stain, not a bit of dried food could be seen on his uniform, front or back. But there was a sour expression on his sharp-featured face — his lips curled down and his pale blue eyes were narrowed.

Davy, who was standing next to the two boys, said with unmistakable contempt in his voice, "That Lieutenant Rawlins got a cork up his ass. Take out that cork he shrivel like a pig bladder with a hole in it. That Rawlins nothin' but a rich, snooty . . ." Davy paused, reaching for an appropriate word, then spat out, ". . . turd."

"He sure is a fancy turd," Luke said in a whisper.

The exchange was interrupted by the arrival of a new man, still in civilian clothing, accompanied by the captain's orderly. The new man stood a little below medium height. He was spare and his clothing hung loose from his muscular frame. His features were those of a Caucasian, except for a long, hooked nose, but his skin was a dark brown, darker than many of the slaves that passed the courthouse square on their way to market.

Most of the men looked at the new recruit with interest because of his exotic appearance. But Lieutenant Rawlins took one look at the man and turned a blotchy red. His hands tightened and his knuckles turned dead white.

"What's that nigger doin' here?" he snarled at the orderly. "No nigger is gonna be part of this company unless he shines boots and cleans the shit house all day!" The new man stiffened. "Get that nigger the hell away from here! He stinks so bad I like to puke all over his fancy suit." The lieutenant spoke loud enough for every member of the company to hear.

The captain's orderly shuffled uneasily from foot to foot.

"Didn't you hear me!" the lieutenant shouted. "Get him away from here!"

"The captain said . . ." the orderly started to say.

"Tell the captain," the lieutenant interrupted, "that some mistake has been made. It's against the regulations to have any nigger as a soldier. Someone must have signed him up during the night when they couldn't see his black skin." Lieutenant Rawlins softened his tone a little. "You tell the captain like I said."

The orderly swallowed hard then said, "The captain says this man is white. The captain says he's Armenian and is counted as white 'spite of his color. The captain jined him up all proper and tol' me to march him out here." The orderly paused to catch his breath. Then he blurted out, "His name is George. Can't rightly say his other name. He's all legal and proper with this outfit." With that, the orderly saluted. Then without waiting for a return salute, he half walked, half ran back to the courthouse, leaving the man called George standing alone.

"You a nigger?" The lieutenant spoke directly to the new arrival. He walked up close and made as if he were inspecting the dark man from head to toe. Some of the soldiers snickered. "You sure you ain't a nigger?" This was asked in a wheedling tone. "Maybe just a leedle, leedle bit nigger? Your mother, huh? Father? One grandfather — just one? You can't tell me that not one of your great-grandfathers wasn't a pure blooded African. If it's only one great-grandparent, ain't nobody gonna say nothin." To all the questions the man named George did not reply. He had lived in the South ever since he had been brought to the United States while still a boy by his father, a rug merchant. He had known insults, even physical attacks, and had learned not to answer back, just to remain as inoffensive as possible until the abuser lost interest. In spite of the pressures he had known, George counted himself a Southerner. Finally, as an act of conscience, he decided to join the Confederate Army. From the moment he reached that decision until now as he stood defenseless in front of the lieutenant, he had known that sooner or later some white man would try his mettle.

"George," the lieutenant said the name in an almost loving manner, "they say you ain't nigger, so you can join this white man's army. Well, maybe that's true and maybe it ain't." The lieutenant paused. Then, spraying droplets of spittle into the new man's face, he shouted, "To me you' a nigger. A low down, no account, thievin', black ass nigger . . ."

The lieutenant's tirade was interrupted by one of the men calling his name.

"Lieutenant Rawlins, Lieutenant Rawlins, sir." The officer turned around to see who was speaking. It was Davy.

"Lieutenant Rawlins, sir," Davy repeated the officer's name a third time. "How come you do that way to a man 'as jined this company all legal and proper? How come you call him nigger when you know he ain't?" Davy spoke softly and evenly. "Seems like we should be glad to get a man as wants to fight and not call him names. Seems like you ain't actin' the way a proper officer is required to act." Davy let his deep, deep Southern accent fill his mouth, not caring about pronunciation, much as the lieutenant had done.

Had it been anyone else except Davy, the officer would not have hesitated a moment in ordering the man arrested. But Davy presented a problem. He was a veteran of several battles. His value as a soldier was established, while the lieutenant had yet to smell the smoke of a gun fired in his direction.

"I know he is not a nigger." Lieutenant Rawlins forced a grin. "Do you really think that I am unable to tell the difference between a white man and one of color?" Now he spoke textbook English in contrast to the slipshod, accented lingo of a few minutes earlier. "We never had fewer than eighty colored on my Daddy's place. I have known the Nigra all my life. I was just testing this man out to see how much rib punching he could take."

Lieutenant Rawlins turned back to the new man. "Just an initiation to see if you could take it. What did they say your name was? George? To be in this outfit you gotta take it. I was only funnin'." The lieutenant slipped back into his accent. Then he offered his hand without, however, removing his glove.

George took his place in the ranks. Davy, in a deliberate way, made room for him. This, more eloquently than any words, declared that George was to be his friend.

Lieutenant Rawlins turned the company over to Sergeant Graves, who had been standing silently in the rear, and walked away quickly. As he crossed the field the young officer felt as if his head would burst. Being shamed in front of his men and being forced to crawl in order to extricate himself had been a bitter experience.

Ever since he could remember he had held sway over groups of men. Even as a child, he had the right to order slaves and white tenant farmers to do his bidding. His father justified this as a means to develop an understanding of authority in the boy.

On dozens of occasions Lieutenant Rawlins had ordered his slaves whipped, often personally participating in the whipping. He himself never knew more than the most superficial discipline. The only rule he obeyed was to be proud and to protect his honor at all times. Yet at

Christmas time he was lavish with gifts for the slaves. And when a slave fell sick he would often attend to him personally, at times staying up half the night inside one of the squalid huts.

Before he reached the security of the courthouse, Lieutenant Rawlins had determined to get rid of Davy. Not by transferring him, but by killing him or somehow arranging for his death. In combat many things would be possible. There, the advantage was all to the officer.

Davy watched the lieutenant as he crossed the field. For a moment he regretted his words; there was no doubt he had made an enemy. Then with a "what the hell," he put the matter out of his mind.

Sergeant Graves, who had witnessed the exchange, would have clapped Davy on the back if he hadn't thought this might serve to break down the company's discipline. Instead he winked at the man. Then setting his face into hard lines he turned to the lined up men and slowly looked them over.

"We full up in strength now!" he said in a booming voice. "We jus' been foolin' 'round waitin' 'til we came to strength." The men who had blistered their feet and worked their muscles until they ached the day before swallowed hard.

"No tellin' how soon you' ass be under fire. So we better get you in shape to stop a minnie ball in proper style." He glowered at the men for several moments then turned them over to the corporals while he stood off to one side and watched.

The men were marched and countermarched. They were taught to crawl on their bellies. They were paired off and shown how to use their rifles as clubs. Then again they were marched and countermarched, at times almost at a run. Until the bugle signaling the noontime meal was blown there was no letup. After lunch it was the same 'til sunset. Before the day was over three men had fainted and had been carried to their tents. But the sergeant's conscience never bothered him when men fell fainting from the ranks. A man stood a much better chance of surviving in battle if he were well trained. Some always fainted at first. It was to be expected.

The training continued through Saturday noon. Until then the men had little time for themselves. Evening meals had to be cooked, clothing needed washing and mending, and rifles required constant cleaning for the daily inspection. But from Saturday noon 'til the bugle blew Monday morning, the men were to be given leave to stay or go as they pleased, and it was a rare soldier who had not developed plans for his thirty-six hours freedom. Montgomery, the great Southern city, spread all about them. And in their clean grey uniforms they were certain to be welcome just about any place they might happen to wander.

# V

The men were lined up tight and stiff as the sun shone directly overhead that Saturday. Even Davy had abandoned his casual stance and was braced as rigidly as the next. For the first time since Josh and Luke had signed the muster rolls, Captain Carter appeared on the field. His uniform was more stained and wrinkled than before. Frowning, he made a detailed inspection of his men, remarking at any item of dress that showed even the slightest defect. For some reason the men didn't resent the captain's inspection in spite of his own unkempt condition.

The thirty minutes of final inspection felt longer than an entire afternoon of another day. The men were not sure they would be turned loose. Some quirk might change their captain's mind, bringing an end to the glorious time they anticipated having during the next day and a half. But as soon as the inspection was completed, the captain said with a broad wink, "Stay out of jail, hear? Don't want none of my boys all messed up. Don't let me catch a one of you locked up come Monday morning."

With that the men scattered, whooping and shouting. In a minute the parade ground was deserted.

Except for one, every man in the company had plans for the half-holiday and the Sabbath. The one exception was George, the newest recruit. He returned to his tent, forgotten for the moment by his new friends, Davy, Luke, and Josh. They were headed for a picnic supper held by the Christian Ladies Aide Society for "The Comfort of Confederate Soldiers Needing Home Cooked Food and the Gentle Ministrations of Women Yet Too Far Away From Their Own Home to Secure These at Their Own Hearth Sides." At church the Sunday before, Davy had been approached by a plump, perspiring young lady who invited him to the supper. He was asked to bring one or two companions that might fit into the "decorous atmosphere of a late afternoon church picnic supper held by ladies of the best families to be found in all Montgomery," a city, Davy was informed, that contained some of the best names in the entire South.

Davy had been approached by the young lady because she and her club sisters were having difficulty in securing a sufficient number of officers. So, they determined to display their spirit of democracy by inviting a select few men from the ranks, it being tacitly understood that these were to be single, young and, if possible, not unattractive.

In spite of the high polish and perfect order of their uniforms during inspection, the boys returned to their tent for a quick brush-up which included several peeks into the looking glass to confirm the slickness of their hair and the special angle of their caps.

The picnic was on the estate of one of the elders of the church, a man who had acquired a large fortune while still quite young and was spending the rest of his days trying to bury any recollection of how his fortune was obtained. Scarcely anyone spoke anymore of the slave trade he had been mired in, thirty years of Christian charity apparently being sufficient to wash the stain from the pile he had accumulated.

The elder's estate consisted of ten acres located in an exclusive section on the outskirts of the city. Every square foot of his land was well tended. The grass had been cut just the right length to provide a velvety touch. The hedges had a delicate sculptured look. Flowers were everywhere.

Neither Josh nor Luke ever had imagined that anywhere in the world a place like this existed. As they stood at the open gate and peered in at the rolling green lawns, the profusion of flowers, dazzling in their colors, the bubbling, bustling, busy young ladies, they froze and held back. Even Davy was impressed, and he counted himself a man of the world. If several of the hostesses had not noticed the boys and hurried over to lead them in, all three might have found some reason to retreat to a less elegant establishment.

Since most of the guests were officers, who were able to start their weekends at an earlier hour, the three friends were the last to arrive. The number of single hostesses had been carefully matched with the number of men expected. Thus, as might be expected, the three ladies who had yet to be selected were somewhat older, somewhat homelier, and perhaps a bit less well groomed than the others. The prospect of spending several hours in the company of these damsels had a sobering effect on the spirits of the three young men. But now being inside the gate there was no help for it.

The boys were steered to a remote portion of the grounds where they joined two other much younger ladies whose charms were such that four soldiers were playing them court. The advantage to be found in the spot where the boys were taken was that once they were in, there was no chance of escape. The bower was bounded at the rear by an artificial fish pond in which great golden carp could be seen slowly gliding. On one side stood a hedge, delicately manicured as if by a pair of lady's scissors, but nonetheless impenetrable. The other side was secured by a white wicker fence well laced with dark green ivy. The space between the fence and the pond that might have offered an escape was blocked by a flowering rose bush bursting with blood red roses defended by hundreds of needle-sharp thorns. The entrance to the arbor itself was defended by five ladies, for the three escorts of the boys had joined the two already there and were now sitting in a semi-circle.

In front of the ladies stood five wicker baskets covered by brightly checkered cloths that concealed their contents, but could not hide the remarkable fragrances that seeped through. Even those less favored amongst the ranks of Southern belles had learned the value of seductive cooking, for it is a widely known fact that a well-fed man has clouds in his eyes.

Davy, Josh, and Luke joined the four other men, and in a moment all seven of them were facing the ladies, the five picnic baskets separating the one sex from the other. The four soldiers who had been present before the arrival of the three friends were aware that now they could no longer cultivate the two lovelies they had followed into this trap. But, having heard that an ugly woman makes a good cook, they expected at least one of their needs to be satisfied.

The three more mature ladies were named Becky, Martha, and Sophie. The other two had been christened Dorothy Lee and Melinda. They sat with their hands demurely folded in their laps, their petticoats billowing out all around, modestly covering their limbs down to the tips of their patent leather shoes. More than a minute passed without a word spoken. Finally Martha, being the oldest, though if charged with the fact she would have hotly denied it, felt it her duty to find a conversational wedge to pry open the silence that was growing oppressive.

"Well," she said brightly, "we certainly are fortunate to be honored by so many fine young gentlemen." The boldness of the statement caused Dorothy Lee to titter and Melinda to blush. Becky and Sophie were past the tittering, blushing stage. To them, picnics and parties were serious skirmishes in the campaign of finding a husband before the grim appellation of spinster permanently attached itself to them.

"The ladies decided it was time and enough we invited some of the poor boys in the ranks," Martha went on, her voice traveling up and down the scale with every sentence. "*They* are just as important as the officers — where would we be if there were no privates at all — just officers? My goodness, it isn't fair the way those fancy lieutenants and captains with all their airs have all the fun! Don't you agree, Sophie?"

Sophie, who sat next to the speaker, nodded vigorously. This wasn't the first time she had been together with Martha, and she knew when the conversational torch was being passed to her. "I should say so!" She snapped her lips. "Those officers parading around in all their braid as if the war was being fought by them alone!" she humphed. When Sophie wanted to give emphasis to something, in addition to her lip snap, she humphed through her nose. "Of course, I'm not talking about Beauregard, Jackson or Lee. They really are our he-roes, but those young upstarts with all their showy ways, just fancy themselves so special." To each word Martha and Becky attested by nods of their heads. And when the names of the three heroic generals were mentioned, the women sat up straighter in a sort of silent salute. Then Sophie added, "Why Miss Becky's own brother signed up as a private soldier." It was tacitly understood that Becky, as the youngest of the three, would always be referred to as Miss Becky.

"Yes, and he stayed a private for three whole months," Miss Becky stated emphatically, her voice taking on a girlish quality. "Why, if Daddy hadn't spoken to the Governor, I 'spect he'd be off fightin' those heathenish Yanks as a private soldier, or maybe," the young lady lowered her voice, "he would be lying somewhere out there in an unmarked grave, a sniper's bullet lodged in his noble breast."

The three ladies bowed their heads for a moment. Without being aware of what they were doing, the men bowed their heads also.

Dorothy Lee and Melinda, who had experienced the arrival of the three other women as sort of an invasion, were totally unable to cope with these senior, more articulate members of their sex. Thus they had no choice other than to remain silent, their annoyance masked by tiny smiles and half-shut eyes.

The baskets still stood untouched; not one of the men could take his eyes off these waiting mysteries that continued to exude the most delicious aromas. But the women showed not the slightest indication that they intended to share their contents.

"Why I'll bet most anything that you boys have seen more of the war than any of them," said Martha with a sweeping gesture as she returned to her topic, a gesture that included all male invited guests at the picnic except the seven directly in front of her. "I'll bet you have killed just lots of Yanks already." The young men, with the exception of Davy, vigorously shook their heads. None had been in the Army for more than a month.

The young lady then concentrated her gaze on Davy. "You've killed more than your fair share of those barbarous Yankees, I can tell." She wagged her finger at him in a teasing manner.

"I knew he had been out there fighting from the very moment I laid eyes on him," Sophie interjected, her lips snapping with style. "There's somethin' 'bout a fightin' man; you just can tell, that's all," she humphed. "He's so young, yet he's seen so much," she added.

Becky, not to be outdone, chimed in, "He's so pale it's easy to see he's really suffered."

Davy grew embarrassed by all this attention. Quite the opposite from Becky's observation, he was not pale, but rather strawberry red.

"Were you ever wounded?" asked Dorothy Lee. "I mean did you ever get hurt or . . .!" The three older ladies froze the questioner with their looks.

"Humph," Sophie exploded through her nose, the sound coming out with such vigor that as soon as she was able to turn her head she made use of her handkerchief.

"Why, that's no question to ask a fighting man." Martha pressed her lips together shaking her head in disgust.

Dorothy Lee wasn't at all sure exactly what she had done that was wrong, but to be scorned in front of seven young men left her at the verge of tears.

"Any soldier who has really seen action and has suffered wounds does not want to be reminded, at least not in public," Martha spoke in a voice that sounded as if this were the hundredth time the young lady had erred.

Then, without any critical reaction from the others, Becky observed, "Of course he has been wounded. You can tell from the look in his eyes. It must still cause him terrible pain — poor boy." Martha and Sophie clucked in sympathy.

Davy felt the hot blood burning his face. He was sure everyone could see his embarrassment.

"My Daddy's cousin's husband never did get over the wounds those monstrous Yanks inflicted on his poor body." Martha looked around to make sure everyone was listening.

"You've often heard me speak about second cousin

Harriett?" The question was directed to Becky and Sophie. Both nodded, obediently. "She's the one went to live right outside of Gulf Port after she married. It was to a Wilson, Samuel, son of old Judge Wilson — a very fine family. They say they was cousins to Andrew Jackson. Well," Martha picked up the thread of her narrative, "Cousin Samuel was in the war from the very start. In spite of being trained for the ministry he felt his duty was in defending his state. Well, his company was captured after they were surrounded by ten times their number of Yanks and instead of treating them like prisoners the Yanks . . .," Martha hesitated, swallowed hard then trying for a real shocker said, "They did those men in such a way that . . . that they will never be able to have children!"

Everyone in the audience expelled a breath in unison. Martha then offered as a parting shot, "Poor, poor cousin Harriett. She says sometimes at night Samuel has the most terrible nightmares. He rolls around in bed shouting 'No! No! No! No!'" With every "no" Martha grimaced, causing each of the seven soldiers, Davy included, to jerk backwards.

The picnic baskets now were no longer the soldiers' center of attention.

"My uncle by marriage had a brother that never did come back," Sophie declared. Then she snapped her lips. After a cautious "humph", she continued, "My uncle's brother, his name was Samuel, too, was doing picket duty when he fell into Yankee hands. The next thing his company knew he was stumbling across a field, his belly slit wide open." Sophie paused to show her embarrassment at mentioning that part of the anatomy, then with a sigh continued. "He came stumbling across the field, his intestines in his bloody hands, screaming in mortal pain. He would drop some of the slippery organs from time to time and they would tangle his feet causing him to trip and fall. Then he would pick himself up with what was left of them and keep coming on, screaming all the while."

Davy, of all the men, was the most deeply affected by the story. He had seen soldiers with their abdomens laid open. He had seen men try to stuff their guts back into themselves. The other six soldiers, grown pale, had lost their appetites. Soon it might be their intestines.

Dorothy Lee and Melinda at first were horrified. But now, not being themselves personally threatened, they began to warm to the tales the likes of which they had never been exposed to in the past. Melinda, in addition to being fascinated, found herself filling with anger, a feeling she hadn't allowed herself to experience ever since she had been told it really wasn't ladylike.

"They had deliberately slit him open with a butcher knife," said Sophie, determined to finish her story. "It took him until sundown to die. They say you could hear the Yank soldiers laughing and whooping hidden as they were in the trees on the other side of the field."

"Why, if I was a man, I'd kill every last one of those terrible people!" Melinda blurted out, her sense of outrage too strong to control. "Any man who won't go and fight those terrible, terrible Yanks, well, I can tell you I don't think much of his . . .," she groped for the right word, ". . .of his spirit." Then as an afterthought, "I certainly wouldn't want any man who wasn't in uniform to come calling at my home!"

Instead of rebuking the young lady for this interruption, the three older women set their faces in agreement. By her response to the two stories, Melinda had ceased to be a competitor and now was an ally.

Sensing her companion's changed status and wanting to obtain the approval that would erase her earlier censure, Dorothy Lee declared, "No man need ever come calling at my house except if he is wearing a butternut uniform. I won't even come downstairs!" With that she had joined the four others and now all five women were united by a common bond. Oddly enough they all felt a growing resentment toward the seven innocent soldiers who were clothed with the proper color of uniform. The ladies would have relished the opportunity to spray some of their venom directly on some unsuspecting civilian. That the soldiers were protected and thus could not be attacked made them objects of irritation, not admiration.

Becky, or Miss Becky as she was referred to by the others, was mildly put out. Try as she would her imagination was not sufficiently fertile to produce a usable story. In a valiant attempt to add emphasis to what had already been said she remarked, "If I was a man I could think of nothing nobler than suffering and dying for my native state." It was weak, but it was better than nothing. Then as a postscript she added with explosive force that came from years of accumulated rage, "You men have all the luck. You men get all the glory while we're expected to suffer in silence!"

As is so often the case with boys still clinging to their teens, or a year or two past, no matter how upset they may be, no matter how distressing their thoughts, if given a good five minutes to recover, their appetites will invariably return with no apparent damage. And so it was with the seven soldiers.

As the ladies began to unpack their hampers, all thoughts of death or dismemberment vanished. These were replaced by anticipatory fantasies of roasted chickens with crisp brown skins still hugging their juicy bodies, of thick slices of soft white bread well buttered on both sides, of little meat pies with savory sauces just the right size for a hungry man, of a profusion of pickles, sweet and tart, cakes and pastries, deviled eggs and good round cuts of tender ham well-flavored with the smoke of slow oak fires. In none of their fantasies were the boys disappointed. All that the South could give her fighting men was packed in those baskets.

They ate until their sides began to ache, then regretfully put down knives and forks, sucking the clinging juices from each finger. So much had been eaten, yet there still was so much left to eat! Tomorrow's plain victuals would be a poor match for those they were forced to leave uneaten.

It was apparent the soldiers considered the older hostesses the better cooks, for their baskets were now nearly empty, those of the young girls still containing enough to feed them all another modest meal.

The meal coming to an end, Martha, Sophie and Becky settled back, daintily wiping the crumbs of the feast from their mouths. Their faces held that certain look that promised an hour, if not two, of uninterrupted story-telling horror. Dorothy Lee and Melinda leaned slightly toward the senior ladies waiting eagerly. But Davy upset all plans by jumping up and proclaiming that it was time they were back to camp. That they all would "catch it" if they were late. The other six, after several bows and "thank you's", followed after Davy as he stepped gingerly between the seated ladies. More than anything else the young soldiers were unwilling to risk losing the meal that was so comfortably packed inside by facing another serving of patriotic gore.

# VI

Although less than enthusiastic church goers, the next day the three boys attended services at a grand, well-kept old church located in the better part of town. At home there had never been any doubt about the necessity of sitting through a long morning of preaching and praying ever Sunday. So, although far from home, each boy that Sabbath dutifully marched to church as if in the tight tow of his mother and father.

The afternoon was spent in sightseeing, which included participation in a hymn-sing under an enormous striped canvas tent, a sing the boys thoroughly enjoyed what with the drum beating, foot stamping, and hundreds of swaying bodies. By sunset, having grown exhausted, they decided to return to camp.

Josh and Luke sat in front of their tent picking at the tufts of grass with their bare toes. All around other men were returning. Some showed by their unsteady step and puffy eyes that tomorrow's drill would be painful, for their mouths would be filled with dry cotton and their heads would ache. Some had that certain look that spoke of satisfying amorous encounters. These fairly reeked of self-satisfaction and their walk was a cross between a skip and a swagger. Some men slid into camp so softly it was plain they wanted to be left alone. These were the ones who had been lonely and homesick. The big city, with all its people, had made them feel isolated. These were the ones who were the willing victims of sharpers and con men. They had traded their money and their watches for friendly words and toothy smiles and never complained that they were losers. Although many returned in twos and threes, the homesick ones were always by themselves.

All over the camp, cook fires sprang up. These, together with the swaying trees and clothing flapping on scores of guy rope, created a flickering effect as if a swarm of giant fireflies had settled there.

A pot of thick stew was being supervised by Davy who never tired of experimenting with items of food. This time he had added, in addition to the standard ingredients, a handfull of watercress to give it a certain sharpness. From time to time he tasted the bubbling mixture, but found it difficult to decide whether his experiment was a success or a failure.

Ordinarily, Davy would have hesitated to ask Sergeant Graves to share their supper. However, the use of watercress in beef stew raised a question that needed answering — the sergeant was an expert eater. Besides, the sergeant's unsteady gait as he approached was a favorable sign. When liquored up Ben Graves was a friendly, almost lovable man.

Sergeant Graves on his part had been hoping to secure an invitation to supper. Building a fire and preparing a meal was beyond his ability in his present condition. It was no accident that he passed close to Davy's cook fire.

The stew was different, but to the sergeant it tasted good. When he started dipping bits of bread into the remaining juice, Davy smiled and began to dream of the new ingredients he would use the next time.

"How was the weekend?" Davy asked when the sergeant was through eating.

"Tolerable," the sergeant replied in a voice that sounded as if he had little interest in talk. But Davy knew that when Sergeant Graves was liquored up there was nothing he enjoyed as much as talking. The sergeant released a meaty belch and Luke, as a mark of respect, responded with a belch of his own and Josh, not to be outdone, joined the chorus. It was a manly exchange.

"This ol' town don' compare with New Orleans," said Sergeant Graves as if the boys' belches had been questions.

"My Pa tol' me New Orleans' one of the sinfullest cities in the whole worl'," said Luke who had often dreamed of that place after his father's lecture.

"Maybe so," said the sergeant. "Plenty of ways for a couple of innocents like you to get in trouble." The sergeant paused. "But you can't hardly get bored in that town.

"It's been quite a time since I was last in New Orleans," the sergeant went on. Davy, Luke and Josh settled back to listen to what was certainly the start of a story. "I've been there three, no, four times in all. One time was only for a few days." Sergeant Graves screwed up his face as he dug into a pocket of his memory. Then he continued, "First time I ever went to that city I was no older'n you," he pointed at Luke. "I was checkin' cargo in Mobile and they sent me to New Orleans. One of our ships sprung a leak and had to make port there. She was so bad damaged that the cargo was pulled and piled in a warehouse. It all was worth close on to a hundred thousan' dollars, and they sent me to watch it and check it out 'til they figured what they was gonna do.

"It took me near on two weeks to check all that lading. Some was ruint by the water, but none was missin'. After checkin' I waited aroun' another month 'fore they decided what to do. It didn' cost me hardly nothin' to live. I slept in the warehouse and my victuals was paid for by the company. Later I hired me two big free niggers to guard that place and started explorin' around the town.

"To tell the truth," the sergeant's face took on a misty look, "I never had been away from home 'til then and I guess I was a little lonely. I didn' know a single soul in that entire place.

"They is parts of that town where they all speak French. 'Nother, Spanish. The niggers talk so's half the time you can't tell what they sayin'. Plenty of cat houses there. Big ones, small ones, some fancier than a church.

"To tell the truth, I never had visited a fancy house up to that time. I had it in mind, but money was scarce at home. 'Sides, I was still pretty young. Hadn' been shavin' a year. But my keep there was less than at home so the money began to pile up in my pocket. It fair burnt a hole in my britches it wanted spendin' so bad.

"Why'nt you try one of them fancy houses, I asked myself. Not one of the big ones with red plush furniture and a shiny black nigger with top hat and brass buttons at the door, no, and not one of them nasty dark lookin' places with busted out windows and gals leanin' out the windows, yoo-hooin' at you. Some place medium. Some place quiet and friendly.

"Half a dollar could buy a tolerable fine wench in those days. Same as you pay dollar and a half today. Best place in all New Orleans didn' cost no more than a dollar, not countin' the whiskey you want to drink before goin' upstairs.

"Well, there was this little place I had my eye on. I seen some men go in and out that looked like they fit my type. So, there's where I went.

"It wasn't fancy inside, but it wasn't all broken down neither. The lady in charge was just as nice as you please and they took my coat, called me 'yes sir,' 'no sir,' as much as I could ever want. They was four girls attached to the place. Two was workin', two waitin' when I walked in. I decided to have me a few shots of spirits to ready me and I figured it would give me the chance to look them other two over, them that was occupied.

"I ain't gonna lie and tell you that I didn't feel skittish when I first walked in. My money was as good as the next, but I hadn' learned the ways of doing the manly things and didn' want to let on and be shamed in front of strangers.

"After three, maybe four or five drinks of the liquor they had, I started feelin' all right and ready like a young bull first time they take him to cover a fresh heifer. All them girls started lookin' purty good; even that fat old whore as ran the place would-a served me fine. Then, this Spanish gal they called Marie came down those stairs.

"She was pattin' down her skirt and bodice and was puffin' on a little black cigar. Never saw a woman do such a thing before. As she passed the lighted lamp, her skirt was made of such a material you could nearly see through. I looked and bugged my eyes as I followed her legs from ankles to the very top. She was somethin' I can tell you. I felt that hot whiskey rise up into my throat and go down again until it filled all parts of my body. I'da paid two dollars hard money for that woman did they ask me.

"When I said I wanted Marie, she smiled. I guess she felt pleasured I chose her over the others. That girl had the whitest teeth you ever saw and her tongue was just as pink and pointed as a kitten's.

"She took me upstairs and I tripped twice goin' up. My legs were shakin' like I don' know what. They was coming loose from my body."

The sergeant paused to light his pipe. Then he took several long puffs.

"What happened then, Sarge?" asked Davy.

The sergeant puffed several more times, examined the pipe, spat into the fire, then continued. "As soon as she got me in that room of hers, she started pullin' the straps off her shoulders and undoin' the ribbons and buttons. It gave me quite a turn, I'll tell you. I didn' know exactly what to expect, but I thought at least I'd get a chance to say howdy-do and ask after her health first.

"I didn' want to let on I was green so I jus' stood and watched never sayin' a word. In less 'an a minute the whole shebang came slidin' to the floor and there she stood naked as a jaybird. It turned my insides upside down and then some.

"'Come on what you waitin' for,' she said.

"She had a heavy Spanish accent. It was the first words she spoke so I was kinda surprised to hear her talk. She put her hands on those nice thick hips and started tappin' her shoe. It gave me quite a turn it did. That gal was the most beautiful thing I ever seen in all my days.

"After I done what I was supposed to, I didn' want to leave that gal. She was almost dressed and was pattin' her hair in place when I decided it was worth another half dollar to stay with her a while more. I didn' want to make free with her again, just wanted to spend some more time. I gave her the money and with a shrug she started tuggin' at her bows. I told her I just wanted to stay and talk. Then she smiled at me in a different way. The way people smile at people.

"'What you want to talk to me for?' she said.

"Only her words sounded plenty different from the way I talk. I couldn' speak like that woman to save my natural soul.

"'You like me, is that why you want to talk, heh?'

"I tol' her I sure did. I tol' her my name and where I come from and she told me she was from the island of

Cuba and her name was Marie. Marie Paulos. It was a pretty name. I thought so then; I still do."

The three listeners nodded. During his year of Army life, Davy had heard other stories about whores and fancy houses, but to Josh and Luke this was all new and fascinating.

"I tol' her lots a-things about myself and she listened good — to ever' word," the sergeant went on. "I even tol' her she was the first woman I ever had anythin' to do with. She nodded like she knowed all the time. I tol' her things I never tol' anyone. It jus' seemed to come natural to talk to her. Hardly no one ever would sit and listen to me before.

"Well, it was soon time and she let me know in a gentle way.

"She said, 'If it was allowed, I'd listen to you longer, but it is not permitted.'

"She picked up my hand and she kissed it; me, yes she kissed my hand. Nothin' like that ever happened before in my life. I tell you that woman was really somethin'; she even called me by my name. Not sweetheart or honey like most fancy girls do."

The sergeant's pipe had gone out and he paused to light it.

"Did you ever go back to that house?" Luke asked.

The sergeant nodded.

"Whatever happened to that girl, that Marie Paulos?" Luke then asked.

The sergeant took several slow puffs then said, "I went back the very next day, and I went back the day after that, too. Couldn't get enough of that gal. Even after I had lain with her I still wanted her. It was the peculiarest thing you ever saw.

"All that fancy house visitin' began to cost me a pretty. So I found me some extra work helpin' check fresh cargo like I did in Mobile.

"After maybe twenty visits I asked that gal could I take her ridin' sometime — maybe in the mornin' before she had to work. But they never would let her go ridin' with me nor walkin' neither.

"After they got to know me real good I could come visit early and talk with Marie downstairs and no one would listen. I would buy a glass of spirits now and then to show I was a sport. Marie could keep her mouth closed pretty good. She scarcely ever talked about her own self, no more than to mention that her folks was dead and she had been taken from Cuba when she was half growed. But that gal could listen and she sure could understand. You could see in her big brown eyes and in her parted lips she was real interested in what you said. If you asked her advice or opinion, she would first say she couldn' say, but if you pressed her she would talk as good as any man and make a hell of a lot more sense than most.

"I was dreadin' goin' back to Mobile, but I had no choice. They finally sold that whole load of cargo right there in New Orleans and I had to go back or lose my job — one. Besides, I was gone a long time and needed to see my people.

"I tol' her goodbye and what do you think — she started to cry. She bust out cryin' right there in that cathouse! It near made me decide to chuck my job and stay. I believe that gal really loved me. I tol' her first chance I get in a month or two maybe I'd be back and see her. She made me promise I wouldn' forget her and she made me promise I would come back.

"I tell you I was really tore up inside when I got on that train. I couldn' get Marie out of my mind, not for a minute. I ain't ashamed to say I wanted to cry for that woman. Had I been a gal I'da busted clear open."

The sergeant cleared his throat several times, then blew his nose. The embers of the fire had burnt themselves into powderey white ashes. Most of the other fires had been covered over with dirt. The soldiers who had sat around those fires were now curled in sleep. The faint drone of their snores could be heard.

"Took me near three months to make it back to New Orleans." As he spoke the sergeant stared into the ashes of the fire. "Had I waited to be sent back to that city, I'd be waitin' yet. So I just picked up and went.

"Train was held up. The track came loose and it took half a day to fix. I near went out of my skin so I jus' got down and dug on the roadbed with the nigger gang that was tryin' to put the tracks back straight. The half a day felt as long as half a month.

"Soon as I got to New Orleans I found me a place to take a bath. I'd taken a good one the day before, but all the sweatin' made me smell like a billy goat. You might-a thought I was fixin' to go to church the way I went at it.

"It was jus' about noon straight up when I got to her place. My heart was goin' in such a way I had to work at catchin' my breath. Darned if I didn' feel skittish as a crappin' jackass. There was that fat smilin' lady of the house jus' the way I'd left her. It felt like I'd been there the day before.

"The moment I saw that fat woman's face I knew somethin' mus' be wrong. She stopped smilin' like she was sorry to see me. Before, she would show me all kinds of friendship with plenty of honey's and dearie's. Now, she jus' looked at me in a certain way and her face wasn' smilin', not a bit. I asked could I see Marie and she made as if she didn' understand what I was sayin'. Then she turned away to talk to another gentleman that came in.

"I felt mighty peculiar; somethin' was wrong, but I didn' know exactly what.

"The other gentleman went upstairs with one a the gals. I noticed that the girl was new. Then the woman turned to me and said right out that Marie was gone. I

thought maybe she was funnin' so I started to grin hopin'
she would grin, too. But she never smiled. 'Where's she
at,' I asked. The woman pulled a jug of whiskey up on
the counter and poured me a full glass.

"'Marie, she ain't here no more. She gone and she
gone for good.' The woman looked more serious than I
ever remember seein' her. Fact was, she looked like she
was sorry for me. 'They sold her to a place in Charleston,
but I 'spect they gonna send her clear up to Washington.
They needs lots of girls in Washington the way that city
is growin'.'

"For a minute I didn' understand what she meant. I
couldn' connect up what she meant when she said Marie
had been sold. But I began to suspicion what she meant.
'She looked to be a white woman,' I said in half as a
question. 'She was fair as me.'

"'Marie was colored, least her mother was counted
as colored. Her mother was a quarter nigger. Made
Marie octoroon.' The fat lady was really trying to tell me
as . . . as nice as she could. Fact was I found out the fat
woman was colored herself. She had bought herself from
her master, least that's what they said.

"Try as I would I couldn' get that woman to tell me
no more. Couldn' get the name of the man who sold her.
He had rented that gal to the whorehouse — taking part
of her earnings as his share. I guess he needed the cash so
he sold her outright to someone else.

"I offered the fat woman five silver dollars if she
would tell me where at I could find Marie. Maybe she
didn' know, but I 'spect she was afraid of somethin'
'cause she wouldn' say a word. Not even for five silver
dollars!

"I was sick inside my guts so bad I wanted to lie
down some place and just die. I couldn' believe I wasn'
gonna see that gal again. I turned to go. Then the fat
lady asked me did I want to go upstairs with her for a lit-

tle while. She said it would make me feel better and she wouldn' charge me nothin' at all. I wanted to punch that fat whore right in her big belly, but I thought better of it. She asked again did I wanna go upstairs to relieve myself. You know somethin', that fat whore was sorry for me. She was bein' as nice as she knew and here I was ready to punch her.

"I stayed in that woman's room all night. Every chance she got she came in and sat with me. That woman treated me nice as anybody ever did 'ceptin' Marie herself. I was pretty young and she said things to give me comfort. To tell the truth my heart was about to break. I was still little more 'an a boy and my heart was ready to break right in half.

"I went back to Mobile the next day. It was a long, sad trip. I jus' tried not to think at all, kept lookin' out the window countin' the farm houses as we passed."

There was a break in the sergeant's story. Thinking he was finished, Luke began to stir around. But Josh and Davy knew that the sergeant was not quite through.

"Every dime I got holt of, I saved," the sergeant went on. Luke settled down. "I did extra work and had me hundred and fifty dollars piled up before you knew it. I tol' the man I worked for I needed three hundred dollars and offered to give him a note binding me to pay it back. With the money I saved and borrowed and with another seventy from sellin' a fine young trotter I had raised and prided in, I took off for Charleston.

"Soon as I had heard that Marie was sold I swore me an oath to find that gal and pay whatever it would take to get her free. I didn' know where at she was at in Charleston, but I was gonna find that gal with the Lord's help."

The Sergeant suddenly kicked at the ground with the heel of his boot. He was completely sober now. He was angry at himself for shooting his mouth off. Embarrassed that the three boys now knew he had loved a whore. Not only a whore, but a Negro slave.

"Sarge," Davy said softly, "buyin' and sellin' people is against the will of God." These were strong words for a soldier of the Confederate Army. Josh and Luke murmured their agreement.

All the embarrassment left the sergeant as suddenly as it came. Davy understood; so did the other two. The bitterness the sergeant felt against slavers had gnawed at him for years.

He had searched out all the houses of prostitution to be found in Charleston. He had visited each and then returned in case by some chance he had missed her. At first the madams were suspicious; when they finally understood what he was after, they were sympathetic. Better than anyone else they understood and they tried to help. If this young man found his Marie, might not each of them be found some day?

From Charleston he traveled to Washington. In Washington, it was the same. No one knew of Marie Paulos. A month later, with a hundred dollars left in his pocket, he returned to Mobile.

"I never connected up with that Cuban girl again," the sergeant said in a hoarse voice. Then he stood up and stretched, emitting an exaggerated yawn. Davy and Josh spontaneously thrust out their hands. The sergeant hesitated a moment then shook each, hard. Luke, overcome by the hour, lay on the ground with his head cradled in his arms — asleep.

After the sergeant left, Davy and Josh lingered a few minutes.

"That Sergeant Graves sure is different 'an I thought," said Josh.

Davy grunted his agreement.

"What you think happened to her?"

Davy had been about to ask the same question. "No

tellin'; maybe she was bought by a man and kept in his house for his own use. Jus' no tellin' at all."

"That sergeant sure is different," Josh repeated. Then he said, forming each word deliberately, "That sergeant is a man."

"He sure is," said Davy. "Best man in the regiment; in the whole damn army, maybe."

# VII

As days and weeks passed, the regiment began to be knitted into a tougher fabric. The new men absorbed their training and some of the battle wisdom of the veterans rubbed off on them. The older soldiers who had been drained by repeated exposure to death regained their strength in the comparative ease and safety of the camp. And during all this time Lieutenant Rawlins concentrated most of his thinking — day and night — on the Armenian. A man black as any Negro had been the cause of his shame. He would find a way to revenge himself.

Lieutenant Rawlins started his campaign carefully. He said nothing negative or insulting to George, nor did he take particular notice of the man when he saw him in ranks. He wanted to make sure that at a later date no one could say that George had been the target of harassment or that the lieutenant "had it in" for the man. The campaign started with the non-commissioned officers, the sergeants and corporals. One by one, with no appearance of deliberation, the lieutenant would sound them out about the Armenian. After speaking about some matter of general interest, the officer, as if in an afterthought, would ask how the new man, the Armenian, was doing. After listening to the report of the sergeant or corporal, the lieutenant would force his face into a troubled look and thank the man for his intelligence as if it fit into some larger pattern that was of vital importance.

In this way the various non-commissioned officers were made to believe that some sort of problem surrounded the new recruit. Even Sergeant Graves began to find himself concerned about the Armenian. He kept alert for any unusual behavior and gradually grew suspicious of actions that ordinarily would have been considered entirely normal.

Sergeant Graves' reaction was much the same as that of the other non-coms, although at first he exercised a greater degree of restraint in forming a judgment. George, in turn, felt himself being watched and studied. This served to stiffen his responses, to make him more cautious, and thus his behavior became less and less like that of the other men.

The lieutenant let his poison spread slowly. He concealed the excitement he felt as he saw pieces of his jigsaw puzzle lock into place. The non-commissioned officers began to report that the dark-skinned man appeared to be acting in a peculiar fashion. That he was ill at ease. Several stated he seemed to be hiding something.

Carefully dropping a word here and an idea there, trusting that they would share with one another, the lieutenant let the sergeants and the corporals know that he had reason to suspect the Armenian of being something other than what he appeared to be. The word spy or agent of the Union forces was not used. These the non-commissioned officers supplied themselves.

Many of the men, who under ordinary circumstances might have been expected to show George at least some degree of friendship, deliberately avoided him. They sensed something was the matter.

The actions of the rank and file soldiers were misinterpreted by George as avoidance because of his color and his foreign ways. As a reaction to this rejection, he made no effort to socialize and even began to rebuff Davy, Josh and Luke when they made overtures of friendship. When asked to join them in cooking or sitting around the fire after dark, he found some excuse to remain in his tent, where he, unlike any of the other soldiers, lived alone.

Some sixteen days after George had been sworn in, Lieutenant Rawlins spoke to Captain Carter about rumors that were circulating through the camp regarding the dark-skinned man. The lieutenant understated his story, declaring that it all might be nothing but ill-founded gossip. The captain had no reason to suspect his lieutenant. In fact, he was impressed by the man's cautious report. For a full day Captain Carter thought about what the lieutenant had said, then decided to speak to the colonel. If any of the suspicions proved to be true, a dangerous situation existed.

While Captain Carter was still thinking about the intelligence he had received, Lieutenant Rawlins occupied himself in the creation of certain documents. These were prepared by the use of a powerful magnifying glass, a sharp needle substituting for a pen, ink that became colorless when dry and tiny squares of white vellum.

Had any man seen the young officer remove a shirt and a pair of trousers that were hanging on the guy ropes of George's tent where they were placed to dry, he might have wondered about this, but no one saw. It was late at night and within an hour both items were returned.

Few of the soldiers were surprised at the events that then took place.

On the eighteenth day of George's enlistment a provost marshal in command of six armed guards arrested George. He was handcuffed, his feet secured with heavy chains while four of the guards stood close, their guns at the ready. In minutes every soldier in camp, except those who lay ill with the fever, were gathered around the prisoner shouting questions which were not answered.

The provost marshal, with the two remaining guards, piled every single item belonging to George into a cart. Then they pulled up the stakes of the tent itself, collapsed the canvas and piled it on top of the rest.

A babble of voices that contained such words as "traitor," "spy," "Judas," washed over George who was numb with fear. From the suddenness of it all he thought he was about to be lynched. When he realized he was not to be killed but only under arrest, the fear lessened. It was all a mistake, one that might be expected during war time. When the investigation was completed, he would be returned to duty with an apology.

The relief he felt caused George to smile. His smile had the unexpected effect of angering the close-crowding men.

"Look at him smile. He's glad."

"The black bastard's gloating. He needs to have that smile wiped off his face."

Each outburst pushed the assembled men closer to action. The provost marshal pulled his revolver and ordered the men back, threatening to put a ball in the brain of the first one that laid hands on his prisoner.

Captain Carter's arrival, together with Lieutenant Rawlins, Sergeant Graves and several of the other sergeants had a quieting effect on the men.

Sergeant Graves, speaking in the name of the captain, ordered all to disperse on pain of arrest for mutiny. The possibility of joining the shackled prisoner in shackles of their own had its effect. The men dispersed. Then George, followed by the cart piled high with his belongings, was marched as quickly as the chains on his legs would allow to the courthouse. There he was secured in a windowless room while two armed soldiers stood guard outside.

Under the direct supervision of the regimental colonel, the provost marshal began a careful examination of George's belongings as soon as the man had been secured. A pair of pants produced a small strip of paper from a tight seam in the waist. A shirt was found to be hiding a like piece of paper stitched into the collar. The two pieces of paper were passed gently over the flame of a candle. In moments tiny lines of writing appeared covering each slip completely.

Within several hours of his arrest, all the camp knew George was a spy. The slips of paper contained information about the number of men and rifles in the regiment, also lists of the various types of artillery and the location of other units in and around Montgomery. Before nightfall, the commanding general himself of the division was questioning the prisoner.

A court-martial was ordered for the following morning. The general consensus among the officers was that George was an officer in the Union army. As the night drew on, his status rose notch by notch until it was firmly believed that he held no lesser rank than that of a lieutenant colonel.

George was questioned by batteries of officers until the very moment of his trial. Now that it was believed he was a high-ranking Union officer, he was treated with careful respect. All his needs were promptly attended to. After a group of questioners had finished their interrogation, although gaining no more information than they had at first, each interrogator would solemnly shake the prisoner's hand.

The belief that George was a high-ranking officer also affected the attitude of the rank and file. The hatred they felt toward one who was thought to be a traitorous fellow soldier was replaced by feelings of respect mingled

with awe. An exciting occurance, the kind they would re-
count to their folks at home, was taking place right in
their midst. A hero from the enemy camp now faced
death, a fate he had gladly risked for his country. Some of
the glamour of the situation rubbed off on Davy, Josh
and Luke. For hadn't they been friends of George? And
they were treated with marks of deference by the other
men. They in turn continued to feel toward George
friendship now heightened by admiration deserved by a
brave enemy officer.

Of all the men in the regiment only Lieutenant
Rawlins knew the truth. Afraid that by some word or
gesture or facial expression he might betray a portion of
the information locked inside him, he took to his bed
with a sudden case of the chills.

# VIII

All the soldiers stationed in and around the city of Montgomery were lined up to witness the execution. Several thousand interested civilians also gathered. They carried boxes to stand on, spy glasses and ample supplies of food and drink.

A gallows had been set up in the center of a large field usually devoted to quarter-mile horse races. The regiment of which the prisoner had been a member was lined up on one side. The two other regiments of the division took their places so that the three together formed the three sides of an enormous square. The fourth side was made up of miscellaneous military companies as well as individual soldiers home on leave. Civilians, except for a few dignitaries who were provided with seats near the foot of the gibbet, were forced to find their places outside the square.

George was led onto the field guarded by no less than eighty armed soldiers. Twenty marched abreast well in front, twenty to the rear, while three ranks of ten each marched directly in front of the condemned man, one rank of ten directly behind. The soldiers with their prisoner, his hands securely bound behind him, slowly marched entirely around the square.

From the moment the court pronounced his doom, George had known that any further protests would be useless. The rapidity of it all, the evidence, the trial, the sentence, numbed his brain. But until the very last minute he did not actually comprehend that he was to be executed. Even as he mounted the wooden steps that led to the waiting noose, he expected them to say it had all been a joke, a test of his manhood.

There was absolute silence as George, assisted by the provost marshal, mounted the scaffold. The provost marshal then read the sentence ordered by the court-martial. Every high-ranking officer in the district stood at rigid attention at the foot of the gallows, in respect for a brother officer who had braved death for his country.

Davy, Josh, and Luke watched with a mixture of sorrow and horror.

All the soldiers stood stiff and silent as the man dropped through the trap door. The snap of his neck-breaking echoed like a pistol shot.

The civilians, aware of the serious attitude of the thousands of soldiers in their full dress uniforms, did not whoop and yell as was their wont during ordinary executions.

Lieutenant Rawlins, still confined to his sickbed, received detailed descriptions of the event. To each report, the officer responded with headshakes and throat sounds that indicated sympathy for the death of a brave man. And as he listened to these reports he thought about Davy, who at the proper time, in the proper place, long after he ceased to suspect the officer of harboring any animosity, would find what manner of man he had crossed that day on the parade grounds.

# IX

With an abruptness that confused many of the recruits, the regiment was ordered to make itself ready for
transport to the North. Jackson's Corps, seriously
depleted, needed immediate replacements. The training
that many of the men still lacked would have to be completed in the ranks or in the field.

"Thought we'd gain a chanct to go home 'fore they sent
us up north," muttered Luke after Sergeant Graves relayed
the order.

Josh shrugged.

"Be nice to show my uniform to my folks 'fore I get
kilt."

Josh started to nod but then just shrugged again.

The train, which was really three trains, attached
together each with its own engine, was loaded with
regimental supplies. The soldiers filled all the remaining
spaces. Some bunked on open flat cars alongside artillery
pieces. Some were camped on the roofs. These were
warned to be alert when approaching tunnels, lest they
be decapitated by the overhang.

The dozen passenger cars were commandeered by
officers and higher ranking noncommissioned officers. A
few privileged civilians with special passes shared the

passenger cars with the officers.

Corporals and the old-timers among the privates had secured all the choice locations inside the freight cars. They lay on top of piles of canvas, on bags of flour, on bundles of uniforms. They avoided cargo that might shift during the jerky starts and stops; they avoided metal objects that would provide no warmth; they avoided the open flat cars, the roofs, and most particularly the freight cars devoted to transporting horses. Horses were known to become dangerous as they grew upset during long train rides. More than one green soldier, counting himself lucky as he lay on a bed of hay, had had his brains kicked out by a panicky horse.

In their scramble to secure a place on board, men from different companies, and even from different battalions, mixed with one another, and during this scramble Josh and Luke were separated from Davy. Had they all remained together, Davy's past train traveling experience might have helped them find a safe secure berth. As it was, they joined a dozen others sprawled between four twelve-pounders lashed to the bed of a wooden flatcar.

Although the night already was edged with a slight chill, the men camped on the flat car hoped they would not suffer too much discomfort. Anyway, as compensation for any physical distress, they would be able to see all the sights on both sides of the track.

Montgomery, with its thousands of lights, slipped by as the train began to gather speed. The old freight cars clashed at their couplings. Wooden cars that had traveled tens of thousands of miles groaned and creaked, protesting yet another long journey. Those soldiers quartered in the open quickly felt the sting of chilled night air. Like frozen fingers, the air searched its way into the soldiers' clothing. Before Montgomery had faded to the rear, the soldiers riding outside were chattering from the cold.

Josh and Luke attempted to relieve their discomfort. A rubber ground cloth was spread on the vibrating wooden platform, and on this they placed a blanket. Both boys then stretched out on the blanket pressed tightly together, using another blanket as a cover, with the second ground cloth on top. Their haversacks proved adequate as makeshift pillows.

Two by two, the soldiers always paired off in cold or wet weather, for this was the only means of survival when they were not in camp. The outcast soldier, the one who could not count a single man his friend, was doomed just as surely as if by the judgment of a court-martial. Sooner or later pneumonia or some other fatal disease would end both his military career and his life.

As the glow of the city faded in the distance the stars took on an added brilliance. A quarter moon provided enough light so that the boys could see the countryside. The train was traveling east. Broad fields and pasture land stretched away on both sides of the right-of-way. Josh propped his head on his hand. The vibration of steel wheels against steel tracks made his body buzz. Every few moments sparks flew from the clashing wheels. The metal grinding against metal produced an odor sharp, yet pleasant. An occasional farmhouse, silhouetted for a moment by moon rays, appeared then disappeared into the darkness. Not a crack of light could be seen coming from these houses. Inside, Josh thought, they're all asleep. The farmer and his woman lying safe, side by side.

Josh thought of his home, of his life with his mother and father. His father, with his own hands, had built the house before Josh was born. Josh's bed stood beneath a window that looked out to the mountains of the northeast. It was more a box than a bed, and was filled with pine needles covered by a hand-stitched quilt. Although there were no springs or webbing, the bed was warm and safe and the sun drenched it with light every morning.

His father knew his duty as a man — ceaselessly working so his wife and children would never whimper from hunger. Josh's mother kept the home comfortable and happy. She cooked and baked, doing her best with the simple foodstuffs available in that part of the country.

As he lay beneath the cold night sky, moving north toward a place that might contain a plot of earth marked as his grave, Josh was filled with loneliness. He missed his parents.

While Josh watched the farmhouses slipping by, Luke hovered between sleep and wakefulness. Warm savory thoughts — almost dreams — formed in his mind. He would suffer a small, moderately painful but rapidly healed wound — in a leg like Davy's, but not quite as ghastly. Pa will look at me and see I'm limpin'. He'll be proud, I'll bet. Ever' place I go they'll say, "Look, there's Luke. He's been away fightin'. Minnie ball caught him in the leg." Walkin' down the church aisle, I'll try not to limp, but a little will show no matter what. They'll whisper, "See how brave he is, poor boy." Luke smiled as he slipped into sleep.

The piercing rays of the sun forced their way through closed lids. Josh and Luke sat up yawning; sharp prickles of pain ran down their backs while their faces burned from the wind brushing they had received during the night. Other men on the flatcar were sitting up also. Most rubbed their gummy eyes with their fists. Some tried to free nostrils stuffed with dust, shirttails providing a ready handkerchief.

All the men were hungry and as they rubbed and yawned the last remnants of sleep away, they grew famished. Biscuits softened with stale water were a miserable substitute for the hot breakfasts enjoyed while in camp. Grime from the smoking engines caked their lips, giving the hardtack a gritty taste as they chewed.

Until the sharp twinges of hunger were dulled a little, few of the soldiers paid attention to the passing scenery. They now were traveling through the heartland of Georgia. On both sides stretching away to the horizon were cotton fields. Although ripe, most of the cotton was still unpicked. The war had seriously disrupted normal plantation life. Now and then a group of bandannaed slaves came into view. Hooked to belts around their middles were open sacks into which their quick fingers stuffed fluffy white balls of cotton. These teams of slaves included not only full grown men and women, but half-grown children as well, each trailing a separate sack. Little children no more than five or six years old walked beside their mothers, picking into their bags. Even toddlers scarcely old enough to walk would pull a piece of cotton now and then.

As the train moved along at a steady twenty-five miles per hour, it passed clusters of huts that served as quarters for the field hands. These were one room affairs, unpainted and windowless, with holes cut in the roofs for chimneys. From time to time, an open door revealed filthy crowded interiors. Often an old slave, withered and twisted, lay on a pile of straw while naked babies crawled about on the dirt floor.

Usually the slaves looked up from their work as the troop train passed. They would shield their eyes, then lower their heads back to the task. A few of the littlest waved but never the adults.

For three days the train slowly moved northward. In the midst of desolate stretches of timberland, it would stop and wait, sometimes for hours.

For those three days, the soldiers scarcely had a chance to wash and never had a chance to prepare a hot meal for themselves. Almost a quarter of the men sickened. Several became so ill they were left behind in some strange town to get well, or die. A number — it was said at least two dozen — failed to reboard the train after its numerous stops and were marked down as deserters.

By the time the troop train reached the outskirts of Richmond, it stank of urine and vomit.

All the men, not excluding the officers, were streaked with grime. They ached and were troubled with constipation — those not afflicted with dysentery. Crawling grey-backs that had found their way on board had been evenly distributed so that scarcely a man was not scratching and slapping. Later, when the men grew more accustomed to the insects, they would stop slapping and instead crush the vigorous little beasts between their fingernails — or when the opportunity presented itself, flip them into the fire.

Any gloss that had adhered to the regiment in Montgomery was completely rubbed off by the time Richmond was sighted. The train shifted from track to track, backing up, then lurching forward, finally coming to a complete halt just north of the capitol city. Tempers were short; a half dozen fights had to be broken up within five minutes after disembarking from the train.

Josh and Luke had not seen Davy during the entire trip, and were not to see him for another day. He had found a tolerably comfortable berth in a freight car loaded with canvas tents. And, lest someone take over this prized place, he remained in the car the entire time. But this inactivity had affected his wounded leg and he walked with a limp. Yet he was in better shape than his friends. Three days on a flat car had left them depressed, sore, and suffering from bad colds. More than anything they yearned for a hot soak, but instead were pressed into unloading supplies without so much as a minute to freshen themselves.

When the supplies were unloaded, the company officers mustered the soldiers into ranks. Then, laden down with knapsack, haversack, blanket roll, and musket, the men marched into the gathering darkness. They were seven hundred miles away from home; hungry, weary, lousy, chilled and depressed, and, as if to make matters completely unbearable, it began to rain — turning the roadway into sticky, sucking mud, soaking clothing down to the skin and stimulating the lice to increase their activity.

Dozens fell out of ranks. Gasping with exhaustion they lay for a few minutes in the ooze, then forced themselves to their feet and joined whatever group of soldiers happened to be passing. No one wanted to be left; they were strangers in a strange state.

The regiment camped fifteen miles northwest of Richmond together with element of Jackson's Corps that had been ordered there to join the main force that was regrouping after recent losses — battle losses and losses due to disease and desertion. No significant concentrations of Yankee troops were reported within twenty miles, but scattered Union bands roamed the area and raided sporadically. The regrouping area itself was judged comparatively safe, but as close as a half a mile from camp, a soldier might come up against one of these bands and then be found the following day shot or bayonetted through the middle. Neither side showed any mercy to stragglers or foragers.

For the first time since leaving Montgomery, a hot meal was available. It was only a soup thickened with hardtack biscuits, yet it was welcome. In spite of their hunger, most of the men ate slowly. Exhaustion caused many to nod between bites. The rain continued, but the men were past caring. All were soaked. After eating, in many cases before finishing the food, the soldiers slept. A number, overwhelmed by exhaustion, lay in the mud, with rain beating down on their unprotected bodies. Some managed to prepare makeshift shelters with their rubber ground sheets. Others bundled together, a ground sheet below, one on top to deflect the rain, and the two blankets for covering. Josh and Luke were among this group. In this way they found sufficient warmth, although it was a wet sticky warmth; a paradise for the lice, but fatigue anesthetized their skin against the bites.

They lay with the rain falling steadily on their exposed faces, yet slept deeply, their breaths wheezing in their cold-infected chests. They slept until four in the morning when they were roused by tugs and curses of the sergeant of the guard. Through some mysterious process, they had been chosen to stand a two-hour watch. Only the sergeant's rank protected him from a physical attack. Both boys reacted the same way — hatred followed by depression and a feeling of helplessness.

A canteen cup of strong hot coffee each was their only compensation before being marched to the edge of the woods bordering the staging area where they were joined by a third man, an experienced veteran. The three soldiers whom they were relieving waited trembling with cold, beating their sides with their arms. After an exchange of passwords, they slogged away toward camp, heads bowed, without a backward glance.

The rain drizzled down steadily. Josh, Luke, and the third man huddled together, their shoulders hunched, trying to keep the water from trickling down their backs.

As soon as the third man found out that his companions were inexperienced soldiers, he pulled a stern face. "You patrol the left," he said pointing at Josh, "you the right," he nodded to Luke. "I'll stand guard back a ways in the field. Do either of you see somethin', give a shout and I'll come runnin'." Both boys nodded dully. "Pace off five hundred long steps, then turn 'round and come back," the veteran continued. "I'll keep close watch all the while. Don' forget, holler out do you have trouble."

The boys started their patrols, but before they got five paces, the other man called out, "Do they find you sleeping on guard duty, they put you 'gainst a wall and shoot you." Then he warned that Yankee patrols had been seen in the district.

The third soldier watched the two greenies until they were lost in the thick, wet night, then he walked back into the field, found himself a slightly raised patch of ground relatively free of water, lay down, wrapped himself in his ground cloth and fell asleep, trusting the boys to wake him if needed, his well-trained ears to rouse him if the sergeant of the guard should come along.

It was too dark for Luke to see anything except the shadow of the woods which served as a boundary line for his patrol. He stumbled every few steps into puddles of mud and knocked his shins from time to time against boulders. He allowed himself very little thinking. It was just a matter of staying awake and keeping moving for two hours. The closest he came to mental activity was a rote count of his steps 'til he reached five hundred. Then he turned around and counted himself back. Within minutes Luke was more animal than human — a plodding ox. He had solved the problem of guard duty.

Josh, unlike Luke, was unable to adjust to the condition he found himself in. Outraged at being required to stand watch in his present state of exhaustion, as he trudged through the dripping blackness counting, he warmed himself with a hatred of army life.

He reached five hundred and stopped. Except for the woods to his right, he could see nothing, and the woods were no more than shadows. Rubbing his eyes he yawned and stretched. Suddenly he realized that if he got turned around, he might pace off another five hundred steps and instead of returning to the starting point be a thousand steps away. The thought panicked him. Then he remembered the woods had been to his right as he walked. He would need to keep them to his left as he returned — or were they to his left and now they must be to his right? He wasn't sure. He thought the woods belonged on the left. He looked to the left to see the woods but there was nothing. He turned around, but turned too far. Still nothing. Josh bit his lip and squeezed his musket to steady himself. "I was to patrol to the left, therefore the woods would be to my right. Now they will be to my left as I return." He carefully turned around almost a full circle until the woods were on his left. A rush of relief brought hot tears to his eyes.

He started the patrol back. The brief confusion had left him uneasy. Then for the first time he considered the possibility of enemy troops nearby.

Exhausted to the point of nausea, feverish from his cold, Josh was a candidate for panic. "What if there are Yanks hiding in the woods," he thought. This gave rise to: "There probably are Yanks hiding in the woods . . ." Then, "The woods are full of Yanks . . . Yankee snipers are taking sight along their rifles barrels . . . I am going to be killed by a Yankee sniper . . .!"

Josh started running crouched low, afraid to call out lest his voice invite gunfire. He had never been this frightened. He fell face down into a puddle as his feet hit against a stump. Picking himself up, he tried to run, but his mud-slicked shoes kicked out from under him and he fell again. This time he just lay in the cold mud gasping, waiting for the bullet that would tear into his brain. He lay full length, every muscle tensed. A minute passed. All he could hear was the splash of raindrops.

Josh slowly got to his feet, his face burning. As he continued the patrol, he angrily muttered to himself, "Scared rabbit. What you gonna do when you smell gunpowder — shit you' pants?"

# X

The next day, Captain Carter's company was organized into a unit once again. A few soldiers didn't straggle in until lunchtime. Several, fallen sick, had been left behind. Three were missing and presumed deserters. The rest, bedraggled and exhausted, lined up for morning roll call. All the men were damp and lousy, their shoes and trousers caked with gluey mud. But then the sun broke through the clouds, lifting their spirits a little. Enough to make the difference between misery and hope. But for Josh and Luke the thing that served to raise their spirits — far more than the return of sunshine — was their reunion with Davy. There he was standing in ranks with all the rest. His face showed traces of pain from his wounded leg, but he smiled and nodded as his two friends walked up.

After roll call, Davy led the two boys to a choice campsite he had secured. It was next to a stone fence and by the use of several "surplus" boards a shelter, not completely dry but tolerable, had been constructed.

The sun now blazing in a cloudless sky, the three boys looked forward to a period of drying out and settling in. But before a decent hot meal could be prepared orders came down from regimental headquarters to be prepared to march within an hour.

Two by two the men streamed out of the staging area onto a dirt road in a long line, until the line extended more than three miles. On both sides of the road rose full-grown evergreen trees. The road was springy to the step. A half day earlier it had been a gummy mess, but the sun had done its work and the ground was almost dry. In another day the same road would answer each footfall with a cloud of choking dust. But that afternoon was perfect for a march and the colonel of the regiment was determined to take full advantage of this.

It was to be a forced march, whose goal was a union with Jackson's main forces massed thirty-five miles to the northwest. This was scheduled for the following morning — the orders from the commanding general were explicit.

Seen from a distance a regiment on the march looks like a giant machine whose parts seem to be in perfect synchronization. But as one approaches, the illusion fades and the differences among individual men become more and more apparent. Some soldiers can march carrying loaded packs, haversacks, and muskets and still have reserves of energy after twelve or fourteen hours. Some soldiers, after two or three hours, find each additional step a torture that sends streaks of fire racing up their legs into the muscles of their backs and shoulders — yet, somehow, they force their feet forward, thinking only of the next step. Some soldiers, after a certain time, are so exhausted their legs turn hot, then cold, as a numbness creeps up from their ankles until all at once they stumble and fall from the ranks. (Most of this group of soldiers, if threatened by an angry officer, will rise gasping and groaning, then stumble on for a mile, fall and again rise.) But some soldiers, when they fall, will not rise even if the muzzle of a musket is pointed at their middle. Of this group, an occasional fallen man will prove the sincerity of his exhaustion by expiring without a word, stretched out full length by the side of the road.

No matter how seasoned the troops, a thirty-five mile forced march has its casualties. But when the march involves a regiment two-thirds of which are green soldiers, the casualties can reach a significant number. But in a sense, the march serves to winnow the troops — better than any board of medical examiners, it eliminates those physically unfit to fight.

As Josh and Luke's regiment swallowed up mile after mile, the selective process began to be put into operation. By midnight many of the men found each additional step almost unbearable. The officers and noncoms kept repeating in hoarse voices, "Close up now — close up — don't lag." By one a.m., eight men had permanently fallen and in spite of threats accompanied by kicks and prods of musket nozzles, they remained where they were, gasping helplessly. More than a score of others also had fallen, but these, after a threat or a kick, wearily rose to their feet and slipped back into ranks. Another hour saw a dozen more fall permanently from the ranks. Then every two or three minutes another man fell.

Josh and Luke were about equal in endurance. Set to work in a field behind a plow, either could have handled the task from morning until night. Five minutes in every hour would be devoted to drinking water, resting, or attending to bodily functions, but the work would get done. Both had spent scores of days in the woods chopping trees, trimming them, then finally splitting them with a wedge. But marching was different. The friends, as was true for many others in the ranks, were relatively unused to wearing shoes. They had never spent more than a few hours at a time walking — most of what had to be done around their homes lay close to hand. Before the night was half over both were suffering.

With each step, Josh clenched his teeth. Soon sparks

of pain jumped from his jaw into the muscles of his neck and from there up into his head. His feet felt as if every square inch had been rubbed with a coarse blacksmith's file. The place where his leg joined his hip became a clot of pain, that expanded and contracted as his weight shifted from foot to foot.

Luke's feet were almost numb. He could scarcely feel the ground as he lurched along. Deep inside his back, tugging down into his hips, was an agonizing pressure that at times grew so severe it rose up into his throat bringing with it a sharp vomit taste.

But Luke and Josh belonged to the group of soldiers that somehow would stay on their feet, would use every last bit of energy and will rather than fall from ranks in disgrace. If asked, the generals would have declared that soldiers like Luke and Josh were the sinews of the army.

The road the regiment traveled was left unmistakably marked after the first ten miles. The green soldiers, feeling the weight of their knapsacks sawing into their shoulders, began to toss away item after item heretofore believed to be absolute necessities. Bayonets, daggers, bowie knives and heavy navy revolvers by the tens of dozens littered the roadway. Extra blankets, books, then tins of dry biscuits fell in an ever increasing shower. Ten sutlers could have stocked their wagons with the items the regiment discarded before the night was over.

At three in the morning the troops halted for a fifteen minute break. Fully thirty men were unable to rise when, "On your feet," was passed up and down the line. These thirty, added to those who had fallen earlier, made a total of seventy. The officers, who were not required to carry knapsacks and muskets, stood over the prostrate men cussing and kicking them, threatening to have them shot as deserters. Then seeing it was hopeless, after imparting the last kick, each fallen man was given an order to rejoin the regiment under pain of death after he had rested.

During the fifteen minutes rest, Josh and Luke tended to their feet as carefully as if they were charges of gunpowder. The painful shoes were removed and thrust into their knapsacks. (The rest of the trip, smooth or rocky, would be without these unnatural coverings.) Each then rubbed his feet slowly with the tips of his fingers. Not a toe was neglected. Blisters had formed, broken, re-formed, and broken again during the course of the night. These were treated with a paste made of urine and earth. There was still much that needed to be done to their feet when they were forced to fall back into ranks.

If asked how they had been able to make it through the rest of the night, neither Josh nor Luke could have answered. Somehow they remained upright — stumbling, groaning, cursing — somehow they, along with hundreds of others who had suffered just as much, forced themselves on.

During the night, two hundred soldiers fell from the regiment. For the next twenty-four hours men would trickle into camp one by one, shame-faced, exaggerating their limps as justifications. More than forty would never return. Most of these melted back into the South — deserters. A few lay sick in hospitals. Three had died as they lay by the side of the road.

Davy too had suffered severely during the night. His leg felt like a thick burning stump. Forced marches were not new to him, but his wound reduced him to the level of the green soldiers. His only advantage over Luke or Josh was his knowledge of what the human body was capable of enduring.

As the sun rose, casting its light on the ranks of tortured men, the regiment reached its goal. But no one, except a handful of armed guards patroling the perimeter of the bivouac, was awake to greet them.

Using their knapsacks as pillows, too exhausted to

untie their blankets, the men sprawled on the ground. So great was the fatigue of most that stones, burrs, or pine cones under their backs were ignored. More than one soldier flopped down on tangible evidence that cows had recently inhabited the field, not caring. Had sparks from a campfire fallen on their hands and faces, many would have been unable to shift away, so complete was their exhaustion.

Josh, Luke, and Davy huddled close together. Josh and Luke were asleep before their bodies stopped twitching. But Davy kept sinking into sleep, then rising to the surface of consciousness as fiery darts of pain shot up from his wounded leg into his back. In an effort to relieve the suffering, he threw his leg over the reclining form of Luke, thus providing it with a soft underbase. Luke did not so much as break the even rhythm of his breathing. Slowly the fire in the wound was banked and Davy gradually slipped into total unconsciousness.

# XI

The sun had almost reached its meridian when the three friends were wakened by sounds of laughter. Grouped around them were a dozen bearded men showing the hollow-eyed look of soldiers that had been in the field for months. The men were laughing and pointing at the three new arrivals who had moved closer and closer for comfort and warmth in their sleep until they lay tangled, arms entwined, heads on backs or rumps, legs laced together — so close it was difficult to tell where one man began and the other left off.

The bearded soldiers, coming in from patrol, were tired and nervous and the sight of three men all twisted together provided relief from their tension. They laughed loudly, slapping each other on the back — coughing and wheezing until spittle sprinkled their matted beards. Davy opened his eyes, then Josh, then Luke. Open-eyed, they lay without moving for several moments despite the laughter. Then realizing their peculiar position, they simultaneously attempted to extricate themselves, each one's efforts frustrating the attempts of the other two so that for a short time they lay squirming and thrashing on the ground.

Luke was the first to get to his feet. The laughter

and mocking faces of the bearded men caused a sudden surge of anger. He rushed at one of the bearded men whose laughter had a peculiarly offensive sucking sound, doubling his fists. But before he reached the man Luke was stopped by a severe kick in the seat of his pants by one of the other men. Enraged he whirled around only to receive another vicious kick. Davy and Josh stumbled to their feet, but were scarcely upright when they too were kicked, lost their balance and fell sprawling. Davy, white with rage, reached inside his blouse and pulled out a hunting knife. He leapt to his feet evading another kick and lunged at one of his tormenters. The man crouched, ducking the thrust while he drew his own knife — a foot-long pig sticker.

By now the fight had attracted a group of spectators, most of whom belonged to the same regiment as the three friends. Outnumbered, the bearded men stopped their laughing and stood aside as Davy and the man with the pig sticker started circling each other.

The soldier spectators formed a ring around the two knife fighters leaving a space twenty feet in diameter where both men kept circling, each man's eyes never turning away from the other's knife. The crowd grew silent.

For a full minute Davy and the other soldier kept circling, each waiting for an advantage. Then like a cougar, Davy leaped in slashing; a streak of red, thin as a pencil mark, appeared on the other soldier extending from shoulder to wrist. The pencil mark broadened until the arm was soaked with blood which began to drip from his fingers. Davy, about to leap in again, held back as his opponent's knife dropped from the bloody hand. The wounded man stood for a moment, gray-faced, then collapsed into the arms of his friends.

The warning: "Officer of the guards!" caused the crowd to disperse. The bearded men, carrying their wounded member, disappeared into the masses of men that choked the camp. Within moments only Josh, Luke and Davy were left.

Davy rolled up his sleeve. To the surprise of Josh and Luke, along the back of his left forearm was a thick line of blood. With a sigh, he started to sew up the gash in his arm as if it were a tear in his trousers. Although handicapped by the use of only one hand, he made a neat job of it, cutting the dangling ends of thread with his knife, the reappearance of which caused both of his friends to shudder.

"You a damn fool, Luke," Davy finally said. "If you don' hol' you'self down ever' time someone starts razzin' you — you gonna be dead 'fore Christmas. An maybe me along with you.

"Don' know what come over me myself," said Davy dropping his voice, "makin' me act so ornery. I'd a killed him if I could." He shook his head. "Take thirty - forty stitches to stitch up that soldier's arm. Don' know what came over me," he said again.

Jackson's Corps, like a sick giant, was resting after the bloody weeks at Harper's Ferry and Sharpsburg. Hundreds would never again answer the roll call; these lay buried in hastily dug trenches or unburied in the woods. Hundreds were no longer fit for duty because of wounds. Hundreds were missing — captured or deserters. And more than a thousand were no longer fit for duty because of disease. The Corps lay panting and weak, nursing itself.

As might be expected of a sick giant, the Corps had spread its waste and pollution all over the countryside where it rested. The grass was scorched brown by ten thousand campfires or pawed up by the hundreds of tethered horses and mules. Piles of refuse lay everywhere: tins that had once held salt beef, underclothing too soiled and moldy to salvage, cartridge cases, bones of beef, sheep and pigs, thousands of bandages stained with brownish blood, coffee grounds, broken crockery and more, much more. And everywhere trenches had been dug in a helter-skelter fashion for the sanitary needs of thirty thousand men.

When it rained, the camp became a thick soup of gluey mud. When it dried, the air filled with clouds of dust. More than anything else, the camp stank. It stank from thousands of unwashed bodies, from sweating, from shitting horses and mules, from sanitary trenches baked by the sun, from countless discarded, pus-filled, bloody bandages, from rotting garbage. When the wind blew in the direction of the neighboring hamlet, the residents covered their noses with vinegar-soaked cloths, or stuffed sweet smelling herbs into their nostrils.

Even the combined forces of Europe commanded by the Duke of Wellington at Waterloo would have scarcely shown a greater variety of uniforms than that displayed by the men of Jackson's Corps. Each soldier felt that his uniform was his own affair, and if the man had been in battle, no officer was prepared to encroach on that feeling. Items from fallen Unionists were in evidence everywhere. Union caps, blouses, and trousers were mixed in a hap-hazard fashion with regulation issue of butternut grey. A pair of fine Yankee brogans was a prize much in demand. Hats so differed one from the other, scarcely two men wore identical head coverings. The common wide slouch hat was dressed up with multicolored bands, was wound with red bandanas or had other ornaments attached. Floppy red caps of the Charleston Zouaves added gashes of color here and there, while men from the Virginia cavalry sported carefully-shaped felts wound with tassels of gold.

Camp discipline was a spotty thing depending for the most part on the attitudes of each group of officers.

Laissez-faire was more the rule than the exception. This often gave rise to situations where the men tested the limits of exactly how much they could get away with. From time to time a breaking point would be reached and the offending soldier would find himself subjected to summary punishment. Scarcely a regiment did not sport its wooden horse — a raised rail held by two saw horses placed on upright packing cases. A misbehaving soldier was forced to sit on the cross rail for half a day or more, his hands and feet tied so that all his energy was required to maintain his balance. More serious offenders were lashed to a cannon wheel and whipped with a leather belt until the shriek of the sufferer could be heard a half a mile away. Occasionally a deserter, who had left before or during a battle, was returned by the provost marshal. When this happened, a court martial was quickly convened. The man stood trial in the evening and was led out into the portion of the camp reserved for burials the following morning. He was forced to dig his own grave, then in the presence of his regiment was shot.

Josh, Luke, Davy and the rest of their regiment were quartered alongside a unit of Virginians. Due to the close proximity to their homes, these soldiers were, for the most part, well supplied with those extra luxuries that make the difference between comfort and austerity. The enlisted men regularly had fresh baskets of food and extra changes of clothing; they often were visited by relatives or friends not excluding ladies — wives, mothers, and sweethearts. Many of the officers, in addition to the advantages enjoyed by their men, were waited on and cared for by slaves supplied by their plantations and homes. The presence of a body slave in camp was a mark of status among the Virginia gentlemen. They would have sooner given away their blooded horses than denied themselves the attention of their black bondsmen. Black men fetching or carrying could be seen moving about the area occupied by the Virginians all during the day and well into the night. They cooked and served their masters and their masters' friends. They washed, sewed, and altered uniforms. They built the fires, prepared the beds, and when required, deloused their masters.

The second day in camp, after the three friends had settled themselves and their belongings, they began to explore the area. During the course of this exploration they reached the adjoining section occupied by a unit from Northern Virginia. Their experience with the bearded South Carolinians fresh in their minds, they kept behind the remnants of an old slate fence that served as a line of demarcation between their own unit and the other — some thirty yards from where a group of junior officers were quartered together.

A number of Negro men, their tight faces revealing the pressure they were under, could be seen hurrying about. When an officer called out, the slave who was his particular property stiffened, calling back without a moment's delay, "Yes sir, master, I'm comin'." The other slaves, when they heard one of their number being paged, showed their tension by a twitch of the face or a jerk of the shoulders. And the young officers felt obliged to keep their slaves "hopping," demanding instant response from the black men, punishing with curses, kicks or punches any who lagged.

"Sons of bitches!" Davy growled as he saw an officer kick the buttocks of a white-haired Negro who had accidently spilled some sudsy water from a bucket he was carrying, while another officer watched, laughing.

"Virginians!" snarled Luke.

"Like to kick they ass one time!" Josh hissed. "That old nigger mus' be near seventy; no call doin' him like that." Josh had half a mind to say something to the officers.

"Hey!" Davy stood up and started in the direction

of the officers. "You can kick a nigger's ass, an ol' darky. Think you can kick a white man you' own age?" Davy approached the two Virginians who were seated on the ground.

"I'm bettin' I can lick the both a you together," said Davy hoarsely. "I'm bettin' that spite of you' braid, this man's gonna whip both you' ass, do you stand up right now."

The two officers sat without moving, their mouths hanging half open. Davy stood directly over them. He waited for several seconds, then spat so that droplets spattered on their boots. "Virginians!" he hissed. "Virginians!" he repeated, the corners of his mouth turned down.

As he walked away, Davy swaggered — every movement an invitation to fight. The officers remained seated. Later they would wonder why they hadn't accepted the challenge. They were healthy and strong. Later they would wonder why at the very least they didn't have that Alabama private arrested for threatening an officer. But as Davy walked away, using each step as a means of provoking them, they were frightened — there was something about the man . . . .

The entire drama lasted no more than two minutes. Josh and Luke had remained seated watching, bug-eyed with fascination. For the second time within two days, Davy had shown an unsuspected side of his personality.

# XII

The boys had been settled in camp for ten days and they, together with thirty thousand others, were busy making preparations to fight the immediate enemy — winter. It was generally known that this camp was not intended to be permanent. But as time passed and the troops remained in the one location, more and more men concluded that there would be no more fighting until spring and thus the Corps might remain where it was for months.

Josh, Luke, and Davy, by the use of low earthen walls, a number of boards, and two tent halves, constructed a permanent shelter. For heat Davy dug a pit in front of the tent, then extended the pit, which was two feet wide by a foot deep, through the shelter to the rear. He laid a three- by four-foot metal slab, which he had somehow acquired, over the extension trench, then covered the still exposed section with pieces of wood. When a fire was built outside the tent, a portion of the heat moved into the trench, heating the metal which in turn kept the shelter warm and comfortable.

All around, others, by use of their inventiveness, were overcoming the increasingly inclement weather. The camp began to take on the appearance of a permanent settlement. From time to time, word came down that the Corps would face the Yanks again before too many days had passed. But, in spite of these warnings, the soldiers continued their domestic operations, gaining each day a greater degree of comfort. And there was little effort made to offer the men any additional training except for the regular half day drill, which was handled in a leisurely fashion.

Because of the general atmosphere of ease and the attendant feeling of remoteness of the war, Josh and Luke were surprised and confused when their company suddenly received orders to prepare to march, combat ready, within an hour. Davy was less surprised; his year in service had conditioned him to expect anything, but he too was confused, having concluded that there would be no more fighting 'til the spring thaw.

Within an hour the company was ready, each man having been issued five days marching rations and forty cartridges. Captain Carter, pale-faced and constantly blinking, walked up and down the lines of men growling his annoyance at the disarray and poor condition of their uniforms. His own was scarcely any cleaner or better cared for, but that didn't seem to matter. As he inspected the soldiers he told a number that upon their return to camp they would face punishment for their sloppy appearance. But since no record was made of these threats, the men, who had developed an understanding of their captain, were not too worried. Lieutenant Rawlins, immaculate, walked directly behind the captain, his face impassive. But every once in a while, when his superior would noisily eject a ripe glob of tobacco juice, a flicker of contempt narrowed the younger officer's eyes.

Captain Carter's company had been selected to do patrol duty of a probing nature. The Yanks were known to be camped some thirty miles away. But General Jackson had reason to suspect that units of enemy soldiers had moved in closer, perhaps in preparation for a major battle. Captain Carter's company, and several other companies from other regiments, were to patrol as far north as they might safely go, searching for the outer fringes of the Federals. If the Federals were planning a major move, an increase of perimeter activity would be a warning of their intentions.

The men were lined up and waiting. Captain Carter, now grown tired of inspecting them, stood to one side, stamping his feet and chewing on a fresh chaw of tobacco. Some of the men also started to stamp their feet. But all instantly froze into regulation rigidity as they caught sight of General Jackson approaching on horseback. He was accompanied by several other general officers and two civilians. With scarcely a glance at the lined-up men, Jackson said a few words to Captain Carter, who then executed a salute more military than anything he had done for the past month. Jackson raised his hand in a half salute which instead of ending on his brow, found its way to his armpit which he then scratched. The two civilians remained behind with the company as the Commander-in-Chief wheeled about and rode away still scratching.

The frost-nipped earth was firm under the soldiers' feet as they marched out of the camp, accompanied by the two civilians. Gusts of wind penetrated their cotton uniforms. With each gust the soldiers tensed and drew their shoulders together. Within a short time all were shivering.

The company bivouacked when it grew too dark to see the road. They had traveled nine miles and were now in an area not under the immediate control of either army. Without being told, the men had lowered their voices and finally ceased to speak as they moved further and further away from the camp. No one, not even the civilian guides, who were from the district, knew if the area concealed Yankee snipers who at any moment might reveal themselves through well-aimed, whistling minnie balls. Within minutes of bivouacking, every man not on guard duty was rolled in his blanket or doubled up with another, seeking relief from the falling temperature and rising wind.

The force of the wind increased during the night so that those soldiers who had managed to fall asleep were awakened by the cutting cold. That night, the late autumn ended and winter set in.

By afternoon of the next day, the company had traveled twenty-five miles in a northerly direction. All, officers included, suffered from the bitter weather. A number of men were coughing.

The two civilians conferred with Captain Carter. From that point on, they informed him, there was a good chance of contacting enemy patrols. Rather than continue on the dirt roads, it was suggested that the company be divided into smaller units, these to take the paths that wound through the woodlands where possibility of ambush would be less.

The company was divided into four, Lieutenant Rawlins commanding the platoon to which Davy, Josh and Luke were assigned. The platoon had traveled less than half a mile when Lieutenant Rawlins, without any display of emotion, ordered Davy, Josh, Luke and a fourth soldier, Jaimey Calcott, a lanky, sandy-haired farm boy, to scout ahead. Davy stared into the officer's face as he received the order. He looked into the man's eyes, then slowly nodded. "You ain't forgot nothin', have you?" he said evenly.

Lieutenant Rawlins stared back at Davy, his mouth forming a tiny smile. "You a most experienced soldier, Davy — no one I trust better'n you. Those three," he gestured toward Josh, Luke and Jaimey, "they s'posed to be first rate marksmen. It's no more than my duty to send my best men ahead to guard the rest of us."

Lieutenant Rawlins spoke softly. He paused, then in a much louder voice said, "You ain't afraid — if you afraid . . ." Davy turned his back to the officer, and with a stiff beckon to the three other men, walked into the woods.

"That bastard has it in for me and there's no mistakin'," said Davy bitterly as soon as they were in the woods. He sighed, then continued, "But someone got to be scoutin' ahead, might as well be us." He turned and faced his three companions. "They's no doubt there's Yanks near — I can almost smell 'em. They don' suspect we is about — I hope — so they may be lying aroun', takin' it easy. Long as we look sharp and be ready, ain't nothin' gonna happen to us!

"You follow me," Davy nodded at Jaimey. "Then comes Luke, then Josh. Jaimey, you and Josh mostly watch the right hand side. Luke an me will take care a the left. Don' go shootin' 'less you see a Yank for sure. Poppin' off at shadows'll bring every Fed for ten miles aroun'." Davy hesitated for several moments. "No use foolin' you, we jus' might run into a mess — this is Yankee country and no tellin' what might come off. So be careful! Keep you' heads, and you can get out of most any jam. Lose you' heads . . ." Davy broke off with a shrug.

The woods covered the base and sloping sides of a large hill that joined another hill. In the valley, separating the two hills, the woods grew dense. The four toiled up the first hill following a path expanded from a deer run, then descended into the valley. The ground here was heavily carpeted with a layer of dead leaves, moss, twigs and most of all pine needles. Although only midafternoon, the forest was deeply shadowed, in places almost dark.

Davy strained all his senses to pick up the slightest indication of danger. His eyes examined the path ahead looking for any disturbance of the ground cover. His ears

were tuned to sounds in the forest — man-made rustle or
creak. And he kept sniffing the air.

They made their way through the woods for more
than an hour. For the first thirty minutes the three green
soldiers experienced a mixture of fear and exhilaration.
But then as nothing happened they settled into the
routine of the patrol.

Rounding a hugh boulder their path was suddenly
blocked by a fallen tree. Davy stopped and held up his
hand. The other three froze, their fear returning in a
rush. Davy looked about carefully. He waited for nearly a
half a minute, then slowly made his way around the fallen tree — the others remaining where they were. Once
on the other side, Davy again searched the forest then
cautiously beckoned his companions to come on.

When Jaimey reached the tree, he hesitated. Suddenly he raised his musket. At that same moment a shot
rang out from the underbrush. The musket dropped from
Jaimey's hand as his face showed a look of surprise. He
stood swaying for a moment then toppled over backwards, the look of surprise still on his face.

Without being told, Josh and Luke plunged into the
woods opposite from where the shot was fired. They lay
close together, their muskets ready, listening.

Both boys shuddered as a second shot cracked out.
They pressed closer to the earth waiting for the next shot,
but instead heard a voice softly call, "Hey, Luke — Josh.
It's me, Davy, I'm comin' round the fallen tree — hey,
you hear me — don' shoot!"

Josh answered in a hoarse whisper, "Davy?"
"Yeh!"

"What's you' las' name?" Josh had his musket
trained on the fallen tree.

"Medlock!"

"Come out real slow and easy."

Davy moved carefully around the end of the broken
tree.

"Here — over here!" Josh whispered.

Davy, half crouched, bounded across the path and in a moment was lying next to them gasping. Both boys squeezed their friend's arms and he squeezed back, trying to catch his breath.

"What about the other shot?" whispered Luke.

Davy, still trying to catch his breath, pointed at himself.

"You get him?" Luke asked.

Davy nodded. Then said hoarsely, between gulps of air, "Didn' know what hit him — right through his throat."

"He dead?" Josh pointed to where Jaimey was lying.

Davy squeezed his eyes shut for several moments. "Yes, he's dead," he finally muttered. "And he won't be the only one if we ain't careful. No tellin' if they is others aroun'. The noise might bring some scouts."

A minute went by as Davy reloaded his musket. It took him twice as long as usual — every movement carefully made so as not to cause a bush or a branch to tremble. The ramrod was scarcely withdrawn when Davy's body suddenly went rigid. The other two boys instantly stiffened, not daring to breathe. There was a faint sound.

Davy slowly turned, guiding his musket until it was trained on the path in the direction from which they had come. Josh and Luke did the same, squinting down their musket barrels, forefingers curled stiffly around the triggers. The sound grew louder. Tiny beads of perspiration formed on Luke's forehead, Josh kept licking his lips. Davy's face had drained of color.

All at once, Davy's body sagged and he lowered his gun. He wiped his forehead with a sleeve and swallowed. Then he turned to the others. "They our men — damn near forgot 'bout 'em," he said in a choked voice. Moments later Lieutenant Rawlins followed by the rest of the platoon came into view.

"Yoo! Lieutenant — it's Davy!" Davy warned in a modulated voice before stepping into view. At that moment the lieutenant noticed the shape sprawled on its back in front of the fallen tree. The lieutenant held up his hand, haltin the platoon.

His face a dead pale, the officer tried to avoid looking at the corpse, but his eyes kept darting back to the still, grey form.

"What the hell happened?" he asked Davy, trying to hold his voice steady.

"Sniper," Davy said roughly.

The lieutenant hunched his head down between his shoulders and bowed. "Where's he at?" he whispered.

Davy grinned. "No need to worry, he ain't gonna shoot you — you safe — I kilt him. He's lyin' in the bushes with a hole big as this in his throat." Dave formed a circle with this forefinger and thumb. "You didn' think I'd leave no sniper around to put a ball a lead into my lieutenant, did you?" The lieutenant avoided Davy's eyes.

After almost a minute of hesitation Lieutenant Rawlins declared, "We gonna go a mile further 'fore circling around back. You three stay here," he nodded at Davy, Josh and Luke, "and keep an eye out for any Yankees that might be trying to flank us. When we come back some of the men will help you carry . . ." The officer pointed at the dead man.

The platoon arched around the fallen man, each soldier staring at the corpse as he passed. Several who had been friendly with Jaimey Calcott had tears in their eyes.

After the platoon had disappeared into the forest, Davy climbed onto the fallen tree and stretched himself out on this belly, his chin propped in one hand, his musket gripped in the other, his eyes scanning the pathway. Luke crouched on the side of the tree away from the corpse where he was partially concealed by some bushes, while Josh squatted near the exposed tree roots less than six feet from the stiffening man. Just before the sounds of the platoon were completely lost, Davy muttered, "He forgot to send some scouts ahead again. Every Fed for ten miles gonna know they comin' . . . That Rawlins, he don' know shit!"

Josh stared at the lifeless man lying almost close enough to touch. There seemed to be a sweetish odor coming from the corpse, an odor that remained Josh of a dead dog he had once seen lying alongside the road, blue-green flies buzzing around its head. Every few seconds Josh looked around, examining the trees and squinting down the path, but be could not keep his eyes away from Jaimey's body. The bullet had caught the young soldier just above the belt; his shirt had two buttons missing and gaped out so that Josh could see the place where the bullet had entered. It was a hole scarcely larger than his thumbnail. It didn't seem big enough or important enough to kill a man.

Josh stared into the dead man's wide-open eyes. They were clear, not glazed over or milky; an uneasy feeling that the eyes were staring back at him took hold of him.

"You crazy as a jaybird," Josh muttered to himself. "That Jaimey was dead 'fore he hit the groun'." But the feeling that the eyes were staring would not go away. Josh forced his eyes back to the brownish wound, then to the shapeless grey trousers, then to the square brogans covered with caked mud. The soles of the shoes had several holes, one of which had worn completely through exposing the dead man's stocking.

Josh decided to focus his eyes on that hole. Not to think about the open eyes. He stared and let his mind wander: Wonder what it feels like to be dead? The thought brought a flicker of a grin. When you dead you don' know nothin' — I sure do think some mighty peculiar thoughts. He glanced away checking the path, then shifted his eyes back to Jaimey's square-toed shoes. Suddenly the right foot jerked. Josh gasped. His heart began to race. The other leg quivered. Josh, almost in a panic, quickly glanced at the corpse's face. The eyes still stared. He was about to jump up when he remembered how it was with other dead creatures. As they stiffen there can be a movement of their limbs that is almost lifelike.

"You sure are actin' like some kind of a fool," he murmured. "That dead man is the safest thing in this forest. Better be lookin' out for some live Yank than worryin' 'bout a dead Reb."

Josh turned away from the corpse and carefully searched the forest for any signs of unnatural movement for more than a minute. But like a crow scenting a dead fawn, he was drawn back to the body. Only one of its hands was visible and it lay on a tuft of dead grass. The hand was covered with dirt, each finger had a half moon of black packed under a ragged split nail. The hand, in spite of its grime, was delicately formed. "More like a woman's than a man's," thought Josh. "How that Jaimey ever worked on a farm with those hands . . ." He turned away from the dead man and looked at his own hands. They were thick, the palms covered with a shiny layer of raised callouses. His fingers were almost all the same length, giving his hands a shovel appearance. They were so different from those of the dead man — wide and well muscled. He liked his hands. In a whisper Josh told the dead man, "Your's look too much like a girl's."

All thoughts of the dead man went out of Josh's mind as Davy softly called out, "You hear anything?" He pointed in the direction the platoon had marched.

Josh cupped his ears and held his breath. Tiny sounds, like the splash of pebbles dropping into a pond, drifted through the trees. Josh nodded. "Sounds purty far away. What you think it is?'

Davy concentrated for several moments. "Fightin'!" Davy took firm hold of his musket and swung down to the ground. "They is fightin' Yanks sure as shoot. Come on — be careful, sounds like all hell is bustin' loose."

Davy led the way toward the sounds which rapidly grew louder. He increased his speed and the boys followed, gasping for breath as they jogged up the forested slope of the other hill. Suddenly Davy veered off to the left of the fighting and pushed through the trees, closely followed by Josh and Luke until they were at the edge of an open field. Davy dropped down to his hands and knees and worked his way until only a few branches separated him from the open space. Josh and Luke edged up to him and they all peered out and saw a score of blue-uniformed soldiers flat on their bellies behind rocks and stumps, firing down at Lieutenant Rawlins' platoon trapped in a rocky basin below.

Davy whispered to both boys to choose a Yank and not to miss then to reload and fire again as fast as possible. The boys nodded. Then he whispered, "Soon's we start to shoot, yell and scream loud as you can — get 'em all stirred around, give the others a chance to attack."

All three took aim and fired. Their targets stationary and scarcely twenty yards away, they could not miss. Shrieking, they reloaded. Before the Yankees could make sense of what was happening, three more were dead. The remaining Federal soldiers, believing that they were flanked by a large force, jumped up in terror and started shooting wildly. On their feet they provided easy targets for the platoon down below. In less than a minute, six more Yanks had fallen and the remaining eight, at a signal from their officer, ran into the woods. The Confederate soldiers fired after the escaping Yanks but didn't pursue them into the woods.

Eleven members of the platoon had been killed, five wounded. The rest were drenched with sweat; most trembled. Davy walked up to the lieutenant and gave an exaggerated salute. Then he said, loud enough for all to hear, "You should-a sent out scouts — would a saved you bein' trapped by some Yanks less'en half you' strength."

The lieutenant looked at Davy, his lips a bluish white, his eyes blinking rapidly. Davy stared full in the lieutenants's face then said in a drawling voice, "You don't know any more about bein' an officer 'an my ass. Whyn't you go back to you' plantation and leave the fightin' to them as has the brains for it."

Lieutenant Rawlins sucked in his breath. "Do you know who you're talkin' to?" he hissed. "Trash like you wouldn't be allowed at my back door. Any more from you and I'll fix you with a court martial or worse!"

Davy took a step closer to the officer. "What you mean 'or worse'?"

Lieutenant Rawlins backed away a fraction. "Keep up the way you are and you'll be charged with mutiny." There was a slight break in the officer's voice.

Davy took another step toward the officer. Less than a foot separated the two men. "You no good rich son-a-bitch," he said carefully enunciating each word. "Ain't a single man in this platoon couldn' be a better officer 'an you. You the poorest excuse for a man I ever seen." Davy spat on the ground, droplets splashing the officer's boots. Then he turned and walked away.

Lieutenant Rawlins had a powerful urge to pull out his navy revolver and shoot the back of Davy's head off, but his hand was frozen by the angry looks of his men. So great was his desire to kill the young private, a pressure formed inside his head causing his ears to ring. It took the officer several minutes before he could trust himself to speak. In the interval, the rest of the men gathered up the dead and prepared stretchers for the wounded.

Without being told Davy, accompanied by Josh and Luke, assumed the position of advance scouts and started leading the platoon back through the woods.

# XIII

The company rendezvoused where it had camped the night before. The other three platoons were already there as Lieutenant Rawlins' men staggered out of the woods, weighted down by five wounded and thirteen corpses — on their way back they had picked up Jaimey Calcott and the dead Union soldier.

Captain Carter and Sergeant Graves, seeing something was wrong, started across the field to meet the platoon. As the captain and sergeant came up, the exhausted men lowered their stiffening burdens to the ground and flopped down beside them.

Captain Carter, tobacco juice dribbling down his chin, grew incoherent as he attempted to question Lieutenant Rawlins. Sergeant Graves then stepped in and, in a controlled voice, asked the lieutenant what had happened. As the young officer, taking care not to put himself into a bad light, started to give an account, his men began to grumble and offer comments of their own.

Sergeant Graves turned and threatened to knock down the next man who interrupted. As he turned back to the lieutenant, he caught Davy's eyes for a fraction of a second. In that fraction there was an exchange of understanding. The lieutenant then continued uninterrupted until he had completed his account.

"Them Feds that got away," Captain Carter said in a choked voice, "they gonna bring trouble. Once they report a bunch of Rebs is messin' aroun' you can bet the Yanks scout out the whole country. And it won't be no company a soldiers lookin' either. Be a brigade, maybe more. They be thinkin' Jackson's army nearby."

Sergeant Graves nodded. "Sure as sin those Feds gonna bring trouble," he said slowly. "Too bad you didn't go after the rest of the blue jackets." He looked directly at the lieutenant.

"We better get the hell out a here," said Captain Carter in a whisper. His hands began to shake and he thrust them in his pockets. "We better put as many miles as we can between us and them Union boys or they gonna cut us up into cat's meat."

The captain glanced at the thirteen bodies lying on the ground and turned to Sergeant Graves, "Better leave them where they is," he murmured. "They can't feel nothin' anymore. They be buried by the Yanks just as good as by us." He hesitated a moment. "Better leave the wounded, too. They gonna slow us up and they be taken care of by the Yanks. 'Sides, the Yanks got better medicines."

Sergeant Graves looked the captain in the eyes, "We gonna take the wounded with us, Captain sir," he said in a flat voice. "An' we best bury them others 'fore we go." The sergeant's features were impassive. Captain Carter looked frightened.

"If you think it's better, Ben," he said softly, dropping his eyes. "Let's be quick about it. We all be dead do they catch us here."

After the dead were buried, the company started back carrying the groaning wounded on rough-made litters. From time to time, imagining they heard distant sounds of Federal cavalry, they speeded up despite their fatigue. No rest breaks were given or asked for. Only toward morning, when they were close to their own main camp, did the men fall out for a short rest.

Just as the sprawling camp began to stir awake, the company marched in. Men came to their shelter doors and stared. Seeing the stretchers and the condition of the marching men, they started cheering. Soon hundreds lined the pathway shouting greetings, asking questions, pounding the exhausted men on their backs.

Josh and Luke, numb with fatigue as they reached their campsite, slipped into their shelter and crawled into their bunks. But neither boy was able to relax enough to sleep. Too much had happened. They twisted and stretched trying to find a comfortable position. Then for a time they talked about Davy, who had gone off with Sergeant Graves.

"That Davy sure is a heller," said Luke in a hoarse voice. "Did he have a reason he'd stand up to General Jackson hisself."

"Rawlins like to bust a gut when Davy tol' him all them things," Josh added. "B'lieve do that Rawlins push him too far, Davy take him out in the field and whip his ass . . ." A fit of coughing interrupted him.

"You know somethin', Josh?" Luke said in a serious voice. "I didn' feel scared hardly at all, not even when we started shootin' at the Yanks. That Davy made me feel nothin' bad could happen to me no matter what. Sure proud he's our friend."

There was a pause. "It don' seem real," said Josh. "It's like it didn' really happen. Like I had a dream and I be about ready to wake up. Yesterday we was in the woods — first Jaimey killed, then we killin'. Now we is here, safe like a chick under a hen. It's so peculiar can't hardly b'lieve it's all true."

"Does seem strange at that," Luke added. "Now that you say it, it's more like some made-up story than anything true."

# XIV

Although rumors of a major move kept circulating through the camp, the soldiers continued to improve the comfort and security of their dwellings until most of them took on the appearance of permanent habitations. It was a rare soldier who did not devote an hour or two each day to some construction task related to his army home.

Ten days after the return to Captain Carter's company, the rumors of a major move metamorphosed into a written order that was read at morning assembly to all units in that vast camp. The army was to march north. Every soldier to ready himself for combat. Rations sufficient for five days and forty rounds of ammunition to be issued to each man. Excess baggage to remain behind.

Both excitement and anger surged through the camp. The prospect of fighting excited those soldiers who had not yet seen any. But many combat veterans were angry at the thought of leaving their snug shelters for the rigors of a winter's bivouac. Sensing the mood of the veteran soldiers, the colonels and generals directed their efforts toward whipping up a fever of patriotism.

Josh, Luke, and Davy got in formation with the rest of the regiment to hear the words of their colonel. Then as the men marched to the parade area, drummers who for months had been idle, rolled martial rhythms.

The colonel stood on a jerry-built platform constructed of powder kegs and slats ripped off provision crates. Having taken the precaution of insulating himself internally with a double ration of rum, he was less discomforted by the oozing rain and unpredictable wind than were his men.

"Soldiers of the Confederacy!" The colonel spoke in a measured, slightly thickened voice. "Soldiers of the Confederacy!" he repeated, adjusting his volume to the opposing wind. "Those of you who have never tested your manhood will soon be given a chance to show what you are made of." The colonel, frowning, searched the faces of his men for any signs of inattention, then continued. "Those of you who still have the taste of your mother's milk on your lips can prepare to taste the flavor of Yankee gunpowder!" He took a deep breath. "If there are any cowards among you, now is the time to step forward — later will be too late! If there are any yellow-livered, stinking bomb proofs in my regiment, let them make themselves known so that all brave, decent men can know who they are and can tell their wives and mothers the names of those too chicken-hearted to defend the state of their birth. If any man standing here has shit in his veins instead of blood, I beg such man to quickly raise his hand so that his brave comrades can properly dispose of him as they would any piece of foul filth. If there is any man among you who would prefer to remain behind warm and safe while his fellow soldiers fight for the honor of the South, I implore that man to answer 'here' so that, without a moment's delay, all can clean their muddy boots on his rotten carcass. I hear no sounds, I see no hands; a pity." The colonel paused and pulled his gleaming sword from its sheath, then pointed the weapon at his audience. "A pity!" he repeated. "For I would rather chase any stinking coward into the woods or throw him into the latrine right now than meet up with such a one on the field of battle." The colonel slashed the air several times, almost losing his balance.

"No need my telling what will happen to any man of this regiment who turns tail to the enemy," the colonel snarled — each breath he took forced the rum further into his brain. "Soldiers of the Confederacy, tomorrow, or the next day, or the day after that, or the next week . . ." The colonel began to have trouble forming his words. "Well, anyhow — soon you will be looking down the barrels of Federal muskets! On that day everyone will know which of you are men that love your mothers and sisters and wives and aunts and so forth and so on, and which of you are willing to have big, black, buck niggers defile the flower of Southern womanhood. The Yankees like nothing better than to have your grandmother or old maiden aunt defiled by a big, hairy nigger. Is that what you want!"

Then the colonel, drawing himself up to his full height shouted, "God is on the side of the South!" and staggered off the platform, assisted by his staff officers, who quickly led him away.

The march north, which took a full day, was slowed by frequent stops. This was no scouting company or regiment on a forced march, it was an entire army on the move. In addition to the thousands of soldiers stretched out for miles in several parallel columns, there were hundreds of pieces of artillery dragged by horses or mules, scores of heavy wagons piled high with provisions and ammunition, and there were the many miscellaneous vehicles that accompany an army on the march — ambulances, sutlers' wagons, water carts. Jackson's corps and the armies of Lee were converging on the little Virginia town of Fredericksburg where they would meet the massed might of the Union Army under the command of Ambrose Burnside.

The wind bored its way through the Confederate cotton uniforms, taking a pincer grip on the soldiers' flesh. The slow march on ice-covered earth tortured the men's feet — some green city boys lost toes from frostbite. There was no time for building fires. Cold water, hard tack and uncooked bacon of the poorest quality was the entire bill of fare.

Evening found the army exhausted, numb with cold and in depressed spirits. A few units immediately took up defensive positions; the rest kept moving, scarcely more than a mile an hour. This movement was more shuffle than march with the soldiers' hands thrust deep into their pockets, their heads bowed, their eyes focused on the ground.

Shortly after ten, the boys' regiment reached its assigned position. Josh, Luke, and Davy, more by lucky chance than any effort of their own, staggered into a sunken area of the field protected from the wind by a thickly overgrown hedge. This location provided an additional advantage which none of the three friends anticipated. Curled together under blankets and ponchos in this depression, they were hidden from view so the sergeant of the guard, as he rousted men from their sleep to stand guard, passed them by.

There was no need for a bugler the morning of December 13, 1862; the hacking cough of Federal artillery did the job far more effectively.

The first cannonade brought Josh halfway to his feet, his eyes frantically searching the darkness. The second propelled Luke and Davy out of their body-warmed burrow into the frosty pre-dawn air. All around, hundreds of soldiers were babbling, glancing in every direction, trying to orient themselves. As they began to make sense out of the booming noise, as the frosty air cleared away the last wisps of sleep, the soldiers started stamping their feet and licking their whitish lips with tongues thickened and sour from their night's sleep. Clouds of steam rose from the men's mouths and noses — many cupped their hands to catch the vapor for whatever warmth it might provide to frost-nipped ears and cheeks.

Toward the west the black sky was still thick with stars. The east showed a sliver of light tightly clinging to the tops of the trees. To the north the Federal guns again and again exposed their reddened throats for an instant, before their sharp growls could be heard.

It was still too dark to allow for any camp fires — Union gunners found Rebel campfires irresistible. Thus there was no relief from the cold. Then a little later, as the sun rose, the men were mustered into battle formation. Whatever warmth they would find would come from physical exertion.

The regiment set off in a northwesterly direction. As they marched the men saw preparations for battle everywhere. Officers digging spurs into blood-flecked horses' flanks dashing up and down the road. Parrott guns bouncing wildly, racing toward the front. Knots of soldiers under tense-faced commanders, marching and countermarching. And the sound of the cannonading grew louder.

As the regiment descended into the valley of the Rappahannock River the clear air of the highland was left behind and the men were quickly swallowed up in a chill, wet fog so dense they were unable to see the ground under their feet. The fog, as if it were so much cotton, dulled the noise of combat yet at the same time confused the sound, making it difficult to determine its location. After a few hundred yards in the fog the soldiers' sense of direction grew twisted. Many found their ability to maintain balance affected as their legs were swallowed up in the curling vapor. Men tripped, fell, staggered to their feet, then fell again before they had traveled another dozen yards. It grew evident the regiment could not continue on without the chance of a serious mishap. So an order was passed along to squat down and wait until it was again possible to proceed.

Josh, Luke, and Davy had lost track of one another in the fog. Each sat alone as the regiment waited. Davy quickly settled down, making good use of the unexpected rest — after a few minutes with no lessening of the fog, he stretched out and in moments was asleep.

Luke also made good use of the fog. His bowels had been nagging for relief, but he had been inhibited by the constant presence of others. After attending to his needs, content, he passed the time easily, slipping in and out of a light sleep.

Josh sat, his arms hugging his legs, his chin resting on the knees. He felt uneasy. Ever since the pre-dawn roar of Federal guns had jolted him awake, he had been on edge. Now an awareness that this might be his last day alive caused him to shudder.

"You been through danger already," he whispered to himself. "Out there in the woods with them Yankee soldiers you never felt all funny inside like now." Then came the thought: Before night you gonna be lyin' dead on the ground. They're gonna put you in a hole and you never will see you' Ma or Pa again. Tears filled his eyes.

"You sure a silly calf," he murmured to himself. "Probably won't even get close to fightin'." For a moment he felt relieved. But then the heaviness, now mixed with loneliness, settled on him again. And again his eyes filled with tears.

As the sun rose higher and higher, its rays began to burn off the layers of fog that lay trapped in the river valley. One minute the men were still shrouded under a sheet of thick vapor; the next the vapor dissolved into wisps which then quickly vanished, revealing the gleaming sun above and the sparkling roofs and windows of the town below.

Almost the first person Josh saw as the fog lifted was Davy. The space that separated the two could have been easily covered in two or three moments, yet for more than an hour Josh had felt as if miles separated him from any other human being. He wanted to run over to Davy and pound him on the back. But afraid this might not be understood, he contented himself with a wave, which Davy returned.

From the vantage point of the regiment, the war below looked as if it were being fought by toy soldiers with tin cannons. Because the air was now crystal clear, objects ordinarily too distant for human eyesight came into focus. It all appeared to be a game being played on the outskirts of a little dollhouse town.

The men of the regiment were strangely affected by the toy-like quality of the battle. Everything seemed so unreal. How could anyone be hurt?

The regiment moved forward, marching easily and in good order. For a time the smoking guns and exploding shells seemed to remain at a constant distance, in spite of their advance. A gentle breeze blowing in the direction of the battle wafted sounds away, leaving only a muffled rumble.

A shift of wind carried the din of two great armies tearing at each other directly to the regiment. This sudden burst of noise jolted the regiment out of its near hypnotic state. Moments later the men found themselves in the vortex of swirling masses of soldiers. Hums of minnie balls, howls of cannon balls and shrieks of wounded horses choked the air.

Under frantic orders from officers waving revolvers or sabers, the regiment spread out and prepared to charge. The captains and lieutenants screamed commands in voices that bordered on panic, and any soldier who showed even the slightest hesitation was struck full force on his back with the flat of a saber or the heavy muzzle of a revolver.

Sergeant Graves, having assumed command of Captain Carter's company, bellowed orders which were affirmed by continuous nods of the pasty-faced captain. Apparently oblivious to the whine of the minnie balls, the sergeant strode up and down followed by the captain, who seemed to have shrunk, so deeply was his head sunk between his shoulders. Tobacco juice covered the captain's lips and chin and had dribbled down onto his neck. He followed the sergeant so closely it appeared as if he believed the bulk of the man would provide protection from any stray bullets.

At a barked order from the sergeant, the soldiers fired their muskets in the general direction of the enemy. At a second order, they extracted a new paper cartridge from their pockets, bit off an edge to expose the powder, placed the cartridge in the breech of the gun, and rammed a bullet and a scrap of wadding down the barrel. At a third order they fired again. Standing there amidst the growing noise and confusion, the soldiers welcomed the absorption loading and firing demanded. Few had any idea whether they were shooting too high or too low. It was enough to be shooting. The systematic firing continued until some of the green soldiers, growing frantic, rammed more than one round in at a time. Not noticing that their gun misfired, they rammed in another round, and then another. A few soldiers in their growing anxiety forgot to remove the ramrod and shot it out or, if less lucky, had their muskets blow up in their faces.

The regiment stood its ground. Every few seconds, a dull thud signaled another minnie ball had found a human target. Some men fell with a grunt, some gasped, others shrieked. But most just fell with little more than a sigh. Those who were only wounded often lay wide-eyed on the ground a few minutes, amazed at what had happened to them. The shock of the bullet's impact fended off the pain for a time, and men lay with torn limbs, crushed chests, and ripped bellies, trying to understand — not really believing that *it* had actually happened to them.

Few of those mortally wounded knew that they were dying. They felt weak and strange. They were surprised and some even felt silly. But most were not able to comprehend that the rapidly increasing weakness, the numbness, the sinking feeling, were all signs of approaching death.

The colonel, his hat missing, raced up to where the company was grouped. "We're gonna attack, we're gonna attack," he screamed, his eyes glistening. "We're gonna shoot the balls off them Yankee bastards —" He reached down from his foam-drenched horse and gave Captain Carter a powerful thump on the back that nearly threw the officer to the ground; then the colonel wheeled his mount around and raced to the next company.

"Attack! Attack!" sounded up and down the regimental line. Those soldiers who still carried bayonets affixed them to their guns. The rest took a tight grip on their muskets, holding them at belt level and all started moving forward. Ahead there was little to be seen except smoke and dust and an occasional figure that appeared for an instant, then dropped away out of sight. As they moved, their speed accelerating moment by moment, they began to yell. Each man had his own special sound that rose up from the deep of his chest and tore out of his throat. Some shrieked like frightened horses. Others yelled as if at a cock fight. Still others bellowed as men fighting each other with fists will bellow.

Josh screamed a gutteral sound that hurt his throat, but one he was unable to control. At the order to attack, he had started forward with the rest but the deliberate-

ness of the forward motion unnerved him so he quick-
kened his pace. Other men must have felt the same, for
he did not find himself out in front. The movement
turned into a jog, into a trot, and then into a run.

To his left a man disintegrated, splashing globs of
red matter all over him. Josh did not understand what
had happened. He just brushed the sticky mass from his
face and hair.

As the speed of the soldiers increased, complex feelings reduced themselves to mindless rage. Killing
whatever was out there in front of them became the most
important task on earth.

Without their realizing it, the regiment was upon
the enemy. Facing them in the smoke and dust were
creatures clothed in blue. Creatures not human, not real
— horrible alien beings that must be pulled to pieces.

Josh, shrieking with excitement, rushed at one. He
dodged a wild blow from the man's gun and with every
atom of his strength swung his own weapon, striking the
side of his head with a sound like that made by a melon
dropped on a rock. The soldier fell, his brains splattering
like balls of stained cotton. Josh raised his musket and
smashed down, pulping the man's face into an unrecog-
nizable mass.

Still shrieking, Josh started to run again, but the
blue enemy was gone, and the repeated order to halt and
regroup brought him to a reluctant stop.

The soldiers hysterically laughed and yelled at one
another. Most were so hoarse they scarcely could be understood. Many shook and jerked as if ravaged by fever.
A few vomited. All, including those who were shaking or
vomiting, had a wild, excited cast to their eyes. Everyone
stank from sweat, some from shit.

Josh looked around for Luke. He wasn't there. The
skin on the back of Josh's neck tightened. He zigzagged
through the groups of men calling out the name of his

friend. Choking fear rose up from the pit of his stomach into his throat. Then off to one side he saw Luke, his eyes frantic, his face almost black from gun powder that had sprayed out as he tore the edges of cartridges with his teeth.

"Luke! Luke!" Josh ran toward his friend, his arms wide open, his face flushed with relief.

"There you be!" Luke expelled a lungful of air. "There you be! Thought they might a got you."

"You ol' hoss!" Josh hugged Luke with all his strength while Luke pounded back, laughing hysterically.

"Kicked the shit out-a them Feds, didn't we!" Luke gasped, between bouts of laughter. "We showed them what we is make of and that's for sure." Suddenly Josh pulled away and squinted, trying to see through the smoke and dust.

"Christ!" whispered Luke. "You think somethin' . . .?"

Josh shook his head and continued to strain his eyes. Finally he muttered, "Davy can take care of hisself." Luke tensed. "He been through plenty — no cause for us to fret."

They stared at each other for several moments, then started searching. There were dozens of gray bundles sprawled on the ground. Some still twitched, others lay still. One by one they examined the faces of the dead and dying men. Would the next one be . . .? Both boys avoided putting their thoughts into words.

A gust of wind cleared away a portion of the smoke and dust and there behind a rock, his shoe in his hand, sat their missing friend. He was repairing a tear in the upper done by a nearly spent minnie ball. At first all three men grinned at one another and for a short time acted shy — Josh and Luke actually blushing. Then just as they were ready to launch into accounts of their adventures — Luke had cleared his throat as preparation — the bugle to assemble blew.

"What the hell?" Josh groaned.

"Gonna take 'nother crack at 'em," said Davy, pulling himself wearily to his feet.

"Damn!" growled Luke.

"One time was enough," Josh pleaded. "We ran them Yankees off; why they want to make us charge again?"

Davy shrugged and with a sideways jerk of his head had the boys follow him.

As the regiment regrouped, the enemy, recovered from the shock of the assault, began to pour a murderously accurate fire of musket balls, grape, and cannister at them. The Confederate troops now were pinned down and lay flat on the ground or crouched behind boulders and stumps. Screams of the badly wounded blended with the jarring thumps of exploding shells and the whistle of minnie balls.

Josh sprawled full length, his face pressed against the earth, his hands shielding the back of his head. He could hear and almost feel the movement of the bits of hot metal as they hurtled through the air. The wild exaltation that had filled him scarcely half an hour earlier was replaced by a certainty that he lay under a sentence of death, that at any moment . . . at any moment . . . yet there was no chance of running away. If he rose up from his prone position as little as half a foot, so thick was the enemy fire, he would be torn in half. He could only remain where he was, holding on to the earth, waiting for a scrap of steel to rip through his body. Certain that in a minute or in two he would be dead he began to weep in long, gasping sobs.

The Federals shifted their fire to another sector, and all at once the swarm of iron insects were no longer hissing through the air.

A dozen bugles blasted out attack. Officers shouted, threatening any soldier who appeared to be lagging.

The flat side of a saber stung Josh's rump as he scrambled to his feet. A red-eyed, bearded officer cursed him, ordering him to get moving before he put a revolver ball through his head. Josh dumbly nodded. For a split second he considered turning his musket on the officer. But what difference did it make? In a few minutes both of them would be dead.

In contrast to the earlier attack, this time the soldiers did not start running forward. Most were exhausted. Many had been badly shaken by the thundering bombardment. Some were partially disabled by sprained ankles, specks of dirt in their eyes, pulled tendons. They advanced at a slow yet steady pace. Smoke and dust again hid the movements of the enemy, but the screaming musket balls and the flashes of their guns left no doubt that they were there.

A trick wind whipped away the smoke and haze just as the Confederate troops were within a hundred yards of the Union lines. The men on both sides hesitated for an instant, seeing each other clearly for the first time. Then the Seccesh soldiers, with a roar, rushed toward the Northern troops, their muskets held as clubs. The Federals, instead of standing their ground or slowly retreating, answered with a forward rush of their own.

The soldiers met midpoint and hacked and clubbed at each other, shrieking and cursing and grunting. Both sides used every means available to gouge, maim, or kill the other: muskets swung by their barrels, sabers, bowie knives, rocks, fists, teeth, and nails.

A fresh battalion of Federal troops came running across the field. Some Rebel soldiers closest to the enemy, seeing the gleaming bayonets and shiny musket barrels of the oncoming Feds, panicked, whirled around and ran. At this, other Confederates close by backed away from the men they were fighting, hesitated several moments, then joined in the escape. In a minute, the entire regiment, officers included, was in a wild rout.

Josh, seeing a group of men from his company racing away, parried a blow from a Federal soldier who had been fighting him with a broken artillery ramrod, kicked the soldier in the groin, then turned and ran, his body hunched down close to the ground. At any second he expected to feel the thrust of a Union bayonet into his back or the rip of musket ball. He forced every atom of energy he could muster into his churning legs.

A sergeant, brandishing an officer's saber, tried to stop him. Josh ducked around the man, dodging a blow from the flat of the sword; then he kicked the sergeant with all his strength, his heavy shoe catching the other man in the stomach, doubling him up.

Josh ran until he was unable to squeeze another breath into his lungs. He fell headlong on the ground behind a clump of bushes where he lay gasping and choking. The sounds of battle were dim. He had survived. Tears of gratitude filled his eyes. It was almost as if he had been born again. A miracle! Then, as he rested, Josh detected within himself a tiny pin-point of shame. This spread until his face was a fiery red. He was a coward. An image of his father rose up in his mind. A coward.

With his cheek pressed against the cold earth, Josh lay for a time with both eyes tightly shut. The chill from the ground seeped into his skull, bringing with it a dull ache. He opened one eye, the closer to the ground. Things appeared magnified and distorted. Tiny bits of stone gradually grew larger until they were boulders. Dried weed stalks became wintry trees. An elephant-sized ant, frantically searching for something, ran in a jerking fashion, temporarily hemmed in by the bulk of a being ten thousand times its size. Josh moved his hand until it was poised directly over the insect; he brought it closer, extending one finger. A tiny pressure of the finger and the insect would stop its frantic movements forever. Josh watched the gyrations of the insect, then withdrew his hand. Very gently, by the use of a withered leaf, he helped the ant to freedom.

With the weary movements of an old man, Josh slowly pulled himself to his feet. Mechanically he searched for his musket, but he had dropped it. His haversack was missing as was his cartridge case. Empty-handed, exhausted, and filled with shame, Josh started back toward his regiment. He walked slowly.

He was not alone. Other men were walking in the same direction, avoiding the company of their companions, their heads hanging. Half of the regiment had run. Not all as far as Josh. Not all as successfully. Several dozen lay on the field, facing away from the enemy.

As Josh eased his way into camp, he was not conspicuous. Things were in a confused state. The wounded lay everywhere. More were carted in each minute. Who cared about another battle-stained private shuffling in?

Josh didn't want to face Davy or Luke. For half an hour he hesitated, squatting unnoticed near a fire belonging to men from another company. His knees began to ache but he remained squatting. When it was dark, he forced himself up and started looking for his friends.

Dancing reflections of orange firelight, combined with odd-shaped shadows, confused the soldiers' features. Josh glanced at the men as he threaded his way through dozens of campsites, but the faces always were distorted. As he passed a small fire tended by two twisted-looking men, one yelled out his name. Josh grunted in surprise.

"Can't you see who you' passin'?" said Luke, reaching his hand out for his friend.

"You look different— the fire does somethin'." Josh

kept his voice under control.

"Saw you runnin' 'cross the field!" laughed Luke. "Tried to catch up, but you was too fast. Got all blowed out and you still goin'."

Josh stared at his friend's face smiling at him across the fire.

"Most a the regiment took off when them fresh Yankee troops came down," Luke went on. "Danged lucky we was able to get away," he added.

"Bunch a cowards — we was all scared chickens, no excuse to show our ass to them Yanks," said Josh harshly. He fought the urge to kick the fire — to send sparks and embers flying. "Nothin' but cowards."

"Tha's the biggest pack a shit I ever heard," said Davy, who had been half asleep when Josh arrived and now was yawning. "Not a damn thing wrong do you run to save you' life. If the colonel wants to stand, let him. I'll run any time I know I'm licked."

Josh tried to make out Davy's shadow-draped face. "You run?" Josh asked.

"You' damn right I ran; ran like a billy goat; lucky I wasn't kilt. Lucky we all wasn't kilt. Had them fresh Yanks kept comin' after us we more 'an likely be out there right now dead as mutton." Davy shook his head and snorted. Then he snarled, "I'm sick of this damn war! Don' know what the hell it's all about — half a notion to take off; done more 'an my fair share. It's all rotten; it stinks like a burned out shithouse." He paused.

Josh and Luke, sensing there was something else Davy wanted to say, kept silent, waiting for him to continue.

Davy picked up his musket and started to inspect its firing mechanism. He pulled a dirty handkerchief from his pocket and worked a corner of the cloth into the breach. For several minutes he appeared to be deeply absorbed in the gun cleaning operation. Then, without looking up, he started to speak again. This time his voice was soft. "Ol' Sergeant Graves — he's dead."

Josh gasped; Luke's mouth fell open, but he remained silent.

"Sniper got him clean through the neck." Davy pointed at his throat. "Never knowed what hit him," Davy said half to himself. "He was a damn good sergeant!"

Josh silently nodded, trying to absorb the horror of the man's death. Luke's mouth stayed open and he began to tug at his lower lip, exposing his teeth to their roots.

Davy sighed deeply then muttered, "Don' know what Cap'n Carter is gonna do without Graves to tell him when to eat and when to crap. Without old Graves, the Cap'n ain't worth a gnat's ass."

Josh was too choked up to speak. Luke just kept tugging at his lip.

"Best man in the regiment." Davy let his musket fall to the ground — the first time he had ever done this. Several minutes passed in silence with one or another of the three friends idly poking at the fire.

"That time he tol' us 'bout New Orleans," Josh softly broke the silence, "The way he looked for that gal — Marie. Carryin' all that money to buy her freedom. . ."

"They is others should a been kilt 'stead a him!" Luke said in an unsteady voice. "Piss on that Lieutenant Rawlins' grave do he ever get kilt — twice a day do I get the chance. Gonna miss that old sergeant . . ."

"Me, too," murmured Josh. "Without Graves, this company's gonna be pure hell. Rawlins be runnin' it to suit hisself."

Rawlins' kind never gets kilt," said Davy, his eyes narrowing. He picked up his musket. "Never knew a really mean officer to catch any lead. It's them sweet kind as gets shot ever' time. Rawlins and the colonel be alive and fit after ever' man in this regiment be dead or wounded. Mean sons-a-bitches is always safe as in bed here in the war. Rawlins and the colonel, they too mean for any bullet to have they name written on. Like to kill both of them bastards my own self." He snapped the firing mechanism of his musket.

"Wonder what it's all about?" said Josh, looking up at the stars. The other two made questioning sounds. "What was you 'fore you ever born? I mean you jus' don' start from nothin' then grow and be born."

"What you talkin' about?" said Luke, disturbed by his friend. "'Fore you born it is jus' like after you' dead; you' soul be in heaven." Luke paused, frowning. "Come to think on it, never heard much 'bout before you born; mostly they is preachin' where you headed after you dead."

"Don't b'lieve in none a that; when you dead, you rot!" Davy said with finality.

"How 'bout you' soul?" Josh softly asked.

"Soul — shit!" Davy spat out. "Seen plenty a men kilt; never saw no soul floatin' aroun'."

"They invisible!" Luke defended.

"Invisible — shit!" Davy laughed. "You b'lieve in invisible souls, you nothin' but a simple asshole."

"You mean Sergeant Graves is dead and gonna lie out there forever — never have his soul rise to heaven?" said Josh in a choked voice.

"Damn right! By spring he be so rotted you can't tell him from the next man." Davy swallowed hard, opened his mouth again, but instead of words, there was a burst of sobs. The eyes of his two friends filled with tears.

"Don' know why . . . I spoke in such a fashion . . . 'bout ol' Graves." Davy was scarcely able to force the words through his sobs. "Been feelin' like I lost one a my own family ever since he got hit . . . Hope to God he does have a soul and it goes someplace safe and warm."

"Hope he gets to find Marie." Luke pressed his hands over his eyes. Josh and Davy wordlessly nodded.

# XV

Most of the men somehow believed that by morning the Federal troops would be gone. Enough blood had been shed for one battle. And besides it was so terribly cold — too cold for fighting. But they awoke to the pounding of enemy artillery. Everywhere they saw reminders of the battle of the day before. Most of the dead lay unburied, their numbers swollen by additions from the ranks of gravely wounded that had not been located before dark and had lain unattended through the winter night.

As he opened his eyes, Josh was the first to see the blue-clad soldier who had joined them during the night. He lay within inches of the dead fire, curled close to absorb warmth from its ashes. His eyes were partially shut and a sucking sound arose from the man as he breathed. The wheezing noise came from the soldier's chest — split open like a rotten tomato along his breastbone, almost to his throat. Josh stared at the man. Then he saw that one of the soldier's hands lay on the ashes and had been burnt a spidery black.

Forcing himself under control, Josh started to pull the charred hand out of the ashes. He hesitated, then stopped. There was nothing left. The hand itself had turned to ashes with only the shape of a hand. Wiping away the cold perspiration that had formed on his forehead with his sleeve, Josh studied the soldier's face. A fine, brownish down darkened the upper lip and along his ears were the beginnings of sideburns, but there was no evidence he had ever needed a razor. "Couldn't be more'n fifteen years, still has his baby fat on his jaws," Josh murmured to himself, still staring at the boy.

Josh was not alone in his staring. Davy and Luke, now awake, looked intently at the Union soldier. "He's nothin' but a boy," Luke softly whispered. "Never knew they was so young," he added, more to himself than to the others.

Suddenly Luke pointed at the blackened hand. He had just noticed it and his face blanched white.

"He don' feel nothin', " Davy said hoarsely. "He's too far gone to be feelin'. A few minutes, an hour at the mos' and he be . . ." Davy broke off with a shrug.

"Poor fellow," murmured Josh as the face of the soldier he had killed the day before rose up in his mind. "They is no call in lettin' boys that young fight." Sickened by the image of the head he had squashed, Josh swallowed hard several times.

"He ain't no soldier," Davy nodded at the blue-clad figure. "Leastways he ain't supposed to fight — he's a drummer boy. Probably ran away from home without his ma or pa knowin'."

Luke eased forward until he was close to the boy. He pulled a woolen blouse from his haversack, folded it, then gently raised the unconscious head a few inches and slipped the makeshift pillow under it. As Luke raised the head, the boy sighed and opened his mouth as if trying to form some words. For a moment his eyes lost their dullness. He looked at Luke, his lids fluttered, then they drooped half shut as he slipped back into unconsciousness. Luke reached for his blanket, keeping his tear-streaked face turned away from his friends. But the blanket was no longer needed. The boy had opened his mouth and with a single cough, stopped breathing. Luke gazed at the eyes, now wide open, trying to understand. Then with careful fingers he pressed the eyelids downward until they remained shut. "Sure glad I didn't get to kill none of 'em yesterday," he murmured. "Sure glad . . . "

All morning the Confederate troops remained crouched in the field. As the Federal artillery barrage increased in intensity, the Rebel soldiers dug trenches or threw up breastworks for protection. Neither side undertook any major offensive action, although an occasional sortie was dispatched to feel out the enemy's position and to see if any change was about to take place.

To men who had participated in two major attacks the day before, an artillery barrage, although fatal from time to time to one or another soldier, was of comparatively little concern. What did concern the Rebel soldiers, to a man, was the lack of water. Except for a few dozen partially filled canteens — these in the hands of the officers — they were completely out. Many men had not had a drink since yesterday. On the other side of the Union lines the swollen Rappahannock River flowed. Although this source of water was only two miles distant, it might as well have been two thousand.

Somehow in the gigantic confusion, the water wagons, always granted the highest priority, had been shunted aside and were now ten miles, and a half a day, away. None of the officers doubted that before night there would be, if not ample water, at least enough to slake the thirst of the soldiers. Nevertheless, the officers, especially those experienced in matters of soldier morale, were worried about the behavior of the troops as the day slowly dragged on and their thirst increased. Thirsty sol-

diers at times become demoralized. Wholesale deser-
tions, even mutinies, were not unheard of.

The artillery barrage slackened and finally ceased.
Then word was passed down from the commanders that
efforts could be made, at the discretion of individual officers, to forage the countryside for water, even though
such efforts might result in the loss of men.

When Lieutenant Rawlins learned of this, unlike officers from other companies who assigned the task to
patrols of five or six men, he ordered Davy to do the job
alone.

Moments after the lieutenant called him over, Davy
realized a dangerous situation was developing. "You the
bes' man in the whole company," the lieutenant said
evenly. "The company is lucky to have a man like you,
Medlock." He nodded. "Gonna send you out ever' time
they is a special task as takes a first-rate man like you.
Don' wanna send no green boy who's gonna get hisself
kilt." A toothy smile masked his face.

Davy held the lieutenant's eyes, his mouth dry with
anger. "You a rotten son of a bitch," said Davy softly.
"You tryin' to get me kilt. Better keep you' eyes out for
you' own self. No tellin' what can happen to an officer
when they is shootin' thick and hard."

"I can report you for a court martial for callin' me a
son of a bitch." The lieutenant, his toothy smile still in
place, had a teasing sound to his voice.

"Go on report me — nothin' 'ud please me more
than goin' on report from such as you."

"Why, Davy Medlock," the lieutenant forced a hurt
sound into his voice, "you know I ain't the one to put you
on report. Not a hero like you! I said I could do it, not I
would. Don' have to worry none, you is safe." The lieutenant broadly winked.

"You nothin' but a chicken bastard. My turd is
more a man 'an you. Take you in the woods any time you

say and show you how a man does. Beat you 'till you kiss my shoe.''

"You talk big, Medlock," the officer sneered. "Here is a chance to show what you really made of. Now get your ass out and find us some water. Do you find any, come back and take six, seven men to help you tote it.''

"Watch you'self, Lieutenant, you pushin' the wrong hoss. I'll find some Goddamn water for you, but you be goin' too far.''

Davy turned his back, walked to his campsite, and snatched his musket from the ground. Without a word to anyone he threaded his way through the camp, moving out in a wide arc to the rear.

The young officer watched the private until he was obscured by the hedges that marked the limits of the field. As he watched, the lieutenant's face hardened and his hands tightened into fists. "Cocky little bastard," he muttered to himself. "Wisht' I had the chance to cut you up some with a wet cat 'fore you die. Damn shame you gonna die so easy.''

The lieutenant waited thirty minutes before putting his plan into operation. During this time he walked around making a big show of inspecting the condition of his men.

When the thirty minutes had passed, he called a hurried meeting of all the sergeants and corporals to brief them about "new developments." As soon as the non-coms were gathered, the lieutenant, in an anxious voice, announced, "They is worried some Yankee scouts is tryin' to work their way into our lines." He pointed vaguely in the direction of general headquarters. "They found out some special troopers have been assigned by Burnside hisself to carry gunpowder into our lines and spike our guns." The faces of the non-coms took on a worried look.

"One of them troopers get through to our supplies

they blow 'em up 'fore we have a chance to do nothin'.'' A young corporal who had been with the regiment almost a year spoke the concern of all the others.

The lieutenant nodded. "Don' want to panic the men but we better keep our eyes open. Mos' likely they come from roun' behind. Them Yankees get too close, they gonna blow some of us up. They is a fiendish bunch."

"Any one of them blue jackets come roun' where I'm at, gonna kill him first, ask questions later. Ain't plannin' to let no gunpowder blow up near me," declared an older man, who had recently received his corporal stripes.

Again Lieutenant Rawlins nodded. "Better keep all the troops in close," he said earnestly. "That way we'll know anyone out there is Yanks. Even if your men have to crap, let 'em dig a hole close by — ain't no women to see."

The non-coms grinned at the reference to women.

"If they gonna try to slip inside our lines, they is certain to try the rear," the officer repeated before dismissing them.

Davy had traveled less than a mile from the campsite when he began to feel acutely uneasy. Something was wrong. It was more than the chance of a Union sniper taking a bead on him. "The Yank bullet ain't been cast as got my name on it," he muttered. His steps grew slower. Finally he stopped and sat down on a stump shielded by a copse of trees. "Why did that son-a-bitch send me out by myself?" Davy mused. "Make more sense goin' with half a dozen others and plenty of canteens. Waste-a time to find water then have to come back to get some men.

"Christ almighty!" Davy exploded. Suddenly it was all clear. "That son-a-bitch done set me up like a turkey at a shoot. It ain't Yankee bullets he hopes will get me. Do

I show my head, I'm gonna catch Rebel lead. Shit!''
Davy kicked with his lame leg at an exposed root, sending a streak of pain racing up. "I let him send me out jus'
as if I was a new-borned babe. That crafty son-a-bitch;
he's tryin' for my ass this day.

"Wonder what he tol' the men so's to make them
shoot." Davy tried to control his anger. "One thing certain he didn't tell 'em he sent me out to hunt for water."
He looked up at the sky. In less than an hour the sun
would set. If he returned after dark, he would be shot to
pieces before he had an opportunity to identify himself. If
he waited the night, a charge of desertion would be filed.
The penalty for desertion when facing the enemy was
death.

"Christ, that man sure put me in a box," Davy
whispered. He couldn't help feeling a certain admiration
for the skill of the man. "Did I wait another hour, my ass
would suck buttermilk." He shook his head several times
then grinned as he got to his feet.

Slowly and carefully Davy snaked his way back
toward his company's position. He took advantage of
every bush and out-cropping of rock. Had he been under
direct enemy fire he couldn't have been more careful.

He crawled closer and closer, parting clumps of
dried grass with great care. Every few feet he stopped
and studied the terrain in front trying to detect any
movement or the reflection of the rays of the dying sun on
gun metal. The last two hundred yards he traveled on his
stomach, using his elbows and knees. The sun was on the
verge of setting by the time Davy was close enough to
hear snatches of conversation, coughs and other sounds
from the men of his company.

Using a large boulder as a shield, Davy called out as
loud as he could, "Cap'n Carter's company!" His shout
dropped a sheet of silence over the men. "Cap'n Carter's
company! It's me, Davy Medlock." There was no

answer, but Davy was reassured by the absence of musket fire. "Hey, it's me, Davy Medlock. I been out lookin' for water."

"Who you' messmates — if you be Davy Medlock?" A voice that Davy recognized as belonging to a young sergeant asked the question.

"Hey Sarge," Davy called out, "I can tell you' voice, Sarge — it's me, Davy. Josh and Luke, they be my messmates."

"Medlock?" the voice came back, "sure soun's like you. Hey, Davy, 'fore I let you come on where at was you wounded?"

"In my leg! For Chris-sakes, let me come; soon's you see me you gonna know."

"Come on out jus' a little and give us a look."

Davy raised his head until it cleared the top of the boulder.

"Come on, man, you sure gave us a turn!" The sergeant waved him in, a relieved expression on his face. "Good thing it was still light; might've plugged you did you come along later."

As soon as he joined the men Davy asked the sergeant why all the men were on alert — the company being located to the rear of the bivouac area away from the enemy. Then Davy moved away. Without stopping at his own campsite, where Josh and Luke were making half-hearted attempts at cooking some salt meat, Davy moved quickly through the camp, his eyes darting in every direction.

Lieutenant Rawlins sat next to the remains of a split rail fence, half concealed by a piece of canvas draped over several rails. A small, well protected fire reflected its warmth into the makeshift shelter and provided enough light to enable him to make his daily entry in the journal he faithfully kept. The journal was propped against his raised knees with his face no more than six inches from the page as he carefully formed the words, his lips telling the letters as he wrote. For the moment the officer was oblivious to all that was around him.

Davy noiselessly eased toward the lieutenant. When he was within five feet of the man, he crouched motionless, listening. Certain that no one else was around he took two steps forward and pressed the muzzle of his musket against the back of the lieutenant's neck.

The unexpected shock of chill metal caused the officer to gasp. After an instant of fear, his thought then was that Captain Carter, drunk, was ragging him. When drunk the captain was known to act peculiar.

"Cap'n?" Lieutenant Rawlins partially turned his head as he started to rise.

"Move and I'll blow you' head into that fire," Davy said softly. The officer stiffened. "Do you make a move or call out, you' a dead man — no matter what happens to me."

The officer inclined his head a fraction.

"You had it all set up for them to kill me jus' like I was a chicken!" said Davy, his voice hoarse with anger. "Well, you ain't quite as smart as this hoss, is you?" Davy thrust the muzzle of his weapon hard against the other's head. "Is you?"

His speech cracking with fear, the lieutenant croaked, "No I ain't." Then he asked in a whisper, "You gonna kill me?" Davy jabbed the gun muzzle against the officer's head again. "Don' kill me!" the officer begged. "Do anythin' you want, but please don' kill me — please."

"You a rotten hateful son-a-bitch, Rawlins." Davy felt a portion of his anger evaporating. "You the closest thing on two feet to a swamp snake I ever saw!"

To this Lieutenant Rawlins softly whimpered, "Don' kill me, man. I'll never trouble you again do you let me off this one time. I give you my solemn word."

"Rawlins," said Davy in a steady voice, "I had it in mind to shoot the top of you' head off and throw you' rotten brain into the fire. Do I tell what you tried to do to me there is not a soul would blame me. But don' give me no shit 'bout you never tryin' to get me no more. First chance you get you give it 'nother try. But next time you better make sure. Else, as God is my witness, I won't kill you, I gonna cut your balls off an' turn you into a capon."

"Won' be no next time. I give you my solemn word — as a gentleman." Sweat and mucus dripped from the officer's nose and chin.

Davy withdrew his musket and stared at the trembling man. "You can shove you' solemn word into you' ass, Rawlins," Davy said evenly. "If I had half the brains I was born with I'd kill you now 'stead of givin' you 'nother chance at me. But I guess I'm jus' a natural fool." With that he turned and sauntered away, whistling tunelessly between his front teeth.

For many minutes after Davy left, Lieutenant Rawlins remained huddled, his body twitching. Finally, in a whisper too soft to be heard by anyone but himself, he said, "I'm gonna see that bastard dead if it's the las' thing I ever do." He suddenly scrambled to his feet and viciously kicked at the campfire, scattering sparks and bits of glowing wood into the black night.

# XVI

Josh and Luke greeted Davy with a proffered chunk of roasted meat as he joined them at their campfire. "Where you been?" Josh asked.

"Jus' out tryin' to find some water," said Davy with his mouth full of partially chewed meat.

"Heard the water wagons be here 'fore mornin'," Luke mumbled. "Sure am gettin' parched; that salt meat only makes it worse." Davy belched in agreement.

"Peculiarest day I ever spent," said Josh, scratching his head. "Lyin' here all day, not fightin' or nothin', with the Yanks 'cross the way. Yesterday we fit like the end of the world was comin'; today, 'cept for some artillery, nothin'."

"You complainin'?" Luke asked, grinning.

"Hell no, had a bellyful a fightin'. Jus' was thinkin' on it. Ain't a man got a right to think?"

Luke nodded.

"Them Federal campfires sure look pretty." Josh pointed to the twinkling light in the distance. "Like a mess a stars sprinkled on the earth."

"Sure do," agreed Luke.

"Wonder what they be doin' over there?" said Josh.

"Same as us," answered Davy. "Eatin', talkin', maybe smokin', same as us. Some be sleepin' by now."

"Wonder if any a them is wonderin' 'bout us?" Josh said softly.

"Sure they thinkin' 'bout us," Davy answered, chuckling. "'Bout how they gonna stick bayonets in our bellies, an' shoot us full a holes first chance they get."

"That ain't what I mean." Josh assumed a weary tone.

"I know," Davy said gently. "I was jus' pullin' on you' leg. They probably studyin' our campfires same as you and askin' questions same as you. They ain't really no difference 'tween them and us, jus' a bunch a boys away from home."

"That drummer boy we found by our campfire favored my cousin Paul," Luke said, moving closer to Josh.

"Danged if he didn't," Josh muttered. "Wisht I could let that boy's folks know or somethin'."

Each sat absorbed in his own reflections, each with his eyes steadily focused on the Federal campfires flickering in the distance. Finally, without another word, all three wrapped themselves in their blankets for sleep.

"Luke," Josh whispered in his friend's ear, taking care not to awaken Davy. Three hours had passed, and the campfire was little more than warm, white ashes. "Luke!" Josh whispered again.

"Chris', can't you let a man sleep?" Luke lifted his head a little.

"Got somethin' to tell you."

Luke sat up, his body swaying gently. "Won't it hold 'til mornin'?"

"Can't sleep for thinkin' 'bout ol' Sergeant Graves." Josh leaned close to Luke.

"About Sergeant Graves?"

"He's been lyin' out there for more 'an a day."

"Maybe he been buried already," Luke yawned.

"They ain't even brought in all the wounded!" said Josh impatiently. "Dead won' be touched for several days yet."

"How you know?" Luke sensed what Josh was getting at and he tried to resist.

"Luke," Josh controlled his irritation, "if someone don' ten' to ol' Graves the rats and varmints gonna be at him."

Luke sighed. "Can't we wait 'til mornin'?" he asked, but he already knew the answer.

"No," Josh said softly. "Be picked off by Yankee sharpshooters do we try in the mornin'." He swallowed. "If we gonna do somethin', we better do it now."

The vast battlefield glowed in the light of the moon. Crystals of frost clinging to dried stubble, rocks, and elongated bundles that had once been men, glistened like polished jewels. The wounded that had shrieked their agony the night before lay silent, their cries frozen in their throats. Some of the stilled soldiers lay face up, their mouths open, forming the shape of a scream, their staring eyes catching the reflection of the winter's moon. Strange shapes of fallen horses whose stiffened legs pointed at the sky added to the horror of the night-shrouded battlefield.

Josh and Luke walked slowly, taking care to examine each portion of earth before placing a foot upon it. Within minutes of starting their exploration, they had learned the need for caution when Luke accidentally stepped on the frozen hand of an infantryman who lay concealed in a patch of dead weeds. The crunch of snapping bones sent waves of nausea through both soldiers. Luke had been so unnerved that he had to struggle to control himself from crying out.

They searched for two hours. The distortions of night made them uncertain of the exact sector where their regiment had fought. Landmarks which would have provided clues during the day were changed by the night's shadows. Distances appeared greater by moon-light and ordinary objects assumed strange shapes.

Corpse after corpse was examined. Those facedown were turned over. Those in the shadows were dragged in-to the moonlight. At first they exercised a certain care as the bodies were moved. But as the number of examina-tions reached into the hundreds, the two friends speeded up their movements. Soon their actions were little dif-ferent from those of farm hands handling sacks of grain.

In time, each new corpse became a source of ir-ritaion when it proved not to be that of Sergeant Graves. Those facedown dead, frozen to the ground — whose massive wounds had caused an icy fusion with the frosty earth — were cursed as the soldiers struggled to pry them free.

Darts of anger stabbed Josh as he moved from dead man to dead man. There seemed to be thousands of them; the chances of locating Sergeant Graves, one man among so many, now appeared remote. Had Josh been alone, he might have given up the search.

It was Luke who finally located the object of their search. The sergeant, lying face up, had already been ex-amined by Josh, who had failed to recognize the death-distorted features. Luke almost passed the man, but noticed the massive head and broad shoulders.

Both friends were bent over their lifeless friend about to take hold of his limbs when a wounded Yankee soldier, seeing two Confederates doing something to a fallen soldier, fired his pistol at them. The report of the gun was followed by a gasp from Luke, who fell forward onto the stiffened body. Josh grabbed Luke's arm and, keeping hunched over, dragged him into a nearby copse of bushes. A sickening swirl of panic urged Josh to run. But instead he tightened his grip on Luke's arm. Yet the panic remained.

Minutes passed with no more shots, the only sound

the wind. The shock of the wound kept Luke from speaking. Josh, now mostly under control, examined his friend, taking care to keep hidden in the thick of the bushes. The wound was in the upper thigh. Josh's probing fingers found two holes, one in front, the other behind. He tore several strips of cloth from his shirt, rolled them into balls, and plugged the holes. As he worked, his thinking cleared.

There had been only one shot. There was no sound of moving men. The enemy lines were at least two miles distant. Almost certainly the single shot was fired by a wounded soldier who somehow had managed to survive the bitter cold.

With all possible caution, Josh crawled in the direction from which the shot had been fired. Moving on his belly, propelling himself forward with his knees and elbows, he approached the Yankee officer, who now lay helpless. Fear and the exertion of aiming and shooting had left him exhausted and on the verge of unconsciousness.

The full light of the moon fell on the wounded officer. He was sprawled, legs apart, his back and head supported by an outcropping of rock. His right hand rested on a double-barreled pistol, but in such a way that Josh knew the man was no longer able to use the weapon. The left arm had no hand. Its jagged end had been thrust into the ground to staunch the flow of blood and was held fixed by its frozen blood. For thirty-six hours the Yankee officer had been shackled in this fashion.

"Hey, Yank!" Josh called out, keeping his body pressed to the ground. The officer opened his eyes and leaned forward a few inches, then fell back with a slight gasp. Josh moved up to the man and kicked away the pistol. He looked at the face of the man who had just shot his friend. The eyes of the officer were opened wide and filled with fear.

"Don' worry, man, I ain't gonna harm you none." Josh picked up the officer's one hand and started to chafe it. "You damn near kilt my friend, but I can't fault you none for shootin'. He be alright, jus' a woun' in his thigh, missed the bone, ball went in and come out the other side."

"Thought...you...was...looters." The officer spoke slowly and with great effort. "Be...much...obliged...if... you...stay." He sucked in his breath, then swallowed. "Won't...be...long...." Several words were unintelligible. "Stay?" the officer repeated.

Josh kept rubbing the other man's hand. "I'll stay — 'til you gone," he said hoarsely. He let go of the man's hand. "I be back in a minute. Jus' want to check on my friend."

The officer showed a flash of fear in his eyes. "Please," he whispered.

"Don' worry." Josh picked up the man's hand again. "I ain't gonna leave you. I promise. Jus' have to tend to my friend."

The officer nodded weakly, then allowed his eyes to close.

When Josh returned from attending to Luke, the dying man was breathing regularly and appeared to be sleeping. It had required several minutes before Luke was able to understand why Josh wanted to stay with the Yank. At first, Luke reacted with hurt and anger.

"You mean you gonna tend to a damn bluebelly that jus' come near killin' me dead?" Luke's eyes filled with tears. "I be near froze and you gonna take care of some stinkin' Yankee — an officer!"

Josh put his arm around his friend. "I give my word," he said softly.

"Shit, man, I'm like to freeze, my leg smarts so I can't think a nothin' else," Luke pleaded.

"I give my word," Josh repeated, holding his friend tighter.

"You got more regard for a Fed 'an for me — 'spite a the fact we was raised together."

"Luke, you got no cause in sayin' such a thing. I don' have no regard for that Yank a-tall. But he's dyin' and he's scared and alone. Can't leave him to die alone."

"Don' leave me, Josh," Luke whispered. "Do you leave me I gonna die my own self — I know I boun' to die, I feel that bad."

Tears also filled Josh's eyes. "Luke, you ain't gonna die. If you was 'bout to pass, I wouldn' leave you 'spite a my word to the Yank. You is feelin' poorly, but they ain't no bones broke and the bullet done pass clean out of you' leg." Luke turned his head away. "That Yankee officer, he's a man jus' like you; how you like to be lyin' out here a day and a half and be dyin' 'thout another human soul nearby to help you to go?"

Luke swallowed several times then whispered, "I'm sorry. Don' know what come over me."

It took the Yankee officer two hours to die. Just before he stopped breathing, he opened his eyes and looked at Josh. Josh had his arms around the man's shoulder and held the man's good hand in his, fingers interlacing. Slowly, with his last spark of energy, the officer whispered, "You been a comfort. God bless you." He sucked in a rattling breath and gasped, "I love you." The rattle turned into a shudder, then the Yankee lay still.

Josh carefully disengaged his hand, his arm still around the man's shoulder. He touched the dead officer's cheek, then touched his hair. For several minutes he remained seated, holding the lifeless body. At last, with a groan, he pulled himself to his feet and walked back to Luke.

# XVII

Without help it took Josh more than three hours to dig a grave then bury Sergeant Graves. Although the cold had worked its way into his wound, sending violent throbs of pain up into his back, Luke clenched his jaw against crying out while Josh worked.

It was dawn by the time the two friends returned to camp. They had made slow progress, Josh carrying Luke on his back. Just as they entered camp, word was passed that the Yanks had pulled out. The area, filled with hundreds of Union campfires the night before, now was deserted.

By the time official confirmation came from the general officers, the Confederate lines were scenes of wild celebration, with men shouting, waving, jumping, running in circles, throwing their hats in the air and most of all, shooting muskets and pistols into the sky. Instead of another terrible battle, they had been given the gift of victory.

Confederate patrols ranged for twenty miles and reported the same thing — the Yankee forces had crossed the Rappahannock and were in full retreat. By the following morning, Captain Carter's company, together with the rest of the regiment, was ordered out of the lines and back to camp.

Except for Davy, who had been told as soon as the boys got back to camp, no one else knew the details surrounding Luke's wound. And so many men had been wounded and so many were still dying that no special attention was paid to Luke. His wound needing no care other than that already given by Josh, Luke's condition was considered minimal by the authorities, thus he was not even granted space in an ambulance and had to make do balanced on the whiffle-tree of a twelve pounder as the regiment made its way back to the permanent camp. But the rough ride, although painful, was also joyful, for Lieutenant Rawlins had informed Luke he was to be allowed a two week furlough home with six additional days for travel. Standing up to Captain Carter's objections, the lieutenant had defended the right of every wounded man in the company to recover "in the bosoms of their various families."

The night before Luke was to leave for home on furlough, he, Josh and Davy sat before their campfire in spite of the severe cold that had driven most of the men into the warmth of their shelters.

Davy had bent his best efforts toward preparing a suitable meal for the occasion. Rations were short and most of the troops had little other than a bit of bacon, some flour and some parched corn. Slapjacks fried in bacon grease had become the standard menu. Yet, somehow Davy had secured the services of a large onion, several wilted carrots, and a strip of jerked beef. These, together with the dried corn and flour, he blended into a glorious stew. A plateful of the concoction, to which had been added a handful of crumbled hardtack, followed by a burning hot cup of coffee, put the three soldiers into a mood of mellowness and contemplation.

They sat as close to the crackling flames as their flesh would allow, secure in the knowledge that if the cold grew too severe they could retreat into their snug hut.

Luke felt like a man who had recently come into a considerable property. Due to his wound, the other men in the company had shown him a deference unlike anything he had ever experienced before. Now that he was on the eve of his furlough, he experienced that peculiar compassion felt only by the rich when they chance to think about the poor — a feeling of: "How sad it is that some must be poor, but how fortunate we are rich."

Josh refused to admit that he was jealous of his friend. Yet all he could look forward to was three or four months of boring hibernation until the spring campaigns. While Luke faced fourteen exquisite days at home that might be extended if the note of a qualified surgeon attesting to a need for further recouperation could be obtained.

"Tell my Ma that does she include a couple roasted chickens, they be most welcome here." Josh added another item to the list he expected Luke to present to his parents. "If they dip the chickens in lard and wrap 'em good, they sure to hold 'til you get back."

Luke nodded, a serious face hiding the pleasure he felt. Every new request further emphasized his fortunate situation. "Gonna bring a sack of my daddy's bes' apples for you," Luke declared magnanimously. "Some sugar too," he added. "If they is any to be had."

"Bes' thing ever happened to you," said Davy, putting into words what Luke had been thinking. "Wounded bad enough to get home, but not bad enough to really hurt." Davy caught Luke's eyes and grinned. "Never thought ol' Rawlins would stand up to the captain. Maybe you should bring some of them apples for Rawlins — appreciation for your furlough. Surprised the shit out of me, that man did."

"Better make it three chickens," Josh muttered,

poking at the fire. The pokes soon turned into vicious jabs. "And you can ask my folks why they ain't been writin' 'cept once or twice." Luke nodded. "Don't get no notions on stayin' for good," Josh then said in a sharp voice. "When you' time be over, you come back! Hear?"

Luke vigorously nodded. "Don' wanna stay home for good; two weeks is jus' enough to suit this one."

"Wish to hell I was goin' with you — damn!" Josh got up and without warning gave the fire a kick, scattering embers in every direction. Davy laughed. "Damn!" Josh repeated, then without another word, went into the hut.

# XVIII

Luke sat in the musty, dimly lit railroad car, his forehead pressed against the dingy window, his nose flattened on the glass. His eyes were open but his mind scarcely registered the farms, hamlets and winter-wrapped fields that flashed by. His mind raced ahead to the time when the train would reach a certain stop, the only place that mattered to him.

He closed his eyes to sharpen his thinking. It would take a man four, near five hours to walk from where the train stops to the farm. Luke smiled as he reviewed a matter he had gone over a dozen times already. With my leg, better allow an extra hour. Do I push too hard, I be crippled for a week. His smile broadened as he thought about his wounded limb. It was just the sort of wound he had hoped for: not so serious as to require amputation or disable him for life, yet one that would be noticed no matter how hard he tried to cover it up. And he did intend to make every effort to walk in a normal fashion. But he knew that he would be unable to succeed and folks would notice and comment how brave he was, trying to hide the effects of his wound.

"Wonder what Pa is gonna say?" Luke softly whispered, his eyes still closed. "Jus' gonna walk in as

easy as you please — sit down at the table like I jus' come
from milkin' in the barn." He suppressed a laugh. "Better kiss Ma first, she have a fit do I sit down without."

Luke felt a hand on his shoulder shaking him. "Hey,
wake up soldier, come on man, wake up — we is here."
He opened his eyes and saw the whiskey-reddened face of
the conductor — smelled his pungent breath. "Time to
get off the train — can't wait on you forever."

Luke was confused for a moment and started to
shake his head. Then he jumped up, grabbed his haversack and stumbled down the aisle, bumping into several
passengers but not caring.

Both of his parents sat open-mouthed, with their
food half chewed as Luke stepped into the kitchen. His
father spat the mouthful back into his plate, swallowed,
then said in a choked voice, "Jesus Christ!" His mother
kept staring, her mouth still open.

Luke bent over, kissed the woman on her forehead,
then sat down heavily between them both. "Jesus
Christ!" his father said again. His mother resumed her
chewing, not taking her eyes off her son for a second.
Finally, and with some effort, she swallowed.

"Luke?" Her voice had a ring of hesitancy. "You
run away?" Luke shook his head.

"The war ain't over?" said Luke's father, with a rising inflection.

"It sure ain't!" Then in a matter-of-fact voice, Luke
added, "Been wounded."

His mother stiffened, her eyes rapidly searching her
son's face.

Luke grinned at his mother. "No cause to fret; I be
'most as good as new." The heavy warmth of the kitchen
was working its way into his body, soothing his wound.
"Caught a Yankee ball in my leg; hurt some, but it's
near sound by now."

"You home for good?" his mother asked with quickened breathing. "They give you you' discharge?"

Luke shook his head. "Jus' home for a little — long as you got two of ever'thing, they ain't about to send you home for good."

Luke glanced at his father who had turned back to his plate and was spearing pieces of meat with a knife, and stuffing them in his mouth. The man's entire attention was directed toward the plate of greasy food.

"Luke, you hungry?" His mother began ladling from an iron pot that stood nearby. "You look like you could stand some heavy victuals. They feed you good in the army?"

Luke reached over and patted his mother's arm. "They is no food like yours." The woman blushed. "Army food's tolerable, but I ain't had a really decent-cooked meal since I walked out a this very house." The woman turned a deeper scarlet. "Did they feed the boys with your victuals, Ma, the war be over by now and the Yankees whipped." At this Luke's mother lifted her apron, covered her face and laughed, rocking back and forth.

"Luke, you a caution. They learned you to have a silver tongue, they sure did."

For the next few minutes Luke ate in silence, glancing up at his father from time to time trying to catch his eyes. But the older man kept his eyes fastened on his food.

"Been in a big battle outside Fredricksburg," Luke finally said, chewing and swallowing as he talked. "Charged them Yankees twice, kilt plenty. They sent us scurryin' one time — never ran so fast in my life." Luke's mother clucked and made other appropriate sounds. His father grunted just one time. "Lucky I wasn't kilt — plenty was. Lost our sergeant — Graves, Ben Graves — right through the throat. Bes' man in the regiment." Most of Luke's energy was concentrated on his father.

"Be goin' back in two weeks." Luke paused. There was a tightness around his eyes and at the corners of his mouth. "Probably be the las' time you ever see me. This war is boun' to go on for two, three more years." The older man kept his eyes fixed on the now almost empty plate. He reached for a scrap of meat. As he reached out, his hand shook. Luke's face softened.

"Pa," Luke said gently. "Pa," he repeated, waiting for the older man to look up. "Pa, I sure am glad to be home in you' house." The man nodded. "I sure did miss you, Pa; thought on you and Ma ever' day."

Luke's father got up from the table, hitching up his trousers and tucking in his shirt that had worked loose. "You better take care of you'self, hear!" He spoke without looking at his son. "Too much work to be did on the farm for you to get you'self kilt." With a gasp, Luke's father blew his nose into a piece of rag. Then he turned, squared his shoulders, and walked out of the house.

Luke remained seated at the table. His eyes fixed on the door after it had closed.

His mother followed the man out a minute later. She carried an iron kettle and was headed for the pump.

Luke closed his eyes, his head supported in his hands. Gradually his attention was drawn to the mixture of odors that filled the kitchen. It was an aroma that he would have recognized anywhere. More than anything else, it contained the sharpness of ash soap — fat boiled with wood ash until it mysteriously was fat no longer. And there was the mellow, earthy odor of the dirt floor, the flavor of pine timbers, the faint bitterness of hot cast-iron pots.

The door reopened and his mother struggled in, straining under the weight of the filled vessel. She fixed the handle on the iron hook and swung the kettle over the fire to boil.

Luke grinned at his mother; she was breathing

heavily from her exertions. She grinned back, her eyes glistening. "Let's see you' wound!" She pulled Luke half up from the stool. "Come on, let's see where the Yankees plugged you," she giggled.

"Naw," Luke shook his head, his face reddening.

"I be you' own mother, no need to be 'shamed." She tugged at Luke's arm.

"It ain't fittin' — it's too high up on my leg." Luke freed his arm.

"Luke," his mother teased, "how you are. I seen you without a stitch thousan' times. You shamed 'for you' own mother?"

"I'm all growed, Ma. It ain't the same as when I was little."

"My only child comes back wounded and his own mother cain't even see the wound." The woman pretended to be hurt.

"Aw, Ma, it jus' ain't right for me to shuck my pants, I ain't no baby."

"You still my baby!" She placed both hands on her wide hips. "Neighbors be askin' me 'bout you' wound and I won't know what to tell 'em. They gonna think it mighty peculiar that a mother don' know a thing 'bout her own chile's wound. Come on boy, off with you' pants; you can cover up with a towel." As she spoke, his mother pulled a coarse towel from its hook and tossed it into Luke's lap.

"Turn you' head 'til I get the towel in place." Luke undid his britches while his mother tended to the fire, pumping it up with a pair of bellows.

As soon as she saw the shiny purplish patch surrounded by reddened swollen tissue, the woman sank to her knees beside her son and carefully touched the wounded place. Then noticing where the bullet had exited, she touched that place also.

"It must've hurt fierce!" she whispered, her

roughened, swollen fingers following the outline of the injury. "It still give you pain?" She looked up at Luke, her eyes swimming with tears.

Luke rested the palm of his hand against his mother's round cheek. Tears rolled down the woman's sweaty cheeks; they traveled until they reached the corners of her mouth, wetting her coarse, cracked lips. With a convulsive movement, she turned her head so that her face was buried in her son's hand. She held the hand with both of hers, pressing it tight against her face. Her tears found their way between Luke's fingers, then ran down the back of his hand.

His mother stayed where she was after the door opened and Luke's father came in. He stopped and stared, not understanding. Finally he saw the purplish patch. He came up close and inspected the injured tissue. Then for the first time since Luke was a little boy, he placed his hand on his son's head. For several moments the three of them remained together, motionless and silent.

# XIX

The Sunday after Luke arrived home was the coldest day of winter. He awoke early; it still lacked an hour until daybreak. He lay in his bed with its thick, rough wool blankets on top and its feather-stuffed mattress beneath. Indoors the air was nearly as cold as outside. Each breath turned into steam, but the bed was warm and his leg had almost stopped throbbing. Luke snuggled down until almost all his face was hidden by the covers. Only his eyes and the tip of his nose were free. He lay there in the same bed in which he had slept ever since he was taken from his crib, a bed where nothing could hurt him, where everything was good and peaceful. A week and three days were still left to him. Going back seemed strange and remote. A thing not to think about, not yet.

It was the Sabbath. In a few hours he would be walking with his mother and father on the way to church. They would be dressed in their best. His mother had washed and pressed his uniform, but it had been repaired in several places and showed signs of wear. Luke wondered what it would be like to walk into church and be noticed. He couldn't remember ever having been noticed. Josh always had been noticed. Josh was tall and good looking. Whenever he joined a group, people nodded and smiled at him. But today, in church, things would be different. The wound began to throb. He wasn't certain what he should do while being noticed. Maybe he'd just stay home — say his wound couldn't stand the cold. He pulled the blankets over his head.

Luke walked between his parents; it took them almost an hour to reach the church; their progress was slow because his wound had stiffened in the icy air, his uniform being entirely of cotton, but Luke suffered the discomfort in silence. He had chosen to wear his uniform.

As Luke walked up the aisle to the pew, which long usage had assigned to his family, he kept his eyes fixed rigidly in front of him. The tension he felt made his limp more pronounced in spite of efforts to minimize it. He heard the rustle of clothing as people turned to look at him. A few whispers reached his ears, but he gave no sign of having heard them.

"That's Luke, lives over the hill . . ."

". . . wounded, they say, at Fredericksburg."

"They say he killed a bunch of Yankee soldiers."

". . . see how pale he is . . ."

Never in his life had Luke felt as nervous and excited as he did walking up that aisle, but his frozen face masked his feelings.

The preacher, who had been making several preliminary announcements, paused until Luke and his parents found their seats. Then in the same rising and falling voice he used while delivering his sermons, he said, "Praise God, we have with us this day one of our returning soldiers."

Luke felt his face burning. He sat stiff in his seat with both eyes fastened on the center of the lectern.

The minister continued. "One of our brave boys is back within the bosom of his family, back to receive the love and admiration of his friends and neighbors." The minister took a deep breath and increased the volume of his voice. "One of our own number has returned, having been sorely wounded on the noble field of battle, to spend a few, a far too few short days under the tender care of those to whom he gives the name mother and father." The minister paused and searched the faces of his congregation. Then he thundered, "One of our sons is returned from facing death itself in the service of a holy cause! Yet there are those among you, yes, more than a few that I see sitting before me this very day who still refuse to serve Christ. There are men and women, too, -within the sound of my voice who have not yet come to Christ Jesus, who have not yet asked to be saved from the searing fires of hell! While sitting in their midst is a soldier, a boy who has risked his very life for Christ."

Luke sat stunned. This attention was far beyond anything he had ever dared to imagine. In ways it was like his first drink of corn: burning and exciting at the same time.

Without turning his head, Luke glanced first at his father then at his mother. They both sat bolt upright, impassive, their hands carefully folded in their laps, but their shining eyes and quickened breathing told of their pride in him.

When the service was over, before Luke and his parents were able to leave their pew, the minister, instead of hurrying to the door to receive the congregation as was his custom, walked up to Luke and took his hand, giving it a vigorous shake while at the same time patting him on the shoulder.

In the church yard several dozen people waited for Luke. Men and women, young people — boy and girls crowded around, shaking both of his hands and pounding him on the back. Luke's stern face melted into a grin as his neighbors pressed close. Everyone invited him to come and visit. Most, that he come for supper. Questions were asked about the war, but before Luke could answer, there were new questions. For ten minutes he was the center of attention. But then in two's and three's they moved away. Finally Luke, his parents and the minister were left standing alone. And then the minister, with a mumbled excuse, hurried away.

That afternoon Luke decided to go visiting. The invitations he had received were carefully recorded in his mind and as he changed into his warm wool civilian clothing, there being no longer need for his uniform, he studied the merits of each offer.

Even before Luke started to review the list of invitations, he knew which one he would accept first. Yet he went over each carefully, considering the culinary reputation of the lady of the house. But the offer of Abner Monk stood well ahead of the rest. Although Liza Monk was reputed to be only a fair-to-middling cook and Abner was not given to excessive cleanliness nor to displays of generosity, there was their daughter Abigail! Ah yes, their incomparable daughter Abigail, who had just passed her fifteenth birthday.

When Luke reached the Monk farm, it still lacked two hours 'til supper time. His hair was carefully slicked down, his mother having trimmed the ragged edges then greased and combed the rest. In spite of the bitter cold, before dressing Luke had stood half naked before the pump, sloshing icy water on his face and chest, taking care to rub the gray dirt away from his ears and neck. Thus as he knocked on his neighbor's door, he felt tingling clean — fit in every way to go calling.

The door was opened by Abigail, who lowered her eyes and curtsied when she saw who was calling. Then she, together with the Monk's four other children, sat silent in open-mouthed fascination while Luke and their father shared a pipe of tobacco and talked about the war. Mrs. Monk, a rather thin, also none-too-clean personage, heavily addicted to the chewing of snuff, meanwhile clattered around the kitchen preparing the evening meal.

Luke shared his host's pipe, whose mouthpiece was soft and spongy and covered with saliva, which he tried not to think about each time he took his puff.

"How many Yanks you kill?" asked Mr. Monk, without any preliminaries. Luke shrugged modestly. "One? Two?" Mr. Monk paused a moment looking at his guest's face. "Three?" he asked with an edge of admiration in his voice.

Luke remained silent, concentrating on the blue smoke curling from the pipe.

"You kill more'n three Yankees?" Mr. Monk leaned toward Luke. "Five?" he whispered in a tone of almost disbelief.

Again Luke shrugged, then glanced at Abigail, who was listening with an interest as great as that of her father. "Can't say for certain how many of 'em you get," said Luke in a casual, almost bored voice. "Ever'body bangin' away and them blue bellies fallin' all over. Can only be sure of them as you stick with a bayonet or whose head you squash with the musket stock."

"How many — how many you stuck or squashed, Luke?" said Mr. Monk, his face eager and excited. "How many you certain of?"

Luke stroked his chin, his face set in grave lines. "Four." He hesitated. "No, five I reckon." He tugged on one of his ears, carefully estimating his audience. "'Course, they was two others I plugged and I knowed they was mine, and one more as probably b'longed to me."

"Eight!" Mr. Monk totaled the carnage on his fingers. He was so excited he forgot to take back the pipe for his turn.

"Might be others, but can't be sure on them," said Luke casually, his eyes fastened on a fascinating spot on the ceiling.

"You hear that, Liza?" Abner Monk turned to his wife, who had been listening so intently that she added salt three times to the soup she was preparing.

Mrs. Monk shifted her mouthful of snuff, spat a glob on the earthen floor which she automatically rubbed in with her bare foot, then answered, "I heard him; what you think I am, deaf? He kilt eight! Should a kilt eight hundred. They is all fiends and devils, that's what they is." Mrs. Monk spat again, screwing up her thin, snuff-stained lips.

"They ain't fiends, nor devils neither; they men jus' like us," said Luke magnanimously.

"They is fiends!" shouted Mrs. Monk, turning pale.

"Shut you' mouth, woman!" Mr. Monk half rose from his seat. His wife shrank back, then turned away to her cooking. "Yankee soldiers is jus' like us," Mr. Monk called after his wife. "They men jus' like any man in this county and they is no call in sayin' they ain't, 'spite a the color of they uniform. Too bad we gotta kill 'em. But it's the Lord's will."

Mr. Monk turned to Luke, nodding as he ran his eyes over the soldier's tightly knit frame. He caught a glance of his daughter's excited, flushed face. "It still lacks more 'an a hour 'till supper," he declared. "Abigail, why don' you and Luke take a walk. You look peaked and the air will do Luke some good. No need for him sittin' here jawin' with ol' folks when they is a purty girl to go walkin' with."

Abigail turned a deep scarlet and covered her face with both of her hands while Luke, with a boldness completely new to him, stood up and offered the girl his arm.

Once out in the late afternoon sunlight, Luke's self-confidence began to evaporate. Turning to the girl, he tried to ask where she would like to walk, but the words stuck in his throat. There was something about her wide-spaced, large, gray-blue eyes — several moments passed, with their breaths smoking in the frosty air. Then with a determined toss of her head, Abigail tugged him into motion. They walked for a few minutes, Abigail taking care to match her steps with the stiffened gait of her companion.

"How long you get to stay home, Luke?" she finally asked.

"'Leven more days."

"You gonna take me walkin' again 'fore you leave?"

Luke's heart started to pound hard. His hands grew damp with perspiration in spite of the severe cold. A tightness in his throat prevented him from speaking.

"Ain't you goin' to take me walkin' anymore?" Abigail spoke in a hesitant voice, her full, frost-reddened lips trembling.

"Do your folks say yes," Luke finally replied.

The girl tightened her arm in his and leaned closer. They reached an area covered with stumps, which Mr. Monk was trying to clear. They sat down on a stump just large enough for both if they squeezed close together. Abigail's arm was still carefully tucked in Luke's. The sun, now a golden ball, almost touched the trees that lined the crest of the hill. For several minutes neither one of them spoke. Abigail was the first to break the silence.

"Luke?" She turned to the boy so that he felt her warm breath on his cheek. "Did you ever kiss a girl?"

Luke hesitated, swallowed, then shook his head.

"I never kissed a boy neither."

Luke's pounding heart felt as if it had swollen to the size of a melon.

"Luke," Abigail said in a teasing voice, "how come you never kissed no girl? How come?"

"Never met one I wanted to," Luke mumbled.

"Do you want to kiss me?" she asked, squirming a tiny bit closer. "Do you want, you can."

Swallowing hard, Luke turned his head. Her chilled lips touched his. Then her lips parted and there was a warmth and softness — a wild feeling swept through Luke. His heart felt as if it would tear clear out of his body. Abigail took his hand and guided it inside her bosom until his fingers touched her swollen breast. Like a jet of boiling water, the shock of feeling her skin ran down into his groin.

Luke couldn't catch his breath, he tried to free his mouth, but the girl held him hungrily. With a sudden twist of his head, Luke could breath again. Abigail pressed her flushed face and swollen lips against the boy's neck. She took a deep breath then let it out with explosive suddenness, accompanied by a rush of sobs.

"What ever in the worl' mus' you think a me?" Her body shuddered from the force of her sobbing. "I — I never did nothin' like this before — can't help myself." Luke's fingers still touched her breast as her elbow pressed tightly against his arm, holding his hand in place. He moved his hand a little, stroking the breast which had the feel of a willow branch after the bark is stripped away. As his hand moved, Abigail choked back her sobs and pressed against Luke. Then she whispered, "Oh, Luke, you make me feel like I could do anythin' for you — if you was to ask me to do somethin' I jus' couldn' help doin' it no matter what."

"There ain't no place to go — to . . ." Luke broke off; his throat was so dry it pained him to speak. He coughed, licked his lips then swallowed. "It sure would pleasure me to — to ah, spend some time alone with you, Abigail."

The girl's large eyes glistened crimson in the light of the sunset. "Do you come to the barn after ever'body's asleep we can be alone," she whispered. Then she convulsively pressed her parted lips against his, her free hand digging its nails into his shoulder.

# XX

Luke struggled through the oversalted meal. From the moment they returned from their walk, Abigail had avoided looking at him. After supper was over, she herded the younger children into the room where they all bunked together and then, without so much as a good night, pulled the burlap curtain closed.

Mrs. Monk made no attempt to clean up the remains of the evening meal. After her children had gone to bed, she wiped her food-stained hands on her apron, sighed, belched, then shuffled over to the box bed that occupied one wall of the kitchen and lay down, face against the wall, her skinny body covered with a decomposing blanket.

As soon as his wife was in bed, Mr. Monk pulled a half-gallon jug from under the table and filled two cups. He tilted his head and with a gulp, downed half the contents of his cup. Luke lifted his cup to his lips, trying not to let the sourish fumes find their way into his nose. Mr. Monk watched with a glint of expectation. Then with a rapid toss, Luke swallowed a mouthful. It was newly distilled corn liberally flavored with pepper and, at the moment, it seemed to Luke, a sprinkling of gun powder. The liquid burned as it went down. Luke gagged. With an effort generated by a combination of pride and orneriness, he swallowed down the sour, burning fluid that rose up from his stomach, then swallowed again and again to rid his mouth of the salty saliva that kept pouring in. And then, just to show the man, Luke downed the rest of the cup.

"'Nother drink?" Mr. Monk pulled the wood stopper and poured without waiting to hear Luke's reply. "Traded for ten dozen eggs." The man tapped the jug with a grin. "Liquor sure is high but is worth it. Only thing as can stop my Missus' miseries." Then acting on his word, he lurched over to his wife and thrust a cup of spirits between her and the wall. Without turning around, almost as if she had eyes in the back of her head, Mrs. Monk reached up and pulled the cup in, taking care not to spill a drop. "Some mornin's, if we didn' have a little corn at hand, that old woman never would make it up; she wakes that stiff with the rhumatiz," Mr. Monk declared as he resumed his seat.

After the gurgling inside his stomach stopped — the alcohol having had a chance to find its way into his bloodstream — Luke brightened up considerably. Examining his host's gaunt, pock-marked face and stringy neck, Luke decided that, in spite of his appearance, Mr. Monk was not a bad sort of a fellow. He was, after all, Abigail's father.

The years that separated the two men were diluted by the effects of the drink, and Luke leaned forward until his face almost touched the other man's. "Monk," said Luke in a tone of familiarity he had never before used to an older man, "Monk, why the hell don' you come 'long with me when I go back to the army?" He brought his fist down on the table, rattling the dirty dishes. "Monk, you know what you be?" Luke waited a few seconds, grinning foolishly, then continued. "You are nothin' but a bomb proof — a stay-at-home slacker. Tha's what you be."

The older man, who had finished a second cup of liquor and was starting on a third, slowly nodded, moisture filling his eyes. "You right, Luke, you entirely right." He sighed. "When you goin' back?"

"'Leven days."

Raising an unsteady hand in the sign of a pledge, Mr. Monk declared, "I be with you when you leave, damned if I won't. Liza!" He turned toward the woman whose face was still against the wall. "I'm goin' to jine the army when Luke goes back. Gonna go with Luke in 'leven days — you hear?"

The woman let out a grunt and pressed herself more closely to the wall.

"You be runnin' the farm 'thout me." Mr. Monk tipped back in his chair and brought a thick fist crashing down on the table. "And I don' want no argumen's from you nor from anyone else, hear?!"

Her voice muffled by her bed clothes, the woman mumbled, "I hear you, Abner, no call shoutin' and wake the cherrin."

"I ain't shoutin'," Mr. Monk roared back. "'Sides, even if I was, it's my house and if I wants to shout, I will."

Luke had almost finished the second cup and had developed a good-natured pity for his host. "Come to think on it, Monk, you too old to fight; better stay home and tend to the farmin'," he said.

With a snarl the older man pushed away from the table and jumped up, both fists raised in a threatening gesture, his face blotched with anger. "Who you say be too ol' to fight!" The man moved a couple of steps until he was directly over Luke. "Why you runty little snot face, I eat two like you for breakfas'!"

"Abner, you keep up that-a-way you be down with the apoplexy!" His wife's words caused the man's raised fists to drop to his sides. Then with a grunt Mr. Monk fell back heavily into his chair.

"Ain't no Yankee been borned as I can't lick," he mumbled half to himself. "You'll see, 'leven days from now I be gone and you can run this damn place you'self." His chin started to drop down to his chest; his eyes closed and his entire body began to sag. Then with an effort that brought with it a tired grunt, Mr. Monk pulled himself up, reeled across the floor and tumbled down on the bed beside his wife. As he stretched out on the bed, the woman pulled herself closer to the wall, keeping several inches between her body and his.

Luke looked at his host, waiting to hear if there was anything else he had to say. The man's snores put an end to his waiting. Like sounds arose from the woman who, overcome by sleep, had turned and draped her arm over her husband.

As Luke walked out into the icy air, he suffered a bout of nausea and dizziness. For several minutes he clutched the door jamb, unwilling to go back indoors, yet unable to go on.

Twenty yards away across a refuse littered yard — punctuated here and there with mounds of steaming manure — stood the barn outlined in the moonlight. A windowless, elongated affair built some fifty years earlier by Mr. Monk's grandfather, the barn was constructed of split logs with curved surfaces turned outward, the cracks between the logs chinked with live moss which had finally covered the entire structure with a perpetual coat of green.

The dizziness having finally passed, Luke made his way to the barn. He hesitated several moments before entering, gulping air. Once inside, Luke encountered a darkness more profound then any he had ever remembered. And the absolute blackness was somehow accentuated by the rush of odors and sounds that met him. Animal smells, hay dust, the sweet aroma of stored grain and dried fruits; the sounds of swishing, stomping, rattling; tiny scratchy sounds of mice, the chumping and gurgling of cattle feeding. And the barn was thick with animal and vegetable warmth.

Tucked in among all the other evidences of life, Luke was able to detect the presence of the girl. Her breathing, the rustle of her clothing, perhaps other more subtle clues led him to her. She lay on a pile of hay in an unused stall, one that served to hold the new born colts in the spring. She had heard the young soldier enter and was waiting. Luke was guided the last few feet by movements of her body as she made room for him. He lay down. Several seconds passed. Suddenly she threw herself on him, gasping and tugging frantically at his clothing. Explosively, Luke responded, groping wildly in the darkness.

They thrashed and struggled, rolling from side to side on the rough wood floor, their grunts and gasps mixing with the dozens of other sounds that surrounded them. When their sweat-drenched bodies were finally still, they held each other with desperate tightness.

"I never knowed a girl in all my life I liked half as much as you," Luke whispered. "Never gonna be 'nother girl for me 'cept you." His voice sounded strange to his ears.

Abigail snuggled closer, tightening her grip on his neck and shoulders.

"Abigail, you as soft as a baby chick." Luke's hand stroked her thigh. "Abigail!" He searched for the right thing to say. "I seen some mighty fine ladies in Montgomery, all painted and corseted — ain't none of them purty as you. Not even some of them ladies riding all smart and all in they carriages with shiny black niggers to drive 'em."

"You have 'nother girl in Montgomery?"

Luke forced a chuckle. "Wouldn' have one of them painted Montgomery gals for a gift, not even with a ten dollar gold piece throwed in to boot."

"You have 'nother girl someplace else?"

"How come you askin' me those sorts of questions, Abby?"

"Jus' to be doin' somethin', Luke, it don' matter to me do you have a dozen girls — nor two dozen for that matter." Abigail edged her body away a little.

"You the first girl I ever had, don' want no other — you 'nough for me do I live a hundred-sixteen years." Luke tried to pull the girl closer to him but she resisted. "I swear on my heart and soul, Abby, you the only one for me; all the girls in Alabama together ain't worth — " Luke hesitated, "they ain't worth one of you' teeth!" Abigail wriggled back into place.

"Tell you somethin'," said Luke in a serious voice. "We gonna be married do I make it through this war. Day I come home to stay I gonna take you straight to the preacher — don't care what you' pa say."

"Oh, Luke! Oh, Luke!" The girl started to sob. "Do you go back to fightin' — do you go back, you — you be killed. I know — I know jus' as sure as I know my name they is gonna kill you 'fore you ever come back."

"You jus' like a big baby, cryin' and frettin' 'bout somethin' you don' know nothin' 'bout," said Luke in his deepest voice. "You stop that cryin', hear! I be back to marry — I promise; they ain't no Yankee in the worl' can kill this one."

"They is gonna kill you, Luke, I got a feelin'," Abigail moaned. "Same feelin' I had when the baby was took with diphtheria; I knowed he was gonna die soon as he came down sick."

"They ain't gonna kill me," Luke declared with finality. "I gotta go back 'til the war's over, then I be comin' home and we are married, and tha's all they is to that!''

"Don' go 'way, Luke, don' leave me, Luke!'' Abigail raised her voice, sending a flash of panic through Luke as he imagined the sound reaching her sleeping father.

"Shissh you shoutin'! You wake you' pa and we both be in a purty!'' Luke roughly pulled the girl to him, muffling her mouth against his shoulder. She squirmed in his arms until her mouth was against his. Luke clutched the girl and within moments they were thrashing wildly, loud gasps and moans coming from their wide-opened mouths.

The night was half over when Abigail finally left the barn. She eased out of the door and ran across the moonlit yard. Standing in the shadow of the barn, Luke watched the girl until she was inside the house. He waited for almost a minute, watching and listening. Then he silently moved around the barn until it separated him from the house. Again he waited, listening. Finally, with a deep sigh, he started for home.

# XXI

The last night of his furlough, Luke lay in his bed unable to sleep. Over and over the thought dug through his brain that when he said goodbye to his parents in the morning, he would never see them again. He tried to turn his thoughts to Abigail, whom he had taken walking twice more — these times in the company of her younger brothers. But he was equally certain he would never see her again. In time she would forget him and marry another local boy. His eyes filled with tears as he muffled a sob. Then he heard the door to his parents' room open. He stiffened and lay still, partially closing his eyes until they were tiny slits — enough to see through, but giving the appearance of being tightly shut. His door eased open and his father, silent in his bare feet, crossed the cold earth floor. He stood over Luke's bed and stared down at his son's face, illuminated by the golden light of the now full moon.

Luke remained motionless, regulating his breathing. After what felt like a very long time, his father sank down onto his knees alongside the bed, pressing his hands together. There was a whisper of words too faint for Luke to understand. As he whispered, the man's body swayed, casting shadows on the opposite wall.

His father left as silently as he had come. Only when Luke heard the door close did he dare move. He shifted a few times, seeking a comfortable position in his bed. Then, filled with peace and a feeling that, after all, he might come home again, he drifted off to sleep and slept deeply until awakened by the crowing rooster.

# XXII

Josh lay in his bunk sweating out the remnants of a chest cold as Luke walked into the overheated, sourish smelling cabin. Davy sat close to the homemade reflector lantern sewing patches on his pants, pursuing a louse from time to time that ventured from its hiding place in the lining.

"Look what the cat dragged in!" Davy grinned and playfully threw his half-patched pants at Luke, who fended them off with his arm.

Josh snatched up a pair of ripe socks and pitched them one at a time at his friend — his efforts rewarded by exclamations of disgust. "Glad to see you, hoss!" Josh croaked, then blew his nose into the tail of his shirt. "Man, you shoulda been here for the excitement," he went on. "Ever'body in camp is all riled up. The Yanks is using nigger soldiers. Thought the lieutenant was gonna bust his gut when he heard 'bout it."

"Chris', the way they actin' you think it was the end a the world," Davy added.

"Some a the soldiers been askin' for the chance to raid the Yankee lines lookin' for them colored troops." Josh's voice cracked and whistled.

Luke, who had anticipated a different sort of reception, then declared, "Don' know why all this fuss is bein' raised." The irritation he felt leaked into his voice. "If I was Ol' Linkum, I'd use ever' nigger I could find, draft him in do he say no. Bet Jeff Davis 'ud use the niggers did he b'lieve he could trust 'em not to run off."

Davy picked up a shoe and skimmed it in Josh's direction, taking care that it went wide of its mark. "Hey man, ain't we a caution." Davy picked up the other shoe and sent it after its mate. "Here is ol' Luke back and we ain't even asked him how he is doin'!"

"Tha's all right," Luke mumbled, as he laid out his belongings on his bunk giving the task exaggerated attention.

"Seems like you wasn't gone no time a-tall." Josh sat up facing Luke. "You see my folks?" Luke nodded. "They all right?" Luke nodded again. "You tell 'em ever'thing I wanted?" Luke turned and handed Josh a small package, then turned back and continued with his unpacking. Josh looked at the package. "This all they sent?"

"The rest is comin'; be here in three, four days, maybe a week."

"How come you didn' bring the rest?"

"'Cause it was too damn heavy to carry — what you think?" Luke snapped back.

"What you gettin' so salty 'bout?"

"Man — jus' leave me 'lone, can't you? Jus' leave me alone!" Luke kept his face turned away.

"Hey, Josh," said Davy with several quick shakes of his head, "all we been doin' is talkin' 'bout what's happenin' here 'stead of what Luke's been up to."

As he realized what he had been doing, Josh colored deeply. "Hey, Luke — sure 'preciate you carryin' part a the stuff with you."

Luke tensed. Then seeing the expression of his friend's face mumbled, "Tha's all right."

From time to time during the rest of the day, Josh attempted to draw Luke out. But Luke responded in monosyllables.

That night Luke lay in his bunk unable to sleep. His trip home seemed like a dream. Thoughts having little relationship to one another flitted through his mind — confusing, depressing thoughts.

"Hey, Luke, you sleepin'?" Josh whispered.

"I'm awake, what you want?" said Luke without turning in Josh's direction.

"Mus' be strange goin' away then comin' back. Thought you might take a notion not to come back a-tall."

"I studied on it," said Luke in a flat voice.

"How come you decided to make it back?"

"Why did I come back?" said Luke. He paused for several moments. "They is more than one reason I guess. Don' know for sure." He paused again. "'Spose more 'an anythin' else — didn' wanna leave you — nor Davy 'neither." His face burned with embarrassment and he swallowed hard.

"Luke," Josh, too, was embarrassed, "you the bes' friend' I got in this whole worl'. You first and Davy next. Don' know what I do did you stay home. 'Spect I might-a took off myself." Josh took in a deep breath. "Been thinkin' 'bout war and fightin'. More I think on it, more I don' know what the hell it's all about."

"Me, too." Luke turned so he faced Josh. "Ever'where you hear them say you gotta fight; it's the manly thing. But I ain't so sure. Don't think my Ma and Pa have much use for war." Luke paused. "You hear people say no girl will look at you if you ain't in uniform. But I was speakin' with Ol' Monk's girl Abigail — at church — she don' have much use for war neither."

Grinning in the dark, Josh said, "That Abigail is about the purtiest girl I ever did see. Any man as gets that girl for a wife be mighty lucky. Yes sir, mighty lucky. Do I have the chance, gonna call on her myself." He pressed a hand over his mouth to hide a chuckle.

Luke laughed out loud. "You jus' a little too late, Josh. You go callin' on Abigail, you have to beat off this hoss first. This hoss gonna kick hell outa whoever goes callin' on Miss Abigail — even if he is the bes' frien' I got in the whole worl'!"

"Don' worry," said Josh, poking his friend. "You think I wanna get kilt? Any man as chanced callin' on you' girl mus' be mighty tired a livin' — and that's one thing sure."

Luke grinned so hard his ears ached. "Josh — " Luke was unable to suppress a giggle, "after I'm married do I have a boy — his name is gonna be Josh and you can be the Godfather."

"Supposin' it's a girl?" asked Josh, laughing.

"You can be the Godfather anyhow and I gonna name her," Luke hesitated, "gonna name her Josephine." Luke joined his friend in laughter. Their noise brought Davy to the edge of consciousness.

"Why 'n the hell don' you both shut up and go to sleep," he mumbled in a sleep-thickened voice.

Josh and Luke responded with bursts of laughter, but then, after a few more isolated chuckles, settled down in their bunks and fell asleep.

The three boys were drawn from the warmth of their cabin into the early morning frost when a soldier stuck his head in their door and gasped between gulps of air, "They bringin' in some nigger sojers — got three a them Yankee niggers!"

Outside, a patrol of twenty Georgians marching like heroes was just passing. Within their midst shuffled three black men, their hands tied behind their backs, a rope strung from one to the other secured about their necks

The forward end of the rope was tightly gripped by the serious-faced lieutenant in charge of the patrol. The other end was equally firmly gripped by a sergeant. Scores of men — in varying stages of dress and undress — followed the patrol. The number following increased by the minute.

The mass of men passed within a foot of the cabin. The press of bodies was so great that the three friends were forced to flatten themselves against the cabin wall. The three black Yankees were dressed in nondescript, non-military clothing, except for their hats and for their outer blouses, which were of standard Union issue. Their dark features showed an ashen cast; their eyes bulged from the pressure of the noose; their breaths rattled and whistled. As the black men passed, the Confederate soldiers standing in front of their cabins grew silent. All along the way the same thing had taken place.

"What you think is gonna happen to them?" Luke asked Davy as the prisoners moved away.

Davy shrugged. "Be sent to prison camp — maybe paroled back to the Yanks in exchange for a few of ours."

"You think they is gonna treat 'em like reg'lar prisoners a war?" said Josh in an uneasy voice.

"They got-ta," Davy answered with just a trace of hesitation. "Black or white, if you is a soldier and you is captured, you a prisoner a war."

"No cause to tie that rope 'round they necks that-a way," said Luke. His face had turned a dead pale. "Got 'em strung like cattle."

A soldier standing nearby turned to Luke and snarled, "Tha's all they is — cattle." Saliva flecked the soldier's lips. "Cattle, and I'm gonna see the slaughter." At this, Luke retreated into the cabin, followed moments later by Josh and Davy.

Several minutes passed with the three friends glancing at one another, from time to time, as they cleaned their muskets.

"If they ain't careful, those colored men be dead 'fore mornin'," Josh finally said.

"They gonna put them colored boys in the stockade," Davy declared, trying to sound certain. "Once they in the stockade they be safe — ain't no one 'bout to try and take a prisoner out a the stockade."

Josh shook his head, then mumbled, "Sure hope you right, Davy — sure do hope you right."

For the rest of the day, the three friends deliberately avoided any further mention of the black soldiers, but all three showed in their features and in their abrupt movements a lingering uneasiness.

They were about to bank their fire for the night and go indoors when a group of ten men, fully dressed against the cold, hurried by. The three friends exchanged uneasy glances. Another group of men passed by — these were breathing hard, their breaths rising in clouds of steam. Then a group of officers, dressed in greatcoats, their hats pulled well over their faces, appeared.

"They fixin' to lynch them soldiers!" choked Josh, his face turning ash gray.

"Come on," Davy growled, grabbing his coat. "Better see what can be did." His hands shook as he put on his coat. "Them sons-a-bitches, them no good, dirty sons-a-bitches!"

Luke, without a word, went inside the cabin and came out carrying his musket, with a Bowie knife stuck in his belt. Davy and Josh hesitated, then they too went inside. A minute later the three boys, fully armed, followed the groups of soldiers that were hurrying in the direction of the stockade.

The stockade enclosed more than an acre of land. It was built of posts eight feet high, sharpened at the tops and lashed together with fence wire. Several rough-hewn buildings were inside the enclosure as were a dozen or more regulation army tents. In front of the main stockade gate, two soldiers stood guard, their faces tight with tension. Inside the fence, as could easily be seen through the spaces separating each post, were some twenty soldiers holding muskets, to which were affixed foot-long bayonets. More than fifty flickering coal oil lanterns were strung around the four sides of the stockade, three times the number usually in use.

By the time Josh, Davy, and Luke reached the stockade, they found themselves among hundreds of soldiers, all pushing and maneuvering to get as close as possible to the gate. More soldiers were arriving each minute.

At both ends of the huge clearing, in the center of which stood the stockade, great bonfires were sending spurts of orange-red flame toward the sky. From time to time the crack of damp wood sent showers of sparks in every direction. The burning piles provided a crazy, distorting light that twisted and enlarged the shapes of the milling men. Those close to the fires were scorched and at times choked by the clouds of smoke that rolled over them when the wind shifted.

At first the crowd appeared to be without a fixed purpose and without a leader or a recognized group of leaders. But then an officer, his rank hidden by an unmarked greatcoat, shouldered his way to the gate ignoring the protests of the two armed sentries. He climbed half way up, securing a hold with one arm, and turned to the throng below him. The irregular illumination distorted the details of the man's sharp-featured face.

The appearance of a man clinging to the gate with his free arm upraised, fingers spread wide apart, drew the attention of the mob, until finally the eyes of the hundreds of men were focused on him. "Soldiers of the South —" The officer's high-pitched, cultured voice rose until it was almost a shriek. "Men of the Confederacy — we have seen today one of the most vile and villainous sights ever a southern-born white man has been called upon to witness!" Except for coughs and the creak of leather boots, the mob fell silent. "The blue-coated sons of Satan have taken into their ranks," the officer sucked in his breath, "more — taken to their bosoms, to their beds, black niggers — you hear me? Hairy, black niggers!" An uneasy murmur passed through the assemblage. The officer lowered his voice a little. "The Yankee generals, together with that devil in human form — Lincoln — have clothed black African apes with the noble garments of war. They are telling us, they are telling the world that niggers are soldiers; the equal of white men!"

The words of the officer, like fish hooks, pulled the mass of men closer. "Well!" the officer drew the word out until it was a howl. "Well! There are some here tonight that says there's no nigger living, nor dead either, as good as any white man; that you put a savage ape into a uniform, you do not have a soldier, only a beast dressed in a man's clothes! There is some here tonight as believes the only way to show the Yankee generals that niggers never can be soldiers is to make an example of them as was brought in today, an example such as Lincoln and his nigger-loving crew will never forget!" Other than a few shouts of agreement, the crowd stayed silent.

A second officer bulled his way out of the crowd, and in spite of his enormous bulk, agilely climbed the fence, taking his place alongside the first. This man spoke in a deep-south voice — Louisiana or Mississippi. "Ah knows the niggah! Ah has bred, raised an' marketed hundreds a prime bucks an' promisin' does. The niggah, if kept under a firm han', is a good an'mal — is a fine an'mal — ain't no one in this crowd gonna tell me a well-raised niggah ain't a pleasure to b'hold!" The words of the bulky officer puzzled most of the assemblage, but they waited to hear him out. "When a niggah ain't raised proper, when he ain't had his fair share a leather as he needs it, when a niggah starts gettin' notions, then that niggah is a dangerous an'mal. No white woman is safe within twenty mile of that niggah. They ain't no cure for a niggah with notions. I'd rayther be faced with a dozen savage lions than with a niggah that's been given notions!''

Then the officer shouted in a savage voice, "What we do this night gonna affect ever' white woman in the South! You' mother — wife, you' sister, you' own precious chile! Do we let the Yanks put niggahs in the war in uniforms, tellin' those niggahs they is soldiers good as any white — within six months half the white women in the Confederacy be polluted an' defiled, an' ever' loyal niggah slave be coaxed away!''

The crowd began to shift and murmur; a few men along the outer edge moved away.

The first officer, realizing that the other had not been effective, took over. "How many of you will be alive this time next year? The question froze the movement of the crowd. "How many of you will be rotting in some stinking hole, your guts shot out of your body before the next cotton picking?'' He paused and glared at the assemblage. "Niggers with guns are more dangerous than any white Yankee soldier. They hate us and are willing to die as long as they can kill a white Southerner first. If we don't stop Lincoln from using black soldiers now, by next spring there'll be thousands of them. If we act now and show the Northern generals that niggers will not be taken prisoners, that every nigger captured will be hanged and burnt — we still may be able to stop them!''

A tall skinny soldier raised both hands over his head and shouted — "I don' want ta fight no black sojers — Praise the Lord!''

Another soldier fired his musket at the sky. He was joined by dozens of other men firing muskets and revolvers, accompanied by shrieks and hoots. Then a soldier began climbing the fence, a second followed, a third, then more and more until the fence was covered with climbing men.

The guards inside the stockade stood confused and tense, unsure of what they should do. The lieutenant in charge ran up, shouting at the climbers to get down, but he was shoved aside as the men began to drop inside the enclosure. They disarmed the guards, who offered no resistance, then opened the gate, letting the rest of the mob pour in.

Several dozen white prisoners, mostly stragglers or deserters awaiting trial or serving sentences, were quickly released by the mob. They in turn directed the way to the building where the three black soldiers were secured. All the remaining guards, including several officers, concerned with their own safety, stayed as inconspicuous as possible while the hooting soldiers swarmed over the stockade, tearing down fences and ripping out posts and walls.

The fence posts and wall boards were stacked in the center of the compound until a pile of wood taller than twice the height of a man had been built. Flaming brands snatched from the other fires and raced through the night, leaving a trail of glowing sparks, were thrust into the pile; then with a rush streaks of fire swirled up, igniting the whole mass of wood.

Fifty men, under the direction of the two officers who had first climbed the fence, surrounded the guardhouse holding the black soldiers. The officers, fearful lest the overeager men might kill the prisoners while dragging them out, shouted warnings and backed up their shouts with blows from the flats of swords.

The black soldiers were brought out of their prison as canoes are carried during portage — up over the heads of the carriers. The victims twisted and bucked, trying with every fiber of their muscles to free themselves, but the struggles of the black men only served to increase the firmness of the hold of the whites.

When the Union soldiers were brought into view, the sight of their dark, struggling bodies affected the waiting men as a fallen deer affects a pack of wolves. They went into a frenzy. They shrieked and jumped up and down. Many pounded the back or punched the arm of the person standing closest, getting in return the same treatment and enjoying the sting of the blows.

Like a water-rotted dam the crowd gave way, letting the three knots of men with their victims through. A screaming soldier ran up to one of the writhing victims and tried to strike at him with his fist. The soldier was instantly felled by a blow from the flat of an officer's sword, and was struck again by a second officer as he rolled on the ground gasping in agony. There were no more like incidents.

By the time the three clusters of soldiers with their victims reached the main gate, three ropes had been affixed to the top cross bar, each rope fitted with the multi-coiled knot of the hangman. A cavalry officer, with the air of an old hand, who had taken command of the entire proceedings, pulled three sturdy soldiers out of the mass. These were stationed beneath the dangling nooses, and onto the shoulders of each man, one of the black victims was hoisted. A frantic, pimple-faced youth with the quick nervous movements of a fox terrier scrambled up the side posts and straddled the crosspiece, maintaining his balance with wrap-around legs while his arms remained free. The young soldier bent down, trying to slip a noose over the head of the nearest black man. The man ducked and shifted — struggling to keep his head clear of the noose. Every move of the victim was answered by a counter-move from the frantic youth who screamed down directions to the soldier on whose shoulders the black man rode. Finally, after more than a minute of maneuvering, while the mob watched in fascination, the officer in charge struck the struggling prisoner a blow on the side of the head with the haft of his saber. Stunned, the man stopped his struggling for a moment, long enough for the noose to be put in place.

The second prisoner twisted away with such force that he half slipped off the shoulders of his soldier. Several men pushed the victim back up and before he could continue his fight the noose had been fitted.

The third man sat quite still, offering no resistance. His eyes were shut, his face twisted into a strange smile.

When all three black men had been properly strung, at a signal from the officer each was seized by two soldiers and with a toss they lifted the black men from the shoulders on which they rode then let them go suddenly so they dropped straight down, their feet dangling scarcely a foot from the ground. The strangling men spun round and round like tops. Their untied hands clawed at the shaft of rope, then tore at the contracting noose — their fingernails gouging bloody furrows into their throats. Finally, with violent shudders followed by a series of kicks, their hands fell to their sides, as their swollen tongues pushed out of their wide-open mouths.

Only after the three black men were still did the officer in charge, assisted by another man, twist and pull on each body until a sharp snap gave evidence of a breaking neck. Then the officer, with three quick saber strokes, cut the corpes down. Each fell in a jumbled heap on the ground. Then with a raucous laugh and a wave of his saber, he shouted to the tensed mob, "Come on boys, they're yours!" For several moments nobody moved. Then the crowed closed in, grabbing at the corpses, men fighting each other screaming and kicking as they tried to get close to the crumpled bodies. With pocket knives and sharpened bayonets, bits of the corpses were cut away for trophies and pocketed. By the time what remained of the black soldiers was passed hand over hand to the waiting bonfire, ears were missing, as were fingers, toes, private parts, eyes, plus a large portion of skin.

Davy and Luke had watched the proceedings horrified, yet unable to turn their eyes away. Josh, almost from the first, kept his eyes tight shut but had shared in the event through his hearing and then when the dead men were roasted, through his sense of smell, as an acrid odor like that of burnt pork filled his nostrils. Josh felt himself suffocating. In a panic, he shoved and struggled, using elbows, knees and head indiscriminately to clear a pathway — fighting to get away from the choking stench, from the screaming mass of men.

Luke and Davy, seeing the wild struggle of their friend, tried to join him. By flailing and kicking, soon they were right behind him. Finally, they all were free of the screaming, straining press.

Josh, oblivious to the presence of his companions, overwhelmed by his panic, started to run. Once running, he couldn't stop. He had to get away. Behind him Luke and Davy struggled to keep up. They shouted for him to slow down, but their words had no effect. After several hundred yards, Luke found his wound so painful he couldn't go on. Davy lasted only a few more yards; because of his leg, he too was no match for Josh's two sound limbs.

For several minutes the exertion left Luke and Davy gasping, their wounded legs throbbing. Then they hobbled to their feet and followed in the direction Josh had taken. Half a mile away they found him. He lay full length on the ground, his head cradled in his arms, his face pressed against the frozen earth, sobbing.

With no shame or embarrassment, Josh sat up and rubbed his tear-wet face with his hands, leaving streaks of dirt on his forehead and cheeks. A shift of wind brought down sounds of shouts and laughter.

"They nothin' but an'mals," Josh choked. "They like a pack of dogs I once saw foller a little dog down into a gulch and tear that little dog to pieces. All them dogs come up with gore on they snouts — never saw an'mals worse as them — 'til t'night."

Luke limped over to a tree and pressed his forehead hard against its icy bark, remaining motionless in that position.

Davy snapped the firing mechanism of his musket. He was the only one still carrying a weapon; the other two had dropped theirs as they ran. "Takes the heart out of a man — seein' somethin' such as that," he murmured. He turned and raised his gun in a gesture of firing. "'Cept for us, seems like ever'one wanted them nig—," Davy caught himself, "them colored soldiers kilt." He lowered the weapon snapping the firing mechanism again.

"I'm ashamed; I never been so 'shamed in my life," Josh said in an even voice, "to stan' by and not do somethin' — to . . . "

"What the hell you 'spected us to do?" said Davy in a weary voice. "They was so crazy — had we started somethin', they'd a hung us up and served us jus' like they did them black Yankees." He sighed deeply and slowly shook his head. "Never see'd no worse mob in my life. Seen pigs slaughtered more decent!"

"Davy, I'm ashamed," said Josh again. "It ain't only us not doin' somethin' — it's like I'm dirty and nasty from bein' a part of it."

"From bein' in the Goddam army!" Luke yelled, his forehead still pressed against the tree.

"Why'nt we go to the colonel —to the general even?" said Josh.

"You see all them officers?" Davy answered Josh's question with one of his own. "You think the colonel, let alone the general, gonna do anythin' 'bout what they officers been up to? Most of them officers own slaves and they is all stirred up 'bout the chance of losin' niggers do the word get out that the Feds are usin' blacks for soldiers.''

"Saw that son-a-bitch Rawlins.'' Luke left the tree and dropped down beside the other two. "He was hollerin' and carryin' on with the others. Thought he'd piss his pants the way he was doin'!''

"Rotten son of a bitch,'' muttered Davy.

"You know somethin'?'' said Josh, looking first at Davy then at Luke. "I feel like I gotta have a bath — I feel all grimy and dirty and the graybacks is bitin' worse 'an ever.''

"Ain't thought none 'bout takin' a bath, but come to think on it — it's been a while — seems like a good notion.'' Davy started scratching, finally capturing a louse which he crushed under his thumbnail.

"We can use the mess kettle and fill it with water — still got some soap from my mother,'' said Luke.

The three friends stood up, trembling a little from the cold. Then they turned and walked toward their camp, taking care to skirt the vicinity of the stockade, although this added an extra half a mile to the trip.

# XXIII

The lynching of the three Negro soldiers hung over the camp like a blanket of stale air and a rigid taboo relating to the incident was enforced. No one spoke of the occurance; not the slightest reference to it was made.

Although it was forbidden to speak of the grim night, individual soldiers from time to time slipped away to place tree-green pine boughs on the common grave where the charred corpses lay buried. In time flowers fashioned from colored paper and wire were added. It gradually developed that a number of soldiers who had had a share in the killings assumed responsibility for maintaining the burial place. Some days the paper flowers and boughs were so numerous that they blanketed the mound completely.

# XXIV

Jackson's Army suffered during the cold, wet winter of 1863, as did other armies under other commanders, North and South. Although muskets were stacked and cannons were covered with tarpaulins, casualties equalled those of the most bloody battles — disease disabled and killed thousands. So general was sickness that at times as many as half the men of various regiments were too weak to line up for the daily roll call. It was a rare soldier who escaped his bout with a head or chest cold, and recurring attacks of diarrhea were universal. Men sickened, sweated and died within their own tents or shelters. The hospitals were full. More than a third of the battle-wounded still lay with swollen, pus-filled wounds in the damp, poorly-heated wards.

The constant presence of disease, which daily became more severe, produced a change in the behavior and attitude of the soldiers. Those regiments less seriously affected shrank into themselves, avoiding with a furious determination any contact with units known to be more severly infected. Armed pickets, angry and frightened, stood guard, ready to repel soldiers from another unit.

Within each regiment, certain companies also maintained isolation, but this was done by avoidance rather than by the use of armed guards. In every company each mess, consisting of from three to ten men, stayed to itself although when severely disabled by disease, several stricken messes would sometimes join forces, the well caring for the sick.

Captain Carter's company was more fortunate than most units as was the regiment of which it was a part. Unlike many companies and regiments recruited from a single district of a state, this regiment was filled with soldiers from all parts of Alabama — with the majority being city-bred boys. Those who had grown up in the cities and larger towns suffered less from the epidemics that spread through the camps, and when actually stricken, recovered more often and more quickly. Companies composed mostly of country boys were hardest hit. The well-tanned, muscular farm boy could not match the resistance and built-up immunity of the less robust city dweller.

Several weeks after the lynching of the three black soldiers, Josh fell sick. He and Luke had suffered through a series of colds and attacks of painful diarrhea, but until that day had been more fortunate than others who also came from the hill country. He sickened during the night. An acute attack of nausea drove him from his cabin. He vomited, but the relief was momentary. He stumbled back into the cabin and a chill deep inside his chest started spreading until the flesh beneath his skin felt frozen. He fell on his bed and lay gasping. With an effort, he pulled the blankets over his trembling body. The coldness, like frozen fingers, found its way into his throat, into his ears, his brain. Then suddenly a suffocating heat raced along every vessel, nerve and bone of his body, tearing into his chest and guts. With a frenzied movement, he threw his blankets off — their pressure on his skin felt like hot ashes. For a few seconds the cold cabin air relieved him, then the heat returned. Josh wanted to run outdoors to cool himself in the icy air where he could breathe. The tiny cabin was closing in and was choking him with its fetid air. He groped for the door, but was confused by the heat that filled his skull. Instead of reaching the door, he stumbled against Davy's bunk and fell forward across his sleeping friend.

For hours Josh hovered on the edge of consciousness. He would slip off, his eyes half open, his mouth forming words that couldn't be understood. Then his eyes would open and with a frenzied effort he would struggle to get up and escape from the cabin. During these episodes, it took the combined strengths of Luke and Davy to hold him down. Toward morning the fever slacked off and Josh sank into a troubled sleep.

For days Josh was desperately sick. He constantly called for water, then after several sips, would vomit. Unable to eat, the flesh fell from his body like fat from a roasting goose.

On the third day of his illness, during one of his brief periods of lucidity, Josh called out for his friends. The desperation in his voice brought them running. His eyes were opened wide, his pupils shifting rapidly from side to side; the cords of his neck stood out and his hands kept plucking at the edge of the blanket. Luke and Davy stood over their sick friend; he tried to talk, but his mouth was so dry he could only produce a croaking sound. They gave him several sips of water, then bathed his face and lips, leaving the damp cloth on his forehead.

Davy took hold of one of Josh's hands and held it between both of his. "What's stirrin' you up, man?" he softly asked. "No need to fret none; you be up on you' feet 'fore long."

Josh shook his head. "I ain't gonna get better!" he croaked. "Never knew a body could feel this bad — gonna die sure as hell." A series of dry sobs shook his body.

"You damn sure are sick as a live, plucked chicken," said Davy with a forced laugh. "You sicker'n hell, but you ain't 'bout to die. You got the swamp fever purty bad, but I seen worse."

"No man can be worse'n me and live," Josh whispered, fresh sobs shaking his body.

"You don' know shit!" snapped Davy. "Been in this army two-three times as long as you—an I seen plenty a men make you' sickness seem like the cough or the colic and those men was up strong as ever in a fortnight."

Josh shook his head again. "Don' really care do I live or die." He focused his glazed eyes on his friends. Then he whispered with trembling lips, "Only thing I'm askin' is don' send me to no hospital. I don' wanna die in some hospital lyin' among strangers."

Davy gently patted Josh's hand. "There you go talkin' 'bout dyin' again. Ain't no one as gets sick don' think he's the sickest chicken in the worl'. Two, three days — a week at the most, you be fine."

"Luke!" Josh leaned a few inches in direction of his other friend. "Don' let them take me to no hospital! Davy won't promise me. I want you' word, Luke, you' word no one is gonna take me to no hospital!"

"Ain't no one gonna take you out from this cabin!" Luke growled. "Ain't no one gonna take you nowhere without they killin' this one first."

At this Davy softly said, "I give my word same as Luke, live or die, you stay here; they have to kill the both of us 'fore they take you through that door."

As if he hadn't heard what they said Josh cried out, "Don' let them come for me. I don' wanna lie in no hospital 'mong strangers and have the doctors cut me open. Don' let them take me, Davy." He gasped for breath. "Luke! Luke!" he called out. Luke leaned close. "Luke! They gonna cut me up and roast me like they did them niggers! Save me, Luke, please save me!'' With a violent shudder, Josh fell back on his bed and slipped into unconsciousness.

# XXV

It was early spring before Josh completely recovered. During the bitter weeks of winter a quarter of
Captain Carter's company had died of the fever. And
Captain Carter was dead. No one in the company knew
exactly when he died. He had been carried off to a hospital where he lay separated from his brandy and cigars. It
was said that the loss of these, rather than the fever, had
killed the officer. Lieutenant Rawlins now commanded
the company. His promotion to captain was expected
any day.

Several days after Lieutenant Rawlins had taken
command of the company, Josh and Luke sat in front of
their cabin, engaged in the endless burden of picking lice
from their store of clothing. Davy lay on his bunk inside.
Both boys were concentrating so hard on their task —
using the points of their knives to free the seams of hiding
insects and of their eggs — that they did not notice the
approach of the new company commander.

They simultaneously became aware of the presence
of the officer and awkwardly scrambled to their feet,
dropping the clothing on the ground. Lieutenant
Rawlins, to the amazement of both, smiled blandly, bent
down and picked up the fallen garments which he

handed to the boys, murmuring something about the lice being worse than ever.

"Medlock around?" he asked in a friendly voice. Josh and Luke nodded, pointing to the cabin. "Would you do me the courtesy of havin' him step out for a moment?" Neither boy had ever heard him address enlisted men so politely.

Davy, having heard the officer, stepped out into the sunlight, blinking and scratching himself with slow deliberation. "You want me, Lieutenant? Or is it Captain already?"

The lieutenant pretended to ignore the sarcasm in Davy's voice and continued to show a bland smile. "Medlock," he said in an exaggerated southern accent, "ah been studyin' the needs of this comp'ny ever since poor Cap'n Carter passed. It's a heavy re-spon-sib-il-ity," the officer dragged the word out, "to command a company of men during wartime. A very heavy re-spon-sib-il-ity. A company commander must put aside all his personal feelin's, all his likes and dislikes and do what is best for his men." The officer wet his lips with his tongue, maintaining his smile all the while. "Medlock," he continued, "no use'n my sayin' I like you, for I don't and you know it and ah know it. No use'n my tellin' you I haven't damned you to hell more than one time — for I have. Yes, although it ain't fittin' for an officer to damn an enlisted man, ah have done so. But!" he eased the smile from his face replacing it with a serious expression, "but," he repeated, "the time has come for me to put aside mah personal dislike and antipathy for you and to think of the welfare of mah company. Medlock, ah am appointin' you sergeant." As he said the words, Lieutenant Rawlins pulled an official looking piece of paper from his breast pocket, which he presented to Davy.

During the lieutenant's entire speech, Davy stood silent, his hands at his sides, looking the officer full in the face. When the officer pulled out the paper, Davy remained still, his hands still at his sides. "Cap'n Rawlins, I mean, Lieutenant Rawlins," Davy spoke in a monotone, mimicking the officer, "ah is much obliged at you' kind offer. Ah appreciate hearin' how important ah am to the welfare of this comp'ny, but ah am forced to decline you' generous offer. Ah am satisfied with mah present condition."

The bland smile returned to the officer's face. "It distresses me to hear you talk in such a way. The welfare of you' comp'ny should weigh stronger than personal desire. But ah anticipated the possibility of a refusal, although ah hoped that this would not be the case. Jus' to avoid any misunderstandin' ah spoke to the colonel 'bout my need for an experienced sergeant and the colonel made you' promotion an official order, an official regimental order — for the good of the regiment!" With that he thrust the order into Davy's hands, wheeled around and walked rapidly away.

"I wonder what that Rawlins has in his mind?" Davy muttered when the officer was out of sight. "He would never had gone to all that trouble did he not have somethin' in his mind."

"You mean he wants you sergeant so's he can do you some hurt?" Luke asked.

Davy gravely nodded. Then he said in a measured voice, "He wants me to be sergeant — all right, might as well take the pay. But, I'll tell you one thing and you remember what I say. If Rawlins tries to pluck this chicken he's gonna find who's the polecat and who's the chicken. And I'm bettin' it's his pin feathers gonna be pulled — and then there won't be no 'nother time after that!"

"Maybe he did promote you for the good a the company," Josh said hesitantly.

"She-it!" Davy snorted. Then he murmured, half to

himself, "He wants me to be sergeant, well tha's jus' fine with me." With that he went inside the cabin.

Josh and Luke looked at one another and shrugged. "Don't make sense the lieutenant promotin' Davy to sergeant if he still has it in for him," said Luke.

"Sure don't," agreed Josh. "I 'spect Davy is wrong — this one time." Luke nodded.

# XXVI

Jackson's Corps and the other units that made up the Army of Northern Virginia curled through the countryside like a river finally freed by early April sunshine from the icy grasp of winter. At first the army flowed in a compact stream as if contained by elevated banks. In time, as if the elevated banks had been worn away, the army spread out like flood waters, covering an area twenty miles long by ten wide. As the army spread out, the regiments were kept bound together by messengers racing their horses from place to place carrying messages or urgent commands.

Along the northern flank of the undulating army, freshet-like patrols of soldiers probed toward the enemy. These felt their way to the very edge of the Yankee picket lines, then reported back the location of the Federal forces.

The Northern Army sent out patrols of its own as it marched, trying to discover the exact position of the Confederates. Day after day, as if drawn by the same huge vortex, the Northern and Southern Armies moved in the direction of Chancellorsville.

But then the movement of the forces slowed, as the thousands of men with their artillery and supply wagons sank into the sticky ooze of fresh Virginia mud as the rains of April, which had held off until the middle of the month, commenced and continued for two weeks with scarcely any relief.

Dirt roads were turned into thick brown streams that sucked at the legs of horses and men, quickly exhausting their energy. Tiny streams that usually could be forded by a single leap swelled until they became obstacles requiring the ingenuity of the engineers to overcome.

For several days after the rains began, the armies continued their forward movement. But with each passing hour communication with headquarters grew more difficult. When communication ended altogether, the various regiments looked to their own welfare and set up temporary camps.

Both officers and men huddled under worn canvas shelters that sweated and dripped. The incessant rain made the normal supply of firewood unusable, and the men ate their rations cold, without so much as a mug of hot coffee to fend off the chill and damp.

As the masses of northern and southern troops camped, poorly protected against the wet, their stomachs upset from uncooked salt beef and pork and from wormy hardtack, suffering from cold and lice that found the damp, sticky climate much to their liking, as they lay trying to cope with an infestation of fleas that competed with the more familiar graybacks, they yearned for the return of the sunshine although that almost certainly would soon be followed by a major confrontation with the enemy and the loss of thousands from their ranks.

As the end of April approached, the rains lessened until finally they stopped. The swollen creeks receded and the churning Rappahannock River, separating the Northern and Southern Armies, settled back into its usual placid ways. Both armies laboriously pulled themselves from the sticky, sucking mud, wiped off their hundred thousand pairs of boots and started marching; the Northern Army readying itself to attack, the Southern prepared to receive the onslaught and turn it back.

Chancellorsville, the place chosen for the slaughter, was a little town that had gained its name from the Chancellor's House that stood in all its southern splendor on the outskirts.

Some great battles start all at once — both sides line up and, with an "on your mark," the troops tear at each other on a single field of battle. Other engagements get under way in a piecemeal fashion — a skirmish here, a skirmish there until at last a general conflict erupts, moving and shifting over dozens of square miles of disputed territory. The Battle of Chancellorsville was one of these latter kinds — little probing clashes finally coalescing into a wild general struggle.

The earth was carpeted with fresh green grass that looked emerald-satin when viewed from a distance. The trees had passed their budding stage and now were adorned with shiny young leaves, whose tiny droplets of clinging moisture sparkled in the rays of the rising sun.

Out of a copse of trees, whose wetness had sprinkled the heads of the soldiers, onto a broad sloping meadow stepped the company commanded by Captain Rawlins — he had gained his promotion the week before. Detached from the rest of the regiment, his company had been assigned to advance patrol duty with orders to engage any patrols of the enemy that might be met and to send back couriers to the regimental headquarters for assistance as soon as contact was made.

While the rest of the company waited at the edge of the meadow, two squads of soldiers started slowly across the field. The squads, one of which was under Davy's supervision and consisted of Josh, Luke and four others, met with no resistance. Reaching the mid-point of the field, they halted and carefully examined the trees on the far side, still some three hundred yards distant. Nothing. Then at a signal, the rest of the company, in four separate platoons, started across the meadow.

The two lead squads were within seventy yards of the far side with the rest of the company a hundred yards behind when Davy's probing eyes saw a reflection of light among the trees. He yelled for the men to get down. The men of the two squads instantly dropped. But before the rest of the company was able to react, the woods erupted with a salvo of gunfire, leaving eleven dead and twice that number wounded. As the men squirmed on their bellies to find protection behind rocks and in slight depressions, Yankee sharpshooters killed five more and an additional six soldiers were added to the ranks of the wounded.

When the Confederates finally were able to answer the Federal gunfire, the returning musketry forced the Yankees several yards back into the woods, reducing their accuracy. Realizing the seriousness of his company's position, Captain Rawlins crawled forward on his belly until he reached Davy.

Flat on their bellies, their faces separated only by inches, the two young men stared at each other. "Medlock, I'm sorry for — everything," the officer finally whispered. Davy nodded. Then, after several moments of hesitation, he ordered Davy to move to the left with his six-man squad, to enter the woods at the extreme left and to flank the enemy — opening a diversionary fire when he got behind them. This maneuver, he said, would enable the rest of the company to attack with some chance of success.

Impressed by the plan and moved by the officer's apology, Davy grinned, then murmured, "I'll give her my bes' shot, Cap'n. Wish me luck!''

Using every effort to avoid drawing the enemy's attention, under the cover of a steady musket fire from the rest of the company, Davy's squad eased through the grass, making use, when possible, of slight depressions and gullies. Finally they reached the far end of the woods and slipped into the shadows, moving in a wide arc. Then exercising all possible caution, each step taken so as not to disturb even a twig, the squad advanced toward the rear of the Yankee troops.

Davy carefully positioned his six men.

Their attention concentrated on the Confederate troops out in the field, the Yanks had no thought about the possibility of attack from the rear.

The first volley from Davy's squad dropped seven Yanks — one for each shot fired. The second produced the momentary panic among the enemy Davy had anticipated. As the third volley was fired, he expected to hear the yells of counter-attacking Confederates. Instead, there was an end to the Confederate gunfire. And there were no yells. Captain Rawlins had retreated, leaving Davy and his men to the mercy of a force twenty times their number.

Moments after the Confederate gunfire ceased, Davy understood what had happened. For several seconds he was paralyzed by rage. Josh and Luke stared at his face which had gone a dead white. "If I ever get out a this — I'm gonna kill that Rawlins — gonna break his neck with my bare hands,'' he hoarsely whispered. "I swear this on my mother —''

The company of Yankees, using the trees as shields, was approaching.

Taking in a deep breath Davy shouted, "We surrender! We surrender!'' at the scores of approaching men. Then he hoarsely whispered, "Josh — Luke — the rest a you throw down you' guns! We ain't gotta chance!''

Then cupping his mouth he yelled, "Hey Yanks, don' shoot, we give — we surrender!" And then, holding his breath, his eyes shut tight against the chance of being shot, Davy stepped out into the open, his hands raised high above his head.

There were no shots. Moments later the other six members of the squad joined their sergeant — hands above their heads, their faces chalky white and wet with perspiration.

All seven men of the Confederate squad gasped and trembled as the Yankee soldiers surrounded them. During the brief flurry of firing, the enemy troops had been just blue blobs to be lined up in gun sights and then picked off. Now these blue blobs were men. A hundred fully uniformed and armed *black* men. Davy counted himself and his men as dead the moment he saw the skin color of the enemy soldiers. He stood rigid, trying not to tremble, his squad behind him, waiting for the killing which he was certain would be done silently with long-bladed knives and bayonets.

A flat-faced, massive soldier wearing the chevrons of a sergeant, stepped forward. In a deep baritone he turned to Davy and declared, "You is safe, mister, we don' kill no unarmed men, you is safe."

Davy looked up, dumbly searching the black sergeant's features. The eyes of the two met. A slow, full smile spread across the black man's face, exposing a magnificent set of gold-notched, gleaming teeth. Davy expelled the lungful of breath he had been holding. Without being completely aware of what he was doing, he thrust out his hand. The black man stared at the proffered hand. Then he slowly advanced his own hand as if he expected the white hand to be withdrawn at any moment. The two hands touched. The hands of both men dropped to their sides at the same moment — it was the first time that either had shaken a hand of the other race.

Josh, Luke, and the rest of the squad stared, bug-eyed, at Davy and the black sergeant. What had just taken place was more a guarantee of their safety than a paper signed by the Yankee president himself. In the space of a few minutes, they had gone from life to death and then back to life. One by one the Confederate soldiers sank down, their legs grown weak. Each fought an urge to cry. Davy pulled out the tail of his shirt, using it to blow his nose until his emotions were back under control.

"You comp'ny run away an' lef' you," said one of the black soldiers to Davy in a puzzled voice.

"We was in trouble when you started shootin'," added the sergeant. "Did they attack 'stead a runnin' back, they might a whupped us good."

To the two statements Davy only shrugged; the rest of the squad remained silent, listening.

A white Yankee lieutenant, unseen until that moment, ordered the sergeant aside for a quick whispered conversation. Then the Yankee officer walked up to Davy. "I'm Lieutenant Franklin," he said in a nervous voice. "You are our prisoners." Fatigue and the residue of fear showed in the man's face. "You will be treated fairly as long as you make no attempt to escape."

"I'm Davy Medlock — ah, Sergeant Medlock — and these here are my men," said Davy. Then with an effort he pulled himself to his feet, stiffened and executed a precise salute. "No need you worryin' 'bout us, Lieutenant. We ain't gonna escape. That cap'n of ours cut out and left us hangin' — we ain't studyin' no escape." Then with a gush of relief, "And we is thankin' the good Lord we is alive, and thankin' you' men for the way we been treated."

The officer nodded. "These here boys are good soldiers. As good as any I ever commanded." The black soldiers grinned. For several moments the officer chewed on his lower lip. "If your captain had attacked," he said carefully, "instead of falling back, the situation might have been reversed and we would be your prisoners. For a minute, after you started firing at our rear, I though we were surrounded. It gave me quite a turn." The lieutenant screwed up his face. "I just don't understand why we weren't attacked; it doesn't make sense."

Deep patches of scarlet showed in Davy's face and his lips grew white. He was tempted to blurt out the truth. But he decided against it, swallowing hard several times.

The black soldiers gathered their dead and wounded, using panchos tied to split-rail fence posts as stretchers. Within thirty minutes the Union Company was ready to move out — a dozen of their number assigned the task of guarding the Confederate prisoners. The company traveled slowly, burdened by the stretchers. After four hours, as the afternoon shadows lengthened into twilight, the officer ordered his men to make camp. With an unexpected show of consideration, the soldiers assigned to guard Davy and his men took up positions sufficiently far away to permit their prisoners to carry on subdued conversations without being overheard.

The seven southerners built their own fire and gathered armfuls of pine boughs for their beds. At first they were hesitant about engaging in any conversation, expecting the guards to move in close at any time. But as the black soldiers gave no indication of moving and as they were preparing several small fires of their own, the members of Davy's squad started conversing. Each man felt a need to declare his wonder at the miraculousness of their survival. For each man secretly felt that it was all a dream — that at any moment his eyes would open and find the horror they had anticipated if captured by Negro troops. Yet if the right words with the right feeling were said again and again — the horror might not come.

Neither the black soldiers nor their officer approached the squad that night. The guards were changed at two hour intervals and they sat watching, cradling their rifles, but not interfering in any way with their prisoners. As the hours passed and the May breeze became tinged with cold, one by one the men of Davy's squad squirmed down into their temporary beds of pine boughs and fell asleep. Finally, only Josh and Davy remained sitting next to the campfire; Luke had been the first to be overcome by exhaustion and he lay nearby in deep sleep, knees to his chest, his arms cradling his head.

The two friends sat close together, almost touching, each leaning forward and resting his chin on his knees. Josh stared into the glowing embers and watched the changing colors — from orange to red with wisps of dancing blue and yellows back to orange. Davy's eyes were shut, but the light of the fire filtered through his eyelids, creating a pattern of colors in his mind almost as real as the actual glow of the coals.

"Sure is strange sittin' here like this," said Josh softly. "Wouldn'a gave a shaved penny for our chances when I seen them black soldiers comin' at us."

"Uh, huh," grunted Davy. "Sure is a strange worl'" we live in, sure is." He sighed deeply. "Guess this war is over for us."

Josh nodded.

"A week or two and we be in some Federal prison camp, with nothin' to do 'cept wait 'til the war be over," Davy went on. He opened his eyes, picked up a stick and began poking at the fire, each poke sending a flurry of sparks into the air. "Hear that some a those prison camps ain't too bad. D'pends where we get sent. Lucky it ain't winter — might be sent someplace freezin' cold; ain't nothin' troubles me more 'an the cold."

"Don' mind a little cold now and again," Josh murmured. "But not freezin' cold. Gets mighty cold to home, but it ain't nothin' to what it must be up north."

"Don' matter," Davy shrugged. "We got five-six months 'fore we need worry 'bout the cold and the war is likely over by then. Or," he lowered his voice to a whisper, "once we is in the prison camp we might be able to cut out and get back home."

Josh grinned. "Here we is talkin' 'bout escapin' and jus' a few hours ago they weren't one a us as thought we would live to see the mornin'." The grin faded. "When I think on the way them three colored soldiers was served and how we is bein' treated . . ." Josh didn't complete his sentence.

"When I think on all them things we was tol' 'bout nigger troops," Davy muttered, "got me to b'lieve it. Should-a had more sense." He paused. "Damn near shit my britches when I seen them black soldiers comin' at us," he laughed. "You know somethin', Josh, I wouldn'a blamed them one damn bid did they cut our throats or string us up. The way they been served by white men in the South, Christ, makes me sick when I think on different things that has been did to some poor colored man or other. And to they women, too. If I was one a those black men I'd a hung us up for the crows!"

"That black sergeant," Josh said hesitantly, glancing at Davy, "to this chicken he is as good, ah, I mean . . ."

"Good as any white man!" Davy interrupted, finishing the sentence for his friend.

"Yes!" said Josh explosively. "And better 'an some as I could mention. And they all ain't enlisted men neither. Some are officers, 'specially one certain cap'n I could mention!"

Davy poked at the fire again. "That no good son-a-bitch. Do I ever get the chanc't," Davy raised his right hand in the sign of the pledge, "I swear by God almighty I gonna kill that man. You take notice, Josh. I gonna carve his liver out his body and feed it to the dogs. That son-a-bitch!''

"After the war!" muttered Josh.

"Yeah, after the war. I'll still be aroun'." An icy grin pulled at Davy's lips. "Don' worry, I'll still be aroun'."

# XXVII

Just before sunrise the Yankee lieutenant came up to where Davy lay sleeping. The brightening sky was clear — not so much as a trace of a cloud — and in spite of the early hour, a breeze heavy with spring warmth had swept away the remnants of the night's chill. The officer bent down and shook Davy, calling his name softly. Davy opened his eyes and stared at the officer; for a moment he was puzzled, then he remembered and scrambled to his feet. With a quick motion of his head, the lieutenant signaled Davy to follow him. When they were several hundred yards from the others, the officer squatted down and after several moments of hesitation Davy joined him.

"Medlock," said the lieutenant with a deep frown, "I've been thinking about you and about your men." He paused and cleared his throat. "I decided I best have a talk with you and, ah, tell you what I have in mind." Without being too obvious about it, Davy studied the man's features.

"It's hard to tell how far we are from the main body of our troops," the lieutenant continued, with forced casualness. "The army is moving and it might be a day or two — even three before we join up."

A rush of excitement swept through Davy. He tried

to regulate his breathing so as not to give himself away. "Both armies is shiftin' 'round," he said with a prolonged yawn. "Can't tell how far away either one is. They might a moved so's they changed places. I seen it happen more 'an onc't."

"That's why I wanted to talk to you," said the lieutenant carefully. "These men of mine are green — in a manner of speaking." He tried to laugh, but it was more a cough. "They're good men and brave, but new! And we're loaded down with wounded and dead."

Davy nodded. Then in a sympathetic voice, "Carryin' stretchers slows you down — and new soldiers can get mighty skittish if you ain't careful. Three-four days with the chance a bein' ambushed any time is a mighty long time."

The officer looked hard at Davy. Davy returned the look.

"Was I in you' shoes," Davy paused and picked up a blade of grass which he stripped down between his teeth, "my duty would be to my men. No one gonna blame nobody for takin' care a his men and gettin' them back safe."

"An officer's first duty is to his men," the lieutenant said hoarsely. It was as if he was reading it from a manual.

"Lieutenant Franklin," said Davy formally in the military manner, "do you grant me a parole I give my word I won't bear arms 'gainst the Union Army until such time as I is *properly* exchanged for a Fedr'l prisoner of equal rank."

The officer assumed a grave look. "Sergeant Medlock, do I understand, if I grant you parole, you will pledge me your sacred word of honor to return to your home and not bear arms against the forces of the United States of America?" Davy nodded. "The only exception being if you are properly and lawfully exchanged for a

Union prisoner of equal rank." Davy nodded again. The officer looked Davy full in the face. "Do you give me your word as one gives his word to another?"

"I don' pledge my word often, Lieutenant. But do I give my word, I won't break it — does it cost my life. I do give you my word."

The officer turned partially away, then without looking at Davy muttered, "All right, take your men and go, and be quick about it."

With a roughness that was unusual with him, Davy woke his men. They sat up rubbing their eyes and clearing their throats. As he ordered the sleepy men to their feet, Davy noticed that the guards were no longer on duty.

"Will you get the hell up and stop draggin' you' ass!" shouted Davy, grabbing several of the men by their collars and pulling them up. Without answering any of their questions, Davy led them away. Josh tried to ask a question but was silenced when Davy snapped back, "Button you' lip; we talk later!"

The black troops were bunched together, their officer standing next to them as Davy and his squad marched by. Without slowing down, Davy executed a full military salute which he held until it was answered by the officer. "Keep you' eyes front — don' look back, not even for a moment," Davy hissed between his teeth. "We ain't out of gunshot yet!" The men quickened their pace.

They kept their precise military formation until they were on the far side of a small hill. Then Davy, with a sweeping arm gesture growled, "Let's run for it; don' wanna give nobody a chanc't to change his mind!" The men broke into a dead run and they ran until they reached a patch of wilderness and were hidden by the trees. Gasping, the men fell to the ground then lay for several minutes, their chests heaving, unable to speak.

Josh was the first to regain his voice. "Davy," he panted, "how were you able — to pull that one off?"

After several swallows and throat clearings Davy croaked, "I give my word — not to bear arms 'gainst the Yankees . . . the lieutenant give me a parole."

"Then how come you had us run 'til we damn near bust our chests?"

Davy winked, then grinned. The grin grew broader. "I give my word," he chuckled, "but none a you give you' word! I'm the only one paroled — the rest a you be free. Didn' say nothin' 'bout you — that officer jus' plain forgot. And I didn' wanna give him the chanc't to rec'lect!"

"Davy!" Luke exclaimed, "you jus' 'bout the slyest hoss in this whole worl'!"

"Hated to do that lieutenant that-a-way, square as he was but . . ." Davy shrugged.

"Better shake the dust a this place off our feet — they is no tellin' what's gonna happen," Davy then said in a tired voice. "I gonna lead you back 'til we sight some Confederate troops, then Josh is gonna take you the rest a the way."

The men looked puzzled. Josh made a questioning sound.

"I give my word and took a parole," Davy explained. "So I'm headin' home 'til they exchange me all legal and proper. When you find our reg'ment, Josh, you tell the colonel what happened and why I ain't with you. Don' bother tryin' to explain to that son-a-bitch Rawlins! Time will come he and me is gonna meet and they is gonna be scores settled up."

"How long you figure to be gone?" asked Luke.

"Three-four months, maybe longer. Takes time to make a proper exchange after a parole. For all I care they can leave me home 'til the day after the war's over. But I 'spect I be back 'fore the end a summer."

After several minutes of discussion as to the probable location of the Southern Army, they started traveling southwest. They trudged for several hours, taking care to scout any open fields before they crossed them and staying clear of all roads. There was little talk and what little there was, Davy discouraged. At any moment attack could come from Yankee units or from their own soldiers mistaking them for the enemy. It was vital that they stay alert.

The sun stood almost directly overhead when the men detected a faint sound in the distance. They moved forward slowly and carefully. After several minutes it was evident that they were moving in the direction of a major battle. With almost no intervals between, they heard the rumble of cannon fire. Less distinct came a brittle sound like wind in the cane fields — the sound of musketry. They moved closer. Soon over the low hill in front of them they saw curls of black smoke and clouds of dust rising.

Davy motioned the men to gather close around him. "This is as far as I can go," he said frowning. "Josh can take you the rest a the way. Watch you'selves." Still frowning, Davy hesitated. "I don' like leavin' you; 'less you be sharp you' asses be shot off. Neither side knows who you is so you gotta stay as careful a the Southern troops as the Feds. You move slow and stay down — holler out 'fore you go boundin' up — hear?" Josh grunted and the rest of the men nodded. "Josh, you in charge, understan' — do somethin' happen to you — Luke is next. But ain't nothin' gonna happen to you if you use the brains God give you!"

"How we know you is a'right?" asked Luke.

"Soon's I get settled — I'll send you my address and tell you how things is turnin' out."

"Wisht I was goin' with you," Josh muttered.

Davy shook his head. "I know how you feel — this

war's a stinkin' mess — but you signed up — you come with me you be a deserter."

Josh shrugged. Then he offered Davy his hand. "Take care — you'self," he said in a hoarse voice.

Luke took Davy's other hand. "You be good, hoss — an' send us where you is at," he said with a catch in his voice.

Davy pulled his hands away with an impatient gesture. "You don' have to worry 'bout me; this chicken can take care a hisself. You jus' make sure you get back without no Yankee minnie ball in you' ass. Nor no Reb ball neither."

Davy started walking then turned around and saw the men still watching him. "What the hell you waitin' on!" he snapped. "Josh, you get goin'!" When the men were finally out of sight, he raised his arm in a sort of a wave, rubbing his eyes with his sleeve as he brought it down. Then with a sigh, he walked rapidly away in the opposite direction.

# XXVIII

Single file, with less than an arm's length between each man, the soldiers followed Josh over the crest of the hill and down the other side. They moved carefully, snaking their way between boulders and around trees, yet taking as direct a path as possible toward the sound and smoke.

An hour's march brought them to a second hill — steeper than the first. After a brief rest they started up, inching the last few yards, hunched over, almost hugging the ground. Then they again rested, panting from the steep climb. Below, the countryside lay like a checkerboard tablecloth on which had been placed tiny houses, clumps of trees and curling silver streams. Objects that ordinarily might have been obscured by the distance stood glistening in the crystal clear air. Soldiers the size of midges and cricket-sized horses crawled leisurely, first in one direction, then in another.

The soldiers strained to see the color of the uniforms worn by the insect men. As they squinted and shaded their eyes, the tiny figures began to sparkle like bits of broken glass, but the dancing light reflecting off their tiny forms was silvery rather than gray or blue.

Perspiration seeped into Josh's arm pits and started

running down his sides as he prepared to lead his men down the slope. The steady throb of artillery had worked its way into his ears then down into his muscles and bones. His body felt stiff and heavy as iron. "We gonna go down there," Josh pointed, "and see can we find where our side is at. Can any a you tell which is blue and which ain't?" The soldiers shook their heads.

"The harder you look at 'em, less you see," Luke muttered, shading his eyes. "Guess we jus' gotta get closer 'fore we know who is which. Sure would be a comfort did we know 'fore we start down into all that noise and shootin'."

"Ain't no help for it," said Josh evenly. "Did we have some spy glasses we could know for sure. Might as well get goin' now; 'least it's bright daylight 'stead a night."

The hill was steep and sprinkled with loosened stones that gave way as the men descended. Every few yards one or another man would misstep and tumble, cursing, grabbing at branches to break the fall. Until they reached the foot of the hill they had little time to think about anything except their skin and bones. And once down it was too late to worry. The line of battle had suddenly shifted and they were trapped; the hill to their rear with the battle being fought directly in front. A thick pall of smoke had piled up against the hill and the shifting gusts of wind at times brought the sound so close that it seemed as if the battle were being waged almost on top of them. Through the dense haze, in almost every direction, came flashes of artillery fire. The air hissed with bullets and bits of hot metal.

"Find cover!" Josh yelled. "Don' know which side is ours — ain't no call walkin' out there and gettin' kilt!"

The men responded instantly, flattening themselves behind boulders, digging depressions for their heads as they lay prone.

A sharp gust of wind cleared a momentary path through the smoke. Scarcely two hundred yards distant, mounted men grasping sabers hacked at one another. The smoke closed back in, but the pounding of hoofs, the clash of metal and the shrieks of the men and animals came through until the hiding soldiers expected in another minute or two the horses would be galloping over their prone bodies. The din grew deafening. Suddenly horses were everywhere, some racing riderless, their mouths frothing with panic, others carrying red-faced, screaming men standing in their stirrups swinging blood-stained sabers or parrying with inverted muskets used as clubs. The shrieks of the men mixed with wild bellows from terrified animals that often as not received the full force of the saber cut intended for their riders. Men, thrown from their horses or on the ground because their mounts had been killed, stabbed at the bellies of the enemy horses, ducking the slash of the rider, trying to bring the man down.

The battle swirled around the boulders protecting Josh's squad. Several of the squad were nicked by the churning hoofs, one came close to being crushed as he managed to scramble away from a falling animal which left him drenched in its blood.

Two cavalrymen, their hands tearing at each other's throats, fell from their horses within a yard of Josh's hiding place. He watched with horror as the men struggled on the ground, each grasping for the other's windpipe. They broke apart and the one who appeared to be the weaker scrambled to his feet and started running, shrieking in fright, pursued by the other. In an instant they were hidden in the billowing clouds of smoke and dust.

With a frantic effort a group of horsemen wheeled around and raced away, followed moments later by another group shouting for them to stand and fight. The sound of pounding hoofs faded into the throb of artillery and the dull thud of distant exploding shells.

Josh and his men were as breathless as if they had taken part in the battle. The terrible violence had held them in so powerful a grip of fascination and terror that they had forgotten to breathe. Even now their breathing was sporadic.

All around lay the results of the battle. Blue and gray coated soldiers with split heads sprawled twitching, blood and brains oozing onto the torn-up earth. Some still carried in their quivering bodies the saber that had killed them — human Christmas pigs with carving knives sunk to the handle in their backs. Dead and dying horses were everywhere. Those not yet dead kicked helplessly as blood spurted out of gaping wounds, staining the ground and the corpses lying around.

For several minutes after the battle had shifted away, the effects of the din kept Josh and his men from hearing the groans of the wounded and the gurgling of the dying. But as soon as their hearing recovered, the sounds of the wounded and dying drew the men out of their hiding places. With strips of cloth torn from the clothing of the dead, they tied off hemorrhaging limbs or stuffed the strips into open chests and abdomens to lessen the flow of blood. Luke systematically went from horse to horse, not differentiating between those wounded and those already dead, and fired a bullet into the brain of each.

Josh, who carried a needle and several spools of thread in his haversack, used these to sew up gashes in scalps and faces.

They worked for nearly an hour, tying and stitching the wounded and easing the dying, not paying attention to the color of the uniform of any of the victims. They had almost reached the point where all that was possible to do with the limited means available had been done, when a party of Confederate stretcher bearers came out of a nearby clump of trees. From them they learned that the main unit of the Confederate Army lay less than a mile away, on the other side of the woods.

Before they entered the camp, Josh gathered his five men about him. They sat down on the grass and rubbed their hands on the earth, trying to remove the blood that had stained their fingers and dried under their nails. "Less talkin' we do the better," said Josh, forming each word carefully. "Some provost marshal spot us, right away he thinks we is deserters or stragglers and puts us under arrest. Best let me answer any questions 'til we find some Alabama outfit. Don't cotton to the idea a gettin' into the hands of no Carolina or Virginia officers!" The men nodded.

# XXIX

The Confederate camp was a mass of confusion — regiments and parts of regiments were scattered helter-skelter over several square miles. Hospital tents, in which lay wounded men waiting their turn under the amputating knife, were pitched any place there was a patch of level, elevated ground. And boxes and barrels of supplies were piled everywhere.

As Josh's squad moved around the edge of a hospital area — a frantic horseman on a lather-flecked horse dashed by, shouting that General Jackson had been shot. Josh shrugged, muttering, "They is always sayin' this one or that one has been shot. Ol' Stonewall's too mean to be kilt; 'sides the battle has been over a considerable while."

Unnoticed in the confusion of men and equipment, the six soldiers trudged from area to area searching for a familiar face, for an accent that would peg its owner as an Alabaman. Again and again they encountered other groups of soldiers likewise searching. The constant shifting movements of these groups of soldiers added to the confusion.

After circling more than halfway around the sprawling army, Josh had almost given up hope. He had selected an unoccupied grassy knoll protected by several large boulders on which to camp when off to one side he saw the unmistakably familiar figure of his company commander. His face completely drained of color, Captain Rawlins stared back at Josh. The captain's hands started to shake as his eyes darted from Josh to the others then back to Josh. Twice he tried to speak, but the words wouldn't come. The impasse was broken when Josh asked the captain the location of regimental headquarters.

"What you want at regimental headquarters?" croaked the officer.

Josh shifted uneasily from foot to foot. "I got somethin' I gotta report to the col'nel," he said, attempting to sound matter-of-fact.

"Don't you know about the chain of command, soldier?" The captain pulled himself up to his full height and stared hard at Josh. Then Captain Rawlins signaled a sergeant to join them.

"Sergeant, tell this boy about army regulations." The sergeant directed a puzzled glance at the officer. "Tell this boy about when you want to see the colonel you first go to the sergeant, then the lieutenant then the captain and on up." The sergeant nodded. "Tell him that a private can be court-martialed does he go direct to the colonel without him getting permission first."

"You gotta go to the sergeant, then the lieutenant . . ."

"That's enough," interrupted the captain, "it's been said already. But I'd be interested in knowin' what business a private soldier, particularly one as has been missin' these thirty-six hours, has with a regimental colonel. Ask him that, sergeant." The sergeant cleared his throat, reluctant to be cut off a second time. "Tell that private," continued Captain Rawlins, "that unless he fancies the idea of being arrested and charged with 'away without leave', he had better inform his company commander of the circumstances of his absence in addition to any and all matters he had planned to communicate to the colonel. His company commander will decide if said matters are to be taken to regimental headquarters — the decision will not be made by some damn private soldier."

Josh felt his face burning. He was angry with himself for having blundered into a difficult situation. Determined not to reveal any information that might be distorted to Davy's disadvantage, Josh's mind raced as he struggled to find the right words for the question he knew was coming.

"Where's Sergeant Medlock?" asked the captain. Josh frowned then, unable to control himself, swallowed hard. "Well, where is he?" the officer demanded.

"Davy — uh, Sergeant Medlock is on parole."

The officer took a step toward Josh. "What do you mean, on parole?"

"We was captured. Davy, er, Sergeant Medlock took us into the woods behind the Yankees . . ."

"Deliberately disobeyin' my orders," snapped the officer.

Josh looked at the captain in surprise. Then realizing what was developing, a wave of weakness swept through him and he began to feel sick.

"Medlock disobeyed my orders and took you behind the Yankee troops, then what?" said the captain in a softer voice. "Then what?" he repeated.

"Well," said Josh carefully, "we started shootin' at them Yanks and the next thing we knowed you — I mean the comp'ny was high tailin' it in the other direction. So we was captured."

In an almost friendly tone the officer commented, "You and the others here didn't know about my orders; of course not. You followed your sergeant like you're supposed to." A tiny, hard smile showed on the man's face. "You don't have nothin' to worry about. What happened after you were captured?"

Josh felt helpless; he had allowed himself to be sucked into a trap. "They was black soldiers and at first we thought we was dead men."

"Black soldiers?" said the captain, his voice hoarse.

"They was black soldiers — 'bout a hundred of 'em — all 'cept they lieutenant — he was a white man."

"Go on," urged the officer gently.

"They put us under guard — then early in the mornin' Sergeant Medlock convinced them to give him a parole. He swore not to bear arms 'til exchanged for some Yankee as is equal in rank."

"Where is Medlock now?" the captain asked carefully.

"He carried us to where we could hear gunfire and see smoke, then he put me in charge and he cut out. Said he was goin' home to wait out his parole 'til he was exchanged. He said once he give his word and took his parole he couldn't go back to the comp'ny. But we could," Josh said eagerly. "Davy really foxed them Yanks. The way he fixed it we didn't give no parole a-tall."

"So Medlock gave his word to a bunch of niggers?" Captain Rawlins' voice had a strange ring to it. "And it all happened because he deliberately disobeyed an order of his superior officer while under fire. Well!" the captain dropped his voice almost to a whisper, "we'll see about Mister Davy Medlock; we'll see about a sergeant that deserts his men and sends them into battle while he goes on home after giving his word to a bunch of Ne-groes."

Josh had the sensation of icewater running inside his body. He stared at the officer but instead of experiencing rage, he felt afraid.

"You boys get some hot food," said the captain

solicitously. "You been through a bad time from the look-a you." He patted Josh on the shoulder and Josh stiffened at his touch.

"You done good, Josh; you carried your squad back. You done what your sergeant was supposed to — maybe you be sergeant before long."

After Josh and the others had moved off in the direction of the cook fire, Captain Rawlins turned to the sergeant. "You heard everything that boy said about the way Sergeant Medlock deserted?" The sergeant made a sound deep in his chest, but it was neither a yes nor a no. ".You have any doubt that Medlock deserted?" The captain's voice took on an unpleasant edge. "You believe that a sergeant as disobeys his captain's orders under fire and gets himself captured, then gives his word to a bunch of niggers didn't desert?" The sergeant made another sound deep in his chest. "He didn't come back into camp 'cause he knew I would have him shot for willful disobedience under fire. Instead, he deserted and sent a squad of green boys alone through the lines not caring if they got killed."

The sergeant carefully considered what his company commander was saying as he assessed the tight expression on the officer's face. "That Medlock be in plenty a trouble do he ever show up here, Captain."

Imitating the sergeant's manner of speaking, Captain Rawlins added, "That Medlock be measured for his grave do he show up, Sergeant." Then he said, "I'm gonna speak to the colonel 'bout what happened. And meanwhile I want you to take a squad and go lookin' for Medlock. I want you to tell every provost marshal you meet about Medlock and give his description. Sergeant," Captain Rawlins assumed a confidential tone, "do you bring back Medlock, I'm gonna make sure you get thirty days leave plus travelin' time. How does that sound to you?"

"I ain't seen my missus for near two years," the sergeant said softly. "I'll bring Medlock if he's anywheres within a hundred miles."

"Eight-ten days travelin' time, Sergeant," Captain Rawlins called after the man, who had started toward the main cook fire. Without turning around, the sergeant nodded.

Two days later Davy was led into camp, his hands lashed tightly behind his back, a long rope attached to a pack mule knotted around his neck. A provost marshal, who had gained a description from the sergeant, spotted Davy at a train station some thirty miles away. Stretched out on a bench in the depot, asleep, he was placed under arrest before he realized what was happening.

# XXX

As soon as he learned of Davy's capture — a mes-
senger had been dispatched with the news — Captain
Rawlins went directly to the colonel who listened atten-
tively to the account of Davy's disobedience and desertion. Expressing concern that unless an example be
made, the other men of the regiment would assume that
desertion and disobedience under fire were matters of no
great moment, the captain then recommended Davy be
court-martialed.

The colonel nodded.

"It will do the men a world of good to see a deserter
shot," the captain declared.

"General Jackson was always a great believer in
makin' an example of a deserter," the colonel growled.
"You have my order to convene a court-martial." He
scribbled several words on a piece of paper and handed it
to the junior officer. "And I urge that it be done at once.
'Justice delayed is no justice at all,' as they say. Besides,
we may be moving in a day or two and a good execution
will stiffen the men — cut down the plague of deser-
tions."

The captain turned to go, his hand was on the flap
of the tent when the colonel's voice stopped him.

"Rawlins!" the captain turned around. "You sure Medlock disobeyed your orders?"

Captain Rawlins squared his shoulders and looked his superior full in the face. "Colonel, I give my word as one gentleman to another."

The colonel examined the other man for several seconds. Finally he said, "Your pa runs a sizeable plantation, doesn't he?" The younger officer nodded. "He keeps eighty-ninety slaves?"

"Never less than eighty," said the captain proudly. "Been as high as hundred and fifteen when the breeding's good."

"Medlock was captured by nigger soldiers, you say?" The colonel kept his eyes on Captain Rawlins' face.

"More than a hundred niggers, under a white lieutenant!"

The colonel shook his head gravely. "We can't let Confederate troops take paroles from niggers . . ." He rubbed his fatigue-reddened eyes with the back of his hand. "My family keeps slaves too, — don't come up to your pa's spread, but we have two dozen of our own out in the fields together with what we hire from neighbors at harvest." The colonel picked up a metal letter opener and started cleaning his nails. "No, Captain," he said, his eyes concentrating on his fingers, "there is no doubt in my mind that Medlock disobeyed your orders — none at all. But," the colonel maneuvered the letter opener skillfully, "we had better have the court-martial ready as soon as they bring him into camp. And, Captain," the colonel paused, "I, er, want you to find someone to defend Medlock." The colonel held the captain's eyes, that looked back without wavering. "We are gonna be sure and try that nigger-lover all legal and proper — do you understand?"

The captain suppressed a smile. "Colonel," he said,

"if you are ever in the neighborhood of my daddy's place — it's five mile east of Daleville — I would count it an honor did you stop with us several days. We got some prime nigger women that are a pleasure to behold."

# XXXI

The first Josh and Luke knew of Davy's capture was when they saw him being led into the company area roped by the neck to the mule. Both boys were so startled by the unexpected appearance of their friend, whom they thought to be hundreds of miles distant, that they sat staring open-mouthed until he was past. But then, as if propelled by a giant spring, they jumped up and ran after the little procession.

Josh grabbed Davy by the shoulder, but before he had a chance to ask any questions, the sergeant jabbed the muzzle of his musket into Josh's side and ordered him to stand clear.

"You makin' mighty free with that gun," snarled Luke, grabbing the sergeant's sleeve and pulling him half around.

The sergeant, his face, livid, swung his weapon around and pointed it at Luke's face. "You step back, man — you start any trouble you be pickin' you' brains off those bushes."

Luke dropped his hands to his sides and stepped back.

"Simmer down, Luke," Josh tugged at Luke's arm. "No call us makin' things any worse 'an they are for Davy."

Davy tried to speak, but the noose made it difficult. Finally he croaked, "Don' worry — be a'right."

The sergeant turned to Davy and gave him a rough push. "You a prisoner and you be still!" he snarled.

Josh fell in step alongside the sergeant. In a controlled voice he said, "Sergeant, you carryin' a musket and you marchin' a prisoner right now, so no one's gonna mess with you. But at night you be lyin' asleep and there's no tellin' what manner a accidents can happen to a sleepin' man. You serve Davy that way again, I'm bettin' some soldier accidently trips over you while you a-sleep and spills a kettle a boilin' water on you' face."

The sergeant grew pale and he almost stumbled. He fingered his musket for several moments then let it hang with its muzzle trailing on the ground. "When I get Medlock secure in a tent, it'll be all right do you want to talk with him. That Captain Rawlins give me orders — " he said haltingly. Then the sergeant reached over and loosened the noose around Davy's neck a little.

Josh and Luke followed until they reached the sergeant's tent. They waited until Davy had been secured with a heavy pair of shackles around his ankles. But as they were about to enter the tent, Captain Rawlins, accompanied by seven officers, rushed up and ordered the sergeant to bring Davy to regimental headquarters.

Two men under the sergeant's supervision carried Davy out of the tent. Once outside, his ankles were freed and he was hurried forward, a soldier on each side holding his arms, with Captain Rawlins and the seven officers following close behind.

"What the hell is goin' on," Josh muttered as he watched the group move rapidly away. "Come on, Luke, we better stick close; they is somethin' mighty peculiar 'bout this."

When the group reached regimental headquarters,

they were joined by three more officers. All the officers, preceded by Davy, entered the large tent. The two soldiers who had held the prisoner's arms, and the sergeant remained outside with orders to guard the tent and refuse admittance to anyone.

Josh walked up to the sergeant and without any preliminaries asked what was happening inside the tent. The sergeant hesitated, shrugged, then said gruffly, "They is havin' a general court-martial for you' friend." Josh sucked in his breath. "They is tryin' him for desertion and disobeyin' an order from a superior while under fire."

Luke tugged Josh's sleeve — motioning him to follow. When they were clear of the sergeant, Luke said with a wink, "They can't try Davy for desertin'. That sergeant is pullin' on you' leg. We was with Davy when he got his parole. That ain't desertin'!"

"That ain't desertin'!" Josh echoed. Frowning, he bit his knuckles as he tried to think the situation through. "And I don't b'lieve Davy disobeyed no order of Captain Rawlins. They must be jus' tryin' to get Davy to say he done somethin' he didn' do." He hesitated, the muscles around his eyes twitching. "Davy ain't gonna say he done somethin' he didn' do. No call us worryin'. They ain't got nothin' to try him for. Do they try to say he deserted or disobeyed an order, I can say the truth — so can you, and so can all the rest of the squad. Shit, Rawlins an' the others jus' tryin' to fool Davy into confessin' and they never gonna get him to do that. 'Spect he's smarter 'an the lot a 'em together."

"They try to do somethin' 'gainst the law, we can go see the colonel — the gen'ral if needs be," Luke added.

"Damn right we can — ain't nothin' gonna happen to Davy long as we is aroun'!"

The two friends walked back to where the sergeant was standing, easier in their minds. The sergeant, who had been brooding about Josh's threat, fixed a smirk on his face and said with a teasing sound to his voice, "I know for certain they is gonna convict Medlock and that he is gonna be shot tomorrer mornin'! Whole regiment is to see him shot, like the time they hanged that Union spy." Both boys stiffened.

"How you know that?" asked Josh, trying to control his voice.

"Never you mind. I know and tha's all."

"I b'lieve you nothin' but a lyin' billy goat!" snapped Josh.

"You think what you want," said the sergeant lightly. "Don't make me no never mind what you think. But they gonna take Medlock out and shoot him full a holes tomorrer and then they gonna throw earth in his face — and it don' matter do you b'lieve me — 'cause I know!"

For two hours Josh and Luke waited outside the regimental tent, determined to wait all night, if need be, for Davy's reappearance. Finally the tent flap was pulled back, revealing a cloud of bluish cigar smoke which obscured the inside. An officer with a drawn saber stepped out, closely followed by two other officers, each holding on to one of Davy's arms. Josh and Luke started forward, but were stopped by the sergeant and his armed guards. Josh shouted out and Davy tried to turn his head but was rushed forward by the two officers.

Suddenly Josh ducked around one of the guards and ran in Davy's direction. The lead officer stepped away from the procession, turned, raised his saber and struck Josh a blow on the shoulder with its flat that knocked him to the ground. Josh tried to get to his hands and knees, but the officer kicked him in the side, sending him sprawling.

"They gonna shoot me in the mornin' — the sons-a-bitches gonna shoot me!" Davy shouted, bucking backwards trying to free his arms.

"I'm goin' to the colonel — " Josh cried out, "don' worry, you ain't done nothin'."

The two officers started to propel Davy rapidly forward. "The colonel's in on it!" Davy gasped. "Go to General Jackson!"

Josh rolled to one side, keeping his eyes on the officer, then scrambled to his feet. "Luke," he shouted, "come on, man, 'fore they try an' stop us!" Luke broke into a run.

The sergeant turned to the officer, a question on his face. "Let 'em be," muttered the officer. "They can't do no harm — gonna see Jackson!" The officer snorted. "They be hogtied and put in the stockade 'fore they get within a hundred yards of the Gen'ral — sick as he is from being shot. Let 'em be."

When several hundred feet of darkness separated them from the others, Josh and Luke stopped to catch their breaths. Josh's shoulder throbbed painfully and his arm hung almost useless by his side. "That officer damn near broke my shoulder," Josh muttered between his teeth.

"Thought he was tryin' to cut you' head off when I saw him swing," said Luke, a catch in his voice. "Thought you was a dead man."

Josh forced his breathing under control. "You hear what Davy said?"

Luke shook his head. "I couldn't exactly make out his words — heard him say somethin' 'bout Jackson, tha's all."

"He said they is gonna shoot him in the mornin'." Luke stiffened. "He said for us to get to Gen'ral Jackson — that the colonel is in on it."

Luke sucked in his breath, held it several moments, then expelled it explosively. "Jesus Christ! I never heard nothin' like this before. They can't shoot Davy — he ain't done nothin'."

"Luke!" Josh swallowed hard. "Luke, they gonna shoot Davy if we don't do somethin'! Don' know if they gonna do it legal or not, but Davy be dead and it won't make no difference!"

"You mean they gonna kill Davy jus' for nothin'?" Luke tried to blink back the tears that were forming in his eyes. "They gonna shoot him jus' b'cause some officer don' like him?"

"Luke," Josh lowered his voice to a whisper, "that Rawlins is pure poison an' he's got the colonel on his side. Davy's a dead man lessen' we do somethin'."

"Jesus Christ!" whispered Luke, blinking hard. "Jesus Christ — did you ever hear the likes a it!"

"Luke," Josh reached out with his good hand and laid it on his friend's shoulder, "we got us some work to do. We got to get to Gen'ral Jackson an' tell him. They say he's been wounded and it won't be easy to get to him."

"Never heard the like of somethin' like this in my life!" Luke murmured. "We sure gotta see Gen'ral Jackson, an' quick."

# XXXII

Not knowing that Stonewall Jackson had been carried to a place many miles distant near Guinea's Station on the Richmond, Federicksburg and Potomac Railroad, Josh and Luke searched the sprawling camp for the general. They went from company to company inquiring of the sergeant of the guard where they could find corps headquarters. Most just shook their heads and shrugged; several offered directions which proved to be incorrect. The boys grew desperate. Finally, a drunken sergeant of the Charleston Zouaves, after insisting they have a pull at his bottle, gave them detailed directions. These proved to be correct.

A middle-aged captain reading dispatches by a coal-oil lantern looked up when Josh and Luke entered the farm house that had been commandeered as headquarters. He was a loose jowled, inoffensive looking man with steel-rimmed glasses perched halfway down his nose.

"We is tryin' to find Gen'ral Jackson, sir," Josh stated politely. "Is this the place he is at?" He tried to conceal his anxiety.

"What you want with the general?" the captain asked in a friendly voice, putting down the sheaf of dispatches.

"Ah," Josh hesitated, searching for the right words, "we got some personal business, ah — I mean they is somethin' we have to ask him."

The captain shook his head slowly. "Nobody sees the general unless he first states his business, 'specially no enlisted men!"

Josh glanced at Luke, who raised his shoulders a fraction then let them fall. "We was sent by our sergeant to see Gen'ral Jackson," said Josh.

The captain picked up one of the dispatches and started to interest himself in the document. "Sergeant Davy Medlock," Josh went on, struggling to control the anxiety that was taking hold of him. "He tol' us to find Gen'ral Jackson and tell the Gen'ral that he — Sergeant Medlock — has been sentenced to be shot for somethin' he didn' do."

The captain put down the dispatch and leaned forward, resting his chin on his hand. "Go on, young man, go on," he urged.

"Tha's all they is to it, sir. Davy said they is gonna shoot him in the mornin'. Can we see the gen'ral now?"

"Why are they planning to shoot the sergeant?" asked the captain, ignoring Josh's request.

"They charged him with desertin' and Captain Rawlins says Davy disobeyed him under fire. But that's nothin' but a lie — and Davy didn't desert. He give his parole to some Yankee soldiers."

"Was the sergeant court-martialed?"

"He was in with some officers in the regimental headquarters for a time," said Josh lamely.

"If he was properly court-martialed and sentenced to death, there is nothin' *you* can do about it." The captain laid emphasis on the word "you". "Besides," he added, after a moment of hesitation, "the general isn't here. He's miles away — they took him out by ambulance yesterday." The captain turned back to his dispatches.

Josh stared at the officer. Several times he opened his mouth as if to speak but the words wouldn't come.

The captain glanced up. "You still here — didn't I tell you the general is gone? Get out 'fore I put you both to work cleaning up this pig sty."

As soon at they were clear of the building Josh exploded. "He was makin' sport of us — askin' all them questions an' knowin' Gen'ral Jackson wasn't there! Son of a bitch!"

"What we gonna do, Josh?" asked Luke in a hollow voice.

"I don' know, hoss, I don' know."

"Who we gonna see now, Josh — Gen'ral Lee?"

Josh gulped and bit down hard on his lower lip. "Come on!" He grabbed Luke by the arm and turned back into the headquarters building.

"You here again?" the captain asked, annoyance showing in his face.

"We want to see Gen'ral Lee," Josh spoke out firmly.

The officer leaned forward again, his chin in his hand. "Gen'ral Lee don't wan-ta see you, sonny. You ain't seein' any generals. If you have something to say, say it to your colonel. If he wants to take it to General Lee, that's another matter. Now get out and don't come back — hear?"

Outside the building both boys stood hunched up as if chilled, although the night was warm and balmy.

"Le's go see the colonel," Luke suggested.

"But Davy said he's in on it," said Josh hopelessly.

"If we tell the colonel what we know — we was with Davy the whole time — if we 'splain how things was, Josh, he'll change his mind. Maybe the colonel jus' don' know."

Josh nodded. "Do we both swear an oath on the Bible, maybe the colonel *will* hold off shootin' Davy and order a new court-martial. Come on!"

# XXXIII

Inside the regimental tent a light still burnt. It was past three in the morning and the camp lay still except for the muffled moans of wounded men, carried down by a warm wind from the hospital tents a half a mile away. In spite of the late hour, the colonel was awake and fully dressed. He sat tipped back in a wooden camp chair, his mud-flecked boots crossed one over the other resting on a square deal table. At the officer's side stood a partially filled crock of rum punch. An unlit, well-chewed black cigar that had dripped a brown dribble into his gray-streaked beard protruded from his lips. The colonel's eyes were half closed and he hummed softly to himself.

The two young soldiers stood stiffly in front of their colonel. They waited several minutes to be recognized; finally the colonel grunted, which caused his cigar to bob up an down, but did not interfere with the tune he was humming.

"Sir, we come to see you 'bout Davy Medlock," said Josh carefully and in as military a manner as possible. "We was with Sergeant Medlock, sir, and we is both ready to swear he didn' disobey no orders and he didn't desert. He give his parole."

Slowly and laboriously, as if requiring a great effort,

the colonel lifted his hand. The two soldiers watched the hand rise until it reached the cigar and then watched it slowly fall back down, the cigar gripped between the thumb and forefinger. "You actually hear Rawlins' orders when he give them to Medlock?" asked the colonel in a thick voice.

Josh and Luke hesitated, glanced at one another, then shook their heads.

"Then how you know if Medlock disobeyed them or not?" Without waiting for an answer, the officer went on. "An' who the hell you pups think you are, sayin' that Medlock didn't desert? He was tried all legal and proper and the court-martial said he deserted!"

"But, Colonel," Josh said desperately, "we was captured and Davy give his parole."

"To niggers?" The colonel snorted. "He gave his parole to a bunch a niggers."

"They was commanded by a white lieutenant," Luke offered.

The colonel partially turned his head and spat — several droplets splashing on the boys' shoes. "Your friend disobeyed orders — and he deserted. One of those charges is reason enough to be shot, and Sergeant Medlock was found guilty of both." The officer lifted his cigar back to his mouth and clamped his teeth around the frayed, soggy end. "Either of you have anything else to say?" he growled out of the corner of his mouth. The two friends shook their heads. "Then get the hell out. Next time you come to regimental headquarters without your captain's permission, you do two weeks in the stockade. Now git!"

They stood outside the tent staring at the light filtering through the worn places in the canvas. Except for the faint glow of several dying campfires, the rest of the camp was dark.

"What we gonna do, Josh?" Luke whispered, twisting his hands together. "'Less we do somethin', it'll be mornin' and Davy be dead."

"Man, I know; you ain't tellin' me somethin' I don' know," Josh said harshly. "How come you always ask me what to do; how come it's always me as is 'sposed to know the answers? Christ, I don' know what to do!"

"Josh — Josh, you really think they gonna shoot him?" Luke's voice cracked.

"What you mean?"

"I mean ain't it jus' possible they is tryin' to give Davy a lesson an' — an' after worryin' him 'bout gettin' shot they is gonna turn him loose?"

Josh's breathing quickened as he felt a tiny tug of hope. "Don' seem likely," he said hesitantly. "Don' seem likely, but then you just don' know. I heard-a stranger things."

"They shoot Davy and we knowin' what we do — and others, too," Luke's voice took on a ring of excitement, "they be in bad trouble do we get to Gen'ral Jackson or Lee. Don' think they'd risk it."

"If I was Rawlins or the colonel," Josh formed his words carefully, "I sure wouldn't go and shoot a man I knowed to be innocent. Not with those as knows the truth still walkin' about."

"They jus' tryin' to put a scare into Davy," Luke pummeled Josh on the arm. "Tha's what they is doin', jus' worryin' him and us and then they gonna let him go!" His excitement grew so great that he hopped from one foot to the other.

"Luke," Josh said his friend's name slowly, "I do b'lieve you right. They ain't so crazy as to go shootin' people for no reason. They is riled 'cause Davy give parole to some colored soldiers, but they know that ain't desertin'."

"How 'bout what Rawlins says — that Davy disobeyed orders?" Luke grew momentarily cautious.

"Did you ever hear of a man disobeyin' orders and attackin'?" Josh answered, overwhelmed by the logic of it all. "They shoot you for runnin' away, or for lyin' down when you is 'sposed to attack. But the one thing they don' shoot you for is goin' up 'gainst the enemy." He paused, then with amazement at the obviousness of his thinking, he exclaimed, "They don' shoot you, they give you a medal!"

"You sayin' they is gonna give Davy a medal?" asked Luke, wonder showing in his face.

"Hell, no. They is sore 'bout them nigger soldiers and they is pushin' on Davy jus' so they don' have to praise him for what he did. 'Sides, they is coverin' for Rawlins, and he is coverin' for hisself — 'cause he ran 'stead-a goin' after them Yankees!"

Luke giggled. "Josh, we been frettin' and runnin' like a turkey at Christmas time. We sure is simple." For the first time since Davy was led back into camp, Luke felt a sense of relief.

"Hoss," Josh turned to his friend, a half smile fixed on his face, "it don' seem likely they is gonna shoot Davy, but," he hesitated, "you never know 'bout a crazy bastard like Rawlins. I ain't worryin' no more, and," Josh hesitated, "I'm smilin' but I ain't laughin' — least not yet."

# XXXIV

The sun had already cleared the tree tops when Josh
was awakened by the harsh voice of the corporal of the
guard. "Get you asses up. They blowed assembly. You
got all night to sleep!"

Josh rubbed his eyes and looked up into the corporal's sullen, red face. The non-com glowered down at
him. "You be in a parcel a trouble if you an' your
sleepin' friend don't get movin'," the man said angrily.
"The whole regiment is assemblin' to see a deserter
shot." Suddenly the corporal's face went white. "Jesus
Christ," he said in a whisper, "don' know how come I
forgot — he was you' messmate. I'm sorry." The man
backed away. "I'm real sorry. They ain't no call you two
comin'. You stay here if you want."

"They gonna — shoot Davy Medlock?" Josh
gasped. It was as if the corporals words had been kicks to
his midsection — he struggled for breath.

"They is formin' the regiment," the corporal said
softly. "It's to be did at eight o'clock." He paused, his
face still drained of color. Then he turned away murmuring, "He's out there right now diggin' his own grave."

Josh grabbed Luke's arm and dug his fingers into
the muscle. Luke's eyes opened for a moment, then flut-

tered shut. Josh squeezed his friend's arm a second time, using all his strength. "Wake up, damn you, wake up. They is gettin' ready to shoot Davy — they gonna kill him at eight o'clock!"

Luke opened his eyes and tried to focus them. Suddenly he sat up. "What —," he asked. "How you know?"

"Luke!" Josh's voice grew frantic. "Davy is out there — out there right now diggin' his grave — and we is here. God-a mighty, Luke!"

Luke dug wildly in his pocket and pulled out his father's watch. "Ten minutes to eight," he whispered, staring at the time piece.

With a choked cry, Josh jumped up and ran in the direction the corporal had taken. Luke followed, his hands frantically trying to button his pants.

The regiment was gathering on a gently sloping field directly behind a row of hospital tents. In past years the field had been planted with corn, but now lay fallow. Here and there in the dry stubble a green stalk grew from some forgotten seed. In the center of the field a full platoon of soldiers carrying bayoneted muskets formed an open square. Four officers, each holding an unsheathed saber, were lined up shoulder to shoulder inside the square. In the very middle, his sleeves rolled up, his body obscured to the waist by the trench in which he stood, Davy worked, throwing spadefuls of earth up onto a mound.

The soldiers of the regiment had been ordered into a box-like, three-sided formation so that all would be able to see what took place on the fourth side. Curious onlookers from other regiments were scattered in a haphazard fashion outside the regimental formation. Captain Rawlins' company had taken a position along the back line most distant from, but directly facing, the place of execution.

As soon as Josh and Luke reached the edge of the field, (which was obscured from the rest of the camp by the row of hospital tents) they stood panting, trying to orient themselves to what was taking place.

"Oh, my God — there's Davy!" gasped Luke. A hundred yards away he could see the bent-over torso of his friend throwing up shovelfuls of earth. "They really makin' him dig his own grave!" He choked back a sob.

Josh stared out at the field, his eyes wide open. The sun's dazzle filled them, but he didn't blink. The horror of what was about to happen had numbed him.

Luke opened his mouth wide but made no sound. Then with his mouth still open he ran toward Davy. Arms thrashing, he burst through the line of men from his company, ducked around two officers that tried to stop him and kept running. The shock of Luke's action whipped away Josh's numbness and he too plunged through the line of soldiers. The two officers that had missed seizing Luke grabbed Josh, who fought back desperately but with the help of a third officer they managed to throw him to the ground.

Moments later one of the men guarding Davy cracked Luke in the ribs with the butt of his musket. At the commotion, Davy looked up and saw Luke's frantic face just as the musket butt smashed him to the ground. A shudder ran through Davy's body. Then without opening his tightly pressed lips, he turned back to his digging.

Under orders of Captain Rawlins, Josh and Luke were put under arrest, their hands tied behind their backs, their ankles lashed together. He then ordered several soldiers to hold the boys erect so that they would witness the execution.

Accompanied by the provost marshal and two majors in full-dress uniform, the colonel marched to where Davy was digging. Then the colonel read the death warrant in a booming voice, enunciating each word carefully. During this, Davy didn't look up but just continued to dig. The colonel and the two majors stepped away as the provost marshal beckoned to Davy to climb up out of the trench. He wearily laid down the shovel, paused for several seconds, then climbed up, assisted by two of the officers with drawn sabers who took hold of his arms. These two officers guided him to a place directly in front of the grave. One of the officers asked Davy something. He vigorously shook his head. The other officer hesitated, then impulsively grabbed Davy's hand and gave it a single shake. The armed soldiers by this time were drawn up in two ranks, the first down on one knee, the second standing erect.

The two flanking officers stepped back, leaving the condemned man standing alone. Slowly and with great deliberation, forcing his hands steady, Davy rolled down his sleeves and fastened their buttons. Then he straightened his body and nodded his head, biting down on his lower lip. At a command from the provost marshal the soldiers fired and Davy, as if struck by a heavy piece of timber, fell backwards and toppled into his grave. One of his feet held onto the ground for several moments then slid down as the body settled into the earth.

Line by line the soldiers of the regiment were marched up to view the dead soldier. Under orders of Captain Rawlins, Luke and Josh were carried to the lip of the grave. Both kept their eyes squeezed tight shut but at the last moment Josh opened his and saw Davy lying face up on the fresh brown earth. His eyes were wide open, his lip still tightly held by his teeth. Josh closed his eyes. From under the lids tears squeezed out and rolled one by one down his cheeks.

Captain Rawlins came up and, without a word about their violent behavior, ordered that Josh and Luke be untied. He watched as they were being freed and as soon as the ropes were off, he grinned as he motioned them to be on their way. Then, still grinning, the captain turned and walked away, nodding at the officers and enlisted men he passed.

# XXXV

All that day until it was dark, Josh and Luke lay under their canvas half-tent, wrapped in their blankets despite the balmy May weather. A passerby seeing the two young soldiers might have thought that they were stricken with typhus or typhoid, for every few minutes, one or the other would start twitching and gagging. But there were no passersby, for the other soldiers of the company carefully avoided the patch of ground on which the two boys had constructed their temporary campsite.

All during the day Josh and Luke lay without saying a word to one another. Finally when all but the sentries were asleep and the fires were reduced to piles of glowing coals, the two friends sat up and faced each other in the dark. Minutes passed.

"I ain't never gonna forget Davy," Luke finally murmured. He shuddered and pulled the blanket close around his shoulders. "If I live to a hundred, I won't forget what they done to him. I swear I won't forget."

"I ain't mad," whispered Josh. "Thought I would be, but I ain't. Jus' sick inside like a shovel full a worms is crawlin' roun' my belly."

"Josh, 'member that night when they lynched them soldiers? That time I felt all bad and dirty like they throwed me in the san'tary trench. I had to wash and wash so's I was clean again." Luke stopped speaking and a silence of almost a minute intervened. Then he said, "Ain't no water as can make me clean this time. The dirt is inside. Ain't no water in this army can clean me, not do I wash for ten days together."

"Let's go some place away from here, Luke." Josh reached out and rested his hand on the other's arm. "Let's jus' leave ever'thin' and go 'way and never come back."

"Where we go?" asked Luke in a lifeless voice.

Josh shrugged, then realizing that his friend could not see him in the dark whispered, "Don' know — I jus' don' know."

"Think we should call on Captain Rawlins and leave him a rememberance?" said Luke in a flat voice.

Josh pressed his hand over his eyes. "We can if you want, but it don' really matter none. They all the same. 'Nother officer will take his place. It won' bring back Davy."

Luke nodded and repeated in his same flat voice, "It won' bring back Davy."

# XXXVI

A week later Josh's father awoke to find a carefully folded note slipped under the door. Standing in his night shirt, using his finger as a guide, he slowly spelled out the words.

Pa Ma I couldn't stick with the army no more. Maybe out west in California or Nevada I can have a new life. I am sorry if what I done brings shame on you. The best thing for the both of you is to just forget about me. Your son Josh

The man read the note through a second time then, without saying a word to his wife, thrust it deep into the coals of the fire.

That same morning when Luke's father went to the barn to milk he found the watch he had given his son, still ticking, hanging on a peg alongside the milk pail. After several minutes of deep thought, during which he carefully polished the watch with his shirt tail, he walked out to the well, dropped the watch in, then went back to the barn and started milking.